BETRAYAL ON ARUBA WINDS

October 2018
For Tom, a
man who is always
in his write mind
May the winds of good
fortune carry you
Tracy Novinger ☺
TN

Tracy Novinger

Morpho Publishing, Inc. 2018

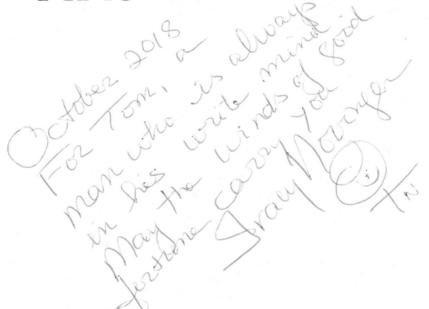

ISBN: 1983723894
ISBN 13: 9781983723896
Library of Congress Control Number: 2018900367
Morpho Publishing, Inc.
Texas, USA

Books by Tracy Novinger:

"Intercultural Communication: A Practical Guide"
"Communicating with Brazilians: When 'Yes' Means 'No'"

For Glen

Mi ta stima bo

# ACKNOWLEDGEMENTS

I first wish to thank friends who allowed me to inflict on them very early, very rough drafts of this book--you know who you are and to express my appreciation to author Amanda Eyre Ward, who is so generous in sharing her knowledge and talent. To Glen, my husband, *gracias, obrigada, merci* for your support for all my schemes, no matter how eccentric, and for your forbearance during the many hours I mentally disappeared into writing this book. Very special thanks to Candace Kane, my talented sister, and to dear friends, Adela Etcharren and Elvira Chavaria, for your interest and comments on the almost-final draft of this story.

If history were taught in the form of stories, it would never be forgotten.

–Kipling

The disaster that was visited upon the island of Aruba by the long reach of World War II, is little known to outsiders. But since this is a work of fiction, any resemblance of the story's characters to real persons living or dead, of entities to real entities, or of incidents to real occurrences other than those of obvious historic record is coincidental, a fictitious use, or perhaps a weaving of the reader's fertile imagination.

Historical images related to this story: *arubawinds.blogspot.com*

In *Betrayal on Aruba Winds*, Tracy Novinger has captured the essence of a unique place in the world through personal reflection, historical fact, and a finely woven, suspenseful story.

--Elvira Chavaria, Librarian, Nettie Lee Benson Latin American Collection, University of Texas, retired.

Caressed by the cooling trade wind and turquoise lagoons, kissed by the sun, tiny Aruba really did play a crucial role in helping the Allies win WWII. This engaging novel tells the compelling story of Alissia Saxton's search for truths that lie hidden in a cache of past betrayals, lust and treason.

--Willow Wood Books

The author's lavish treatment of historic Aruba and the people who lived there evokes Michener's rich sagas; it sculpts Alissia Saxton's search to redeem herself for her misdeeds. When she returns to the island to delve into secrets, she discovers smoldering betrayals that took place on an exotic and dangerous stage.

--Dustin Blair, Senior Software Engineer, Inspirato, Denver

When distant World War II reaches Aruba's shores, destruction and treachery collide with a tropical paradise. Against this extraordinary backdrop, Tracy Novinger takes us into a sensual world rich with the detail of daily life. Novinger's examination of memory and perception, of guilt and forgiveness, weaves a powerful and enchanting tale of a far-flung place scarred by the storms of war. What I learned from this story will stick with me for quite some time.

--C.F. Yetmen, author of *The Roses Underneath* and *What is Forgiven*

I

Dilemma

Perception is reality.

CHAPTER 1
THE DYNAMICS

1973. Sometimes, when she dared, Alissia would go back to her island of crooked divi-divi trees that bowed to the wind. She had only to close her eyes to return and watch puffy clouds sail by as she curled her toes into fine sand. She tasted the salt of the sea, while warm water lapped at her ankles. Turquoise lagoon, the white froth of small waves on a sliver of reef, the deep blue of the Caribbean. It seemed as if she could really feel her hair brush at her face in the constant wind that tempered the heat of Aruba's tropical sun. With pleasure, she basked in the luminous images that she tried always to hold at the top of her thoughts--but her island had an underside. Dark shadows from that place and time had begun to well up unbidden, menacing memories that were destroying Alissia Aruba Saxton's perfect, present life--the life she had so carefully constructed to buy her right to happiness.

History and geography have a long reach. If carefully examines a map and looks for the Equator and the Tropic of Cancer, between these two markers of latitude one will find, near the east coast of South America where the steady trade wind always blows, the diminutive island that fronts the mouth of Venezuela's brackish Lake Maracaibo, the largest lake in South America, one of the oldest on earth. It was in this region, in the early 1900s, that the world's growing addiction to oil collided with significant facts of place. The shock created a powerful dynamic. In truth, the events of the time were both complex and significant. "Black gold" and World War II fueled what happened. Most on the small island of Aruba enjoyed a hedonistic life then, unaware that a dangerous man schemed. The whole mix finally erupted.

CHAPTER 2
THE ATTACK

The explosion hit at precisely 1:31 a.m. on February 16, 1942, not long before Alissia Saxton was born. While the faithful trade wind blew, what sounded like loud claps of thunder escalated into an eruption of such force that it wrenched sleeping Colony residents from their beds. Heavy booms hurtled through the silence to thud into Stass Saxton's chest, knocking him out of deep sleep. Instantly he could tell that the commotion came from the direction of the refinery. Stumbling into his trousers, Alissia's father hurried out of the bungalow to join people who, drunk with sleep, ran in makeshift states of dress towards the tumult. He watched an expanse of bright orange splash higher and higher into the sky.

CHAPTER 3
TRAGEDY

"What the hell is going on?" yelled Stass. He ran toward the low coral cliffs that overlooked the harbor between the Colony and the Lago Refinery. "That's gotta be a huge fire! Is it the plant?" He reached the overlook where residents had gathered. They stood watching in horror. They couldn't tell if the explosions had come from the ships below or from the adjacent refinery. Or had they heard the sound of big guns?

Red Burns stood frozen in shock. "It's an attack. It has to be German subs," he shouted. "They're torpedoing the harbor and shelling the plant."

Below them two oil tankers torched high in flames. Oil had spilled out of the ships and spread in a black, menacing pool across the water where it ignited. The surface of the water burned with flames.

"It's the SS Pedernales and the Oranjestad tankers," Stass yelled.

"Sweet Jesus! They're fully loaded! They'll torch sky high," shouted Tex.

A realization socked Stass in the gut. "Oh my God. My brother-in-law. Ruddy Gifford's out there. Nessa's brother is crew on the Oranjestad tonight."

Colony residents could clearly see the men on the ships. Figures scrambled around on deck and screamed in terror and pain as flames enveloped them. Those who could make it to the railings of the ship hurled themselves overboard to escape the conflagration, but hot flames raced across the surface of the water as the oil that covered it burned, cremating men trying to swim to safety. The repulsive stench of oil and fire and burning flesh enveloped shocked onlookers.

The catastrophe of that night wounded everyone in the Colony. Many years later, whenever Alissia's Grandma Gifford could bring herself to speak about it, Alissia always saw the deep pain that carved her grandmother's face. Grandma G had lost her son in the attack. Alissia had lost her uncle—the uncle, it would turn out, that she would very much want and need.

In the aftermath of the firestorm, a group of refinery men stood by the refinery entrance gate in shock.

Stass said, "We're lucky the torpedoes didn't hit the tank farm," said Stass. Those tanks are all full, too. The whole refinery could have gone up."

"Bloody basturts!" Red swore. "The ships were loaded, with full crew on board. It was as good as if they had our shipping schedule." Red choked. "Poor devils. What a terrible way to go. Good men. The ones that died are the lucky ones. Did ye see the two they were trying to take to hospital? There was nowhere on their bodies they could touch to put them on a stretcher." Red's Scottish temper erupted—anger was easier to deal with than pain. Clenching his hands, he turned and with fury kicked the chain-link fence. Then he pummeled it with his fists until his knuckles bled. "I'd like to get me hands on one of the basturts that did this. Dear Lord, give me just one."

"Where the hell is Máximo?" said Stass. He looked around, perplexed.

"He should be here, right out front," said Tex. "Them tankers are his job."

In the back of the group, a man piped up. "I saw him a few minutes ago, but he just took a look, then disappeared. Maybe he's got his hands full."

At the comment about Maximo's quick departure, Tex looked around. He appeared to process the fact for a moment, then frowned and rubbed his chin. He shook his head. "I'm gittin too blamed old fer this shit. Ain't a quitter. I'll crank out fuel. But retirement's looking mighty close on my horizon."

The men stood despondently, anger slowly melting into despair. After a few minutes, one by one, they drifted away.

Máximo Hirsch made it home just before dawn that night. He latched both doors to his bungalow from the inside, then went to his bedroom and closed the wooden louvers tight. Whiffles of wind crept through the cracks into the room, the ever-present wind that Arubans said carried news and rumors. He stepped inside the doorway to his large closet, turned on the light and in short staccato bursts rapped out one Morse code message of just five words: TWO SHIPS HIT REFINERY MISSED.

When the tally came in, the Pedernales had lost eight of its crew of twenty-six, with Captain McCall wounded. The report on the Oranjestad was appalling. Of a crew of twenty-two, fifteen men had been killed. To the Gifford family, losing Ruddy was like having a limb ripped off, leaving a bloody hole. Grief overwhelmed them. Nessa, recently married, pregnant with Alissia, was disconsolate. She had adored her older brother.

The bad burn cases that survived the initial attack died slow and agonizing deaths. There was no way to adequately treat them except to give them whatever palliatives for pain that could be found. There was much speculation as to whether the enemy might have received inside information. The refinery men had hard and passionate feelings on the subject.

"If some son-of-a-bitch is responsible, we'll find him and douse him with fuel. I'll personally put a match to it," one known hothead was heard to say.

That night ripped and burned. Who and how the fully-loaded tankers were targeted remained an active question that did not go away. It remained a long-lived and recurring subject of heated discussion in the Colony, becoming as much a part of island landscape as the idyllic climate and fragrant blossoms--a permanent part of daily reality.

After the attack, a few wives and families left the island, but most were committed to their familiar world, even content. Aruba got under the skin of those who lived there. They found the advantages outweighed the disadvantages. As for the Brits, their attitude was that they would rather take their chances in Aruba. England was much too close to Germany and was suffering greatly from the air raids by German bombers. In the meantime, much closer than Europe, more danger prowled the Atlantic and the Caribbean while warm, turquoise lagoons bathed sandy beaches on Aruba's lee shore and jasmine blossoms spread their sweet perfume.

On the little island, over centuries, different people had different experiences of place and time, but the trade wind was always there, always constant. To some, if the person knew just how to listen, the wind seemed to whisper secrets, many of which they would later come to confirm. It often became difficult for the few who could hear the murmured stories to determine the source of what they knew. Did they somehow just piece together what had really happened, adding detail from some unconscious recess of mind? Or had they pulled together fragments from past conversations overheard?

CHAPTER 4
EXPLOSION

The second explosion hit in 1973. Alissia Aruba Saxton was thirty-one years old. She stood facing Tom in his colorless kitchen when he asked a simple question about their wedding arrangements.

"Stop it!" she yelled. "Stop it, Tom. Just leave me alone." The room smelled faintly of disinfectant. Outside the biting Chicago wind began to whistle across a frozen landscape. It whipped up into a shriek.

Alissia had not felt her agitation build and her blast shocked them both. It cracked dangerous fissures in the perfect, safe world she had pieced together, piece by deliberate piece. She was destroying the conventional, controlled life she had painstakingly built--the life she believed would pay for her right to happiness.

Alissia had escaped by excelling. When her father told her that a woman didn't need to go to college, she obtained a scholarship to the University of Chicago. Impressed by her achievement, to his credit, he gave her the money she needed for travel and she made her way from a tiny island of balmy weather to a large city with brutal weather extremes. At school, she worked nights and weekends for spending money, books--and to buy her independence. When she graduated *summa cum laude* with a Bachelor's of Business Administration, an import company promptly hired her. The need for perfection that her father had drilled into her had served her well. Even so, she believed that her success was only a veneer for deep and ugly flaws that she did not want exposed.

Alissia started her new job and made herself set aside her recent growing and recurring desire to be irresponsible, to take off for some exotic new place, to roam free without care or responsibility. Now, after years of schooling and months of long hours captive inside an office, she felt like she would not survive unless she got the outdoor activity to which she had been accustomed growing up. She joined a hiking club and on her first outing the fall foliage astounded her. In the Caribbean nature flaunted such showy colors in flowers. It was on that hike that she met Tom. She had liked his compact and sturdy looks and had noted that he seemed to have a settled manner.

When Tom first saw Alissia, his eyes sparked. *Fit,* he thought. *And sexy.* It did not take long for him to walk over and introduce himself.

With pleasure, Alissia watched Tom approach her. He was an engineer, he said, and he seemed smart. They spoke a few moments and then he asked, "Do you mind if I hike with you?"

Alissia smiled at him. "Not in the least. Please do."

Tom enjoyed Alissia's easy laugh and on subsequent outings she told him stories about the exotic island she came from. The big oil refinery that she said was built in such a small place piqued his professional curiosity.

Tom and Alissia continued to seek each other out on hikes, but when the Chicago winter socked in, they hiked less and began to meet for breakfast on weekends. Finally, even though there was still snow on the ground, signs of spring arrived. Tom invited Alissia for a Saturday outing. "Just the two of us," he said. It was fortunate that each carried a daypack with minimal survival gear because a sudden, blinding snowstorm caught them late in the day. They were a long way from Tom's car and Alissia shivered uncontrollably as they tried to find their way in fading light. This was not warm Caribbean weather. Tom stopped to look at her and put his hand on her forearm. "Are you OK?"

"I, uh… I…" She seemed to search for words. "So---cold." Her speech was beginning to slur.

This is taking too long. She's not used to this, Tom thought. *I grew up with it.* "We need to get into my sleeping bag," Tom said. Alissia hesitated.

"Alissia. You're hypothermic. It's dangerous."

She nodded.

Tom hauled a light down bag out of his pack and found a spot with some shelter from the slicing gusts of wind. He laid the bag out. They crawled into it just as darkness swallowed the sun. The dense black of night pressed down on them and heavy snow muted all sound except for their breathing.

They lay on their sides, Alissia with her back toward Tom. "You know we're stuck here until morning," he said.

"Uh-huh," Alissia murmured. Tom drew the full length of her close against him and folded himself around her. As she melted into his warmth, the clicking of her teeth and her shivering slowly settled. Tom ran his hand over the length of her body and she moved in closer. He asked softly, "Is this OK?" He felt her nod of assent and asked again. "Alissia, are you sure?" He heard only the sibilant *s* of her "yes."

Not long after their unusual first night together, Tom and Alissia announced their engagement. It was sometime after the announcement that Alissia had exploded.

CHAPTER 5
CONFLICTED

They stood facing each other in Tom's kitchen. Tom recoiled at the outburst and threw up his arms in defense. "Jeez, Alissia!"

"Oh, Tom. I'm sorry." Alissia cradled her face in her hands.

Tom stood silent for a moment, then said, "You don't laugh anymore." His voice was full of pebbles. "Lately, you funnel into a manic focus on things. You blow up. I don't recognize you."

Alissia dropped her hands. "I'm so sorry, Tom." Subdued, she said, "I'm having problems."

Tom watched Alissia slip her hands around behind her back. She slid her fingers up until she could reach and touch her shoulder blades. She regained composure.

Tom had seen Alissia make that odd little gesture before when something bothered her. She would place both hands behind her back and contort to slide them up until she could just touch her shoulder blades with her fingertips. The first few times he asked her about it, she looked embarrassed, shook her head and would not respond. Ultimately, one day she explained. "When I was a kid, I really believed that I would grow wings and I used to check to see if they were sprouting, especially when something bothered me. To escape unpleasantness and tension I would imagine myself flying. I would feel high and safe, above everything. And I used to fly in my dreams." She stopped speaking, then mimicked the gesture. "I guess fingering my shoulder-blades became a talisman." She laced her fingers together in front of her, both hands at her waist, and she looked down at them. After a moment, without meeting Tom's eyes, she had told him, "I know. It's silly. I'm a grown woman. But if something distresses me, I finger my shoulder blades unconsciously."

Tom had dropped his arms back down to his sides. He stood stiff. He seemed to try to process Alissia's outburst. He rolled his head around a few times, then put his hand to his neck. Finally, he responded. "What are your problems?" he asked.

Alissia hesitated, then answered. "It's work," she lied. "I lost a lot of money buying French Francs. I was wrong about the exchange trend. MedTech is going to lose on a big shipment." This much was true, but she proffered the mistake as a decoy, cringing to admit the error she had made because anxiety was scattering her usual tight focus. Imperfection was not acceptable in the controlled world she had built.

They had been simply talking about their wedding arrangements when Alissia, competent and organized, consummately contained, catapulted out of control. The impending marriage loomed over her. For some reason, discussing it stirred up her guilt over the past and loosed emotions that thudded like thunder into her chest.

She approached Tom to seek safe haven. He stood rigid, arms pressed tight to sides but softened at her nearness. He pulled her in close and she nestled her face up into the hollow of his shoulder. She inhaled deeply to breathe in the familiar scent of his body.

"Your record at MedTech is good. Maybe you'll come out ahead at year-end." Tom's voice and blonde eyebrows hovered at the end of the sentence.

She sidestepped the implied question. "Maybe so."

They stood silent for a moment, arms around each other. He stroked her soft hair. He was as sturdy as a bear, Alissia slim and sleek as an ocelot.

"Our wedding is in just two months," said Tom.

Alissia jerked away.

His mouth tightened. "You're having second thoughts, aren't you?"

She could see Tom's hurt, his blue eyes turn stony. She made a futile sweep through the air with one arm and did not reply.

"What's your problem?"

"I don't know."

Tom tossed his head with exasperation. "Talk to me."

"The world I come from is my being, it's who I am. You don't understand."

Tom clenched his jaw. She could see the muscles stand out. Then he responded. "You say your island was a paradise but then you veer off into talk of mayhem and death, of international sabotage. And you say you did terrible things. What things? When I ask questions, you clam up. Explain it to me."

"I can't."

"Can't or won't?"

"I can't. I just can't. It's too painful." Alissia's face flushed with agitation and she lifted her hair off her neck and shoulders. "I can't stand the guilt. I'm ashamed. I don't want to talk about it. I can't stand to even *think* about it."

"Well, you're right. I don't understand and you won't--" He caught himself. "You can't tell me." He looked at her, silent. His voice hardened. "We have to pay the deposit for our wedding reception. Deal with this. Now. You have two weeks. You need to commit without reservation or this is over." He pivoted on one heel and marched out.

The Chicago day was cold and ponderous and its gloom smothered Alissia's recollection of redolent frangipani, of the trade wind caressing her skin. The thick, sooty grey sky of this place shrouded the images of luminous, white clouds scudding across sea-and-sky blues that Alissia tried to summon. She wanted to contemplate only a perfect vision of her tropical island. She needed to keep all memory of betrayal, death and disaster of war buried deep under her images of paradise. The impending marriage fanned the fire of her insecurities and flames began to devour the smooth mantle of the life she had put together. It could not be easy for Tom to love her, and she knew it.

The nightmares were getting wilder, more frequent. She now had them almost every night. She didn't know which was worse, jerking up from dead sleep into a sitting position, totally disoriented, or hardly being able to rouse herself from agitated sleep in the morning to get to work. She always could recall the awful dreams in vivid detail and they always started the same way. Alissia would see herself sitting at the gate into the refinery thinking, searching…

Because Aruba had been attacked during the war, there was always the ongoing question about a spy. In the small community, the quest for an answer about espionage was entangled with collective and personal anguish and this emotional legacy had been passed on to Alissia. To deal with her own problems, somehow she needed to unravel the intrigue that resulted in the disastrous attack that injured them all. And there was the—the other thing. To come to terms with herself she would have to deal with her part in making such a despicable thing happen. She should have not broken her mother's Big Rule. She wished she had not been so headstrong--willfulness was a trait she had not outgrown. And, yes, she needed to confront Red's death, the death that stalked and suffocated her. The thought of Red paralyzed her with pain and crushed her with guilt because of the choice she had made. She had put herself first.

Alissia awoke with a start. She sat up and shook her head, trying to clear it. Thoughts of the past mixed with thoughts of the present. The island. What had happened. Work. Her relationship with Tom.

Alissia wished that her exhilarating dreams of flying would come back to her, but instead she flailed in the recurring, distressing nightly visions.

CHAPTER 6
PINNACLE

Alissia put great effort into making her present life perfect. She planned. She organized. She locked every detail of every day into its proper cell, daring any fragment to escape her control. Accomplishments and reliability earned her professional recognition. She made good money. Today was Saturday and she was outside running, addicted to the sense of freedom that it brought her, to the high that kicked in when she began to sail without effort. At this time of year, in this place, she could barely feel the warmth of the sun's watery rays on her skin and she wished for the fierce, fiery globe of the Caribbean. With honey-blonde hair to her shoulders and an island lilt in the way she moved, men's eyes would follow her, flashing their approval.

As Alissia ran through the park, she censored recollection of the mayhem and tragedy. She wanted to contemplate only the best of the past. But in time with her breaths, a disturbing recollection leaked through in fragments.

I was very young. When I decided. I'd have to be. Like him.

She recalled her father's arbitrary dictum and winced. She could still feel the sting.

She must have been about seven years old then. Like most days on the island, the weather was balmy. The wind caressed leaves and kissed the surface of lagoons. The school year had just started and the family sat at the dinner table. Her father eyed the potatoes on his plate with obvious pleasure. Good potatoes were a rare commodity on the island. Alissia wriggled with enthusiasm and made an announcement. "You know what?" She waited for eyes to turn to her. "We're learning multiplication now. And guess what. I know through three-times-twelve already. Three times--"

Her father laid down his fork and looked at her. "You know what? You are not to go out of this house until you have memorized multiplication and division through twelve-times-twelve. Backward and forward. Do you understand?"

"But, Dad, we--"

"Don't talk back! You heard me. I'll check you on it."

Alissia hung her head in silence. Nothing she ever did was good enough.

"What do you say?" His tone was menacing.

"Yes, sir," was her quiet response. Light faded from her face.

Alissia continued her run. *He need not have been harsh*, she mused. *I was a good student. I would have done my homework hanging upside down by my knees from a branch in the Seagrape tree to earn a scrap of his praise.* She thought of the high stack of flash cards her mother helped her make. One-hundred and forty-four. Her father's autocratic requirement gave her a skill that still served her well, she knew, but he had imposed it as an unnecessary and unwarranted punishment. There had been no transgression. What Alissia had needed from him, what she always sought, was some wisp of approval. A dim suspicion faded before it took clear form. *Could his irascibility have been about himself, not me?*

Alissia's feet struck an even rhythm on the dirt as she followed the trail. She crossed an expanse of winter-brown grass and then wound on through leafless trees. She dodged a root. The quick, evasive side-step reminded her of how she tried to dodge her father's attention. There was, however, nothing she could do when she watched him dominate and disparage her mother, Nessa. A thought occurred to her. *What about Tom*? she asked herself. Would he be different? She tried to picture Tom as a husband.

Alissia picked up her running pace for the home stretch and her thoughts picked up pace with her. As a child, she had always needed to be alert to navigate unsafe currents and undertow in the household. Observing her father, she had also decided that of the two routes she could discern in life, domination was better than submission. She had told herself then that when she grew up she would have power, the power to protect herself.

Reflecting further, she recognized that the many pleasures of her island were what made up the core of her identity. She was fortunate that her natural, adventurous proclivities had been well fed by her quirky, loving mother, a woman who both permitted and instigated surprising escapades. The serendipity of having roamed as wild and free as a little goat in a tropical paradise had imprinted on her soul.

Alissia held together her present, ordered world with a tight fist. She tried to ignore how her need to control suffocated valuable gifts that came from a unique time and place. She had toned down her walk, replaced flowered island dresses with crisp white blouses and skirted suits in the sober navy or black that blended into the climate and culture that surrounded her. With competence she managed shipment and payment for all of the instruments MedTech imported and she enjoyed business relationships she had built in Spain and France and Germany. Her contact with stellar companies such as Zeiss and Siemens gratified her. But despite obvious efficacy, she knew that her colleagues still made snide comments.

The thought saddened her. She wanted acceptance. She tried to fit in. Her face tightened when she recalled the conversation she had just overheard. The two men did not realize that she was close behind them as they walked down the hall.

"I just can't stand a know-it-all."

"But she *is* good at what she does, you have to grant her that."

The man shrugged. "I guess so."

"What about that place she says she's from? She says it had big industry."

"I don't believe it. The place was in the middle of nowhere. It sounds like a desert of cactus and donkeys to me. Well, some jackasses sure must have lived there is all I can say."

"Well, she does call the place paradise."

The two men elbowed each other and laughed.

The mockery by her colleagues did more than embarrass Alissia. It made her question what she considered indisputable. Her identity was built on facts undergirded by ancient coral reefs uplifted and hardened into a solid limestone surface. The more she dwelled on the office incident, the more disturbing the dismissive remarks became. She had been secure in her knowledge of place, history and time. They were the foundation of who she was. Uncertainty filled her. *I can't handle this. Not on top of everything else. My problems are like a plague. They just keep spreading.*

Nothing was going right. Her relationship with Tom was falling apart. Her performance at work was suffering. Her colleagues belittled her. Doubts, like rats, scurried into her head from every direction, shrilling questions. She didn't know at which to swat at first. Her running gait became choppy, her breath irregular. She would have to deal with questions about the island that she had never had to ask. Now, along with everything else that happened there, she needed to reconfirm for herself concrete facts of history and geography that supported her reality.

Where am I going? Who am I, really? she asked herself.

Alissia was disturbed. The memories of paradise that she always summoned up for pleasure now brought back with them all that she strove to hide underneath--the tragedy that mauled her family, the guilt that still haunted her. When terrible shame over what she did overwhelmed her, she pushed away what had always been pleasurable recollection. To shut out the dark side of the past, she struggled to focus only on her disciplined, ordered world of the present. Even so, somewhere in her psyche she could still hear Arubans melt mouthfuls of crisp Dutch consonants into soft Papiamento as they intoned the peculiar concoction of their language. She listened to clipped British diction, rapid-fire Spanish, deliberate Norwegian and the broad vowels of North Americans. The throaty voices of Trinidadians washed over her and island music played in her head. In an eclectic environment, Alissia learned quite young how to melt into alien groups for survival--or perhaps from a child's need to blend in. Nonetheless, she had always committed only on her terms, always holding some part back and usually, discreetly, she could get by with this. But now, the uniformed cadre that surrounded her in her professional life--men strutting-sure of themselves--would like to at the least see her married, anchored in a familiar, non-threatening niche. Her engagement to Tom had elicited nods of approval.

Alissia's fiancé was a man's man. He respected her abilities. He admired her successes and spoke of her to others with pride. She and Tom discussed work with each other and, although Tom didn't run with her--he preferred racquetball, they shared their love of hiking. The previous summer she had talked him into joining her in Bordeaux after she finished with business and they hiked in the French Pyrénées.

"I had my own guide and translator," he boasted to friends. "Even when we ended up on the Spanish side."

Tom also liked to hear about Alissia's little-known speck of land in the Caribbean, its surprising importance to the world during a significant window of history. His interest was important to her. She could feel his appreciation. And she knew Tom loved her.

Although Alissia thought she had done everything right, a plaintive note of unhappiness now played in the background of each of her days, a low dirge crescendo that drowned light-hearted melody. The only solution she knew was to exert tighter control. She finished her run and began to stretch. She was determined to make light-hearted spontaneity again sing and dance in her life. But how?

CHAPTER 7

THE BOX

The night was quiet. Tom was not happy to learn that Alissia would not spend the usual weekend at his house. She had begged patience. "I need time to work out my problems," she told him. Now in her apartment she lay on the bed seeking answers. Her parents and younger brother, Duncan, had all died in a car accident. Duncan had been driving when the large, oncoming truck hit them head-on in a blind curve. Her grandmother might have had answers to some of Alissia's questions about what happened in Aruba, but it was too late to ask her. In a phone conversation the year before, Alissia realized that advanced age had dulled Grandma G's once-sharp mind. Maybe her mother's good friend, Rika, could help her. *Ree-kah.* She had been like a beloved auntie to Alissia. Could she somehow find Rika? She had to turn off all these thoughts. It was late. Finally, she rolled over and sank, exhausted, into thrashing sleep.

Alissia awoke too early to a day that again promised cold and grey. Sunrise came late at this time of year. She turned on a lamp and eyed the file box by the bed. It had arrived a few weeks earlier by mail from Grandma G but, busy as usual, Alissia had only glanced inside. She went to make a cup of coffee, then moved a

Dutch Delft tea-set from the dining table to the top of a carved Chinese bookcase where its white-and-blue contrasted with the bold black-and-yellow of Dutch Gouda pottery. Both sets were mementos of her mother. Then she went and got her grandmother's box from the bedroom, placed it in the center of the table and took off the lid. She considered the jumble of loose photographs that filled it and nodded. *Going through all this will help me focus on what happened. I have to make time for it.*

She began to dig through the box and saw there were notes penciled on the back of some of the photos; toward the bottom of the pile, she found an album, two tattered books and some old pamphlets published by Standard Oil. At the very bottom, underneath everything, lay a large, spiral notebook, the one in which she used to see her grandmother write. Alissia had not thought of that habit in years. She picked it up. On the cover, the obvious was written in large, block letters: *NOTEBOOK.* Alissia leafed through the lined pages filled with handwritten observations: anecdotes, descriptions and bits of history interspersed with succinct one-line comments. She turned to the first entry.

> April 7, 1929 - Colette Gifford. We just arrived in Aruba. I was seasick the whole way. We're lucky Gus found work here, otherwise I don't know how we would survive with two kids. Jobs are almost impossible to find. They say this is a worldwide depression. Our house is strange-looking. The wind blows all the time and makes strange noises at night. I have a lot to get used to. This island is so different and my life has changed so much, I have decided to keep these notes. I brought a whole box of books with me. Ruddy didn't want to move but little Nessa seems excited.

Alissia sat in her dining room and read random entries in the notebook. As she plunged into thoughts of the past, she could taste the sea in the air. The trade wind seemed to blow a strand of hair across her face and she tucked it back behind one ear. Goose bumps dappled her skin and she shivered with pleasure. The notebook contained decades of disparate observations, a treasury of scribbled information to add to a communal memory of place and time.

She turned back to the box of photos and, at random, selected one to examine. She and Eddie posed proudly in black and white, each displaying the homemade toy they had invented. It was on several of her solitary early morning forays out wheeling it around the Colony that Alissia observed certain incidents—actions that the people involved thought no one ever saw. Whatever had happened to Eddie, her inseparable playmate, her daily companion in mischief and adventure? He had more serious problems than she could understand at the time. To her he was just Eddie. But there was one thing for certain. She could always trust his tight mouth. He could skulk and keep secrets as well as she. She still felt responsible for him, a dimmed nagging that lived on with her.

She dug further through the photos and came across a photograph of her family's dentist with his wife. Arubans were a handsome people and Miss Jultje was a beauty. Alissia idly wondered how the lovely woman's life had unfolded. She smiled at a photo of a trio: her mother on the left, herself as a small girl in the middle, and on the right her mother's good friend, Hendrika. She contemplated her image with tenderness. *Rika.* Alissia really wanted to see her again. Rummaging further through the stack, a particular photo caught her eye. She picked it up to examine it closely. Alissia's father and a group of refinery men all stood at attention in a line as, with serious expressions, they looked at the camera. One visage still stirred up fear but now it triggered anger, too. In the photo, the man wore the fake smile he used to mask the eyes of a predator. It was Eddie's father--Gil. Gil used to focus that look on Alissia when he thought no one was looking. She bounced over his face quickly, then skipped even more quickly over the next face in line. Red. She did not want to reminisce about Red, the person she had cared for so much and betrayed. Last, at the end of the line she considered a tall, blond man. Máximo. He challenged the camera with hard eyes. Máximo had always provoked troubling questions, questions for which she knew she would have to find answers, even though she didn't quite know why. Unsettled, she thrust the charged photo to the bottom of the pile.

Shuffling further through the stack, Alissia came across an enlargement of a snapshot taken at the memorable party. It had been held in the garden where her mother tended brilliant-colored and perfumed flowers to pleasure the senses. Alissia well recalled that evening. Except for Eddie, all of the players in the immediate world of her childhood had been there. She held the large print in both hands and studied it closely. This was the world of pleasures and tragedies that she must understand to resolve the dilemma of her present.

CHAPTER 8
PHOTOGRAPHS

Alissia examined the old photographs in Grandma G's box and floated in nostalgia. Details from the past squabbled for her attention-- attention that Alissia needed to direct to her crisis of the present. She resurfaced from the warm water of her thoughts and tried to bring with her only the best of her past wonderworld, but too much that was unresolved clung to her. She put her hands behind her back and reached up to touch her shoulder blades. That old, reassuring gesture.

She had to get herself back under the usual, steady control with which she managed her life. She had to make her peace with Tom. Her recent agitation had scattered her attention and her job performance had suffered. She could afford no more mistakes at work. She needed to gain the goodwill of her colleagues because she was the outlier. Hired at MedTech by a long-gone maverick, she was too female, too capable--certainly too attractive—and she had been hired for a position several men coveted. She could calculate exchange rates in her head faster than most of them could with a calculator and they resented it. Instead of winning allies as she expected, her abilities distanced her. When her co-workers heard her speak with suppliers in languages they did not understand, she could see them frown. "*Parfait. Envoyez-nous tous ce que vous pouvez nous fournir,*" she might say on the phone, agreeing to take all the merchandise available from a supplier.

In attempting to make friendly office small-talk, Alissia spoke of where she had lived, of foods that she liked. It all sounded too exotic, but it is what she knew. Trying to conform to a spoken and unspoken office code, she curbed some of her usual inclinations but, even so, she was still seen as the interloper. If she further excelled at her job, she thought, maybe then they would accept her. She worked even harder.

Alissia never imagined that the same issues that alienated her at work might distance solid, caring Tom. Her passions and interests had once attracted him to her, but now they seemed only to cause him frustration. She cared so much for Tom, but he did not understand how she loved the sea or how exotic places ignited her desires. He did not relate when she spoke of the ecstasy of biting into a plump slice of fried plantain, redolent of rum, voluptuous in her mouth. He liked potatoes, with butter please, and some meat would be good. She saw the discrete details that undergirded his stability, but she tried to ignore the conventional structure that the parts built when she put them all together. As their wedding date approached, Alissia's disquiet grew and, because she was conscientious and reliable to a fault, her misgivings shocked her. Her feelings loomed over them both. Tom was right to question her. His unhappiness pressed down on her. She felt responsible, a burden too familiar, too similar to weights of the past. Tom did not know what had happened in her tropical world.

Every day Alissia paid for the perfect life she had built and every day she tried to ignore the particle of self that sifted away, one more grain of sand falling through a random crack. She discounted her needs for physical freedom, for adventure, to cavort and wander without thought. She had earned respect for professional accomplishments, that much was good, but still she didn't fit. And she still felt flawed. She believed she had defects of character that were deep and ugly and she did not want them exposed. She could not let anyone know what happened, what she had done. She needed more than professional success to feel that she was whole. If she would also marry, she thought, if she would make this final commitment to the traditional norm, she could buy redemption. *But what I really want,* she thought, *is to flee this city. I want to trade my perfect life for carefree escape. But then will I ever find my place?*

CHAPTER 9
QUANDARY

Tom had issued an ultimatum and Alissia had still not resolved her problem. For a week, every day, the past commanded her present. Perturbing issues warred for attention. They consumed her. She could not afford another mistake at MedTech. Even though she did not match her usual driving pace, she pulled off an acceptable purchase of Deutschmark futures. For Alissia foreign exchange was a game of expertise and skill. She played to win, but the purchase made the dollar cost of a large shipment only a little better than break-even—it was not up to her usual profit performance and MedTech's president told her so. Nothing was going well.

Alissia cradled her face in her hands, ignoring the file folders for orders and shipments strewn across her desk in disarray. Ordinarily they sat arranged in neat stacks, sorted with care by priority. After a moment, she got up and went to the break-room for coffee. *This space is like a watering-hole in the wild,* she thought. She never knew who would show up. She poured herself coffee. It smelled good, but she groaned to herself when a co-worker peacocked into the room. Richard had delusions of irresistibility. She put a hand up and rubbed one of her pink-gold earrings between thumb and forefinger. She could not stand this bird-brain. Richard's pomaded hair matched the sheen of his shoes. He selected a coffee mug and without preamble suggested they get together after work.

"You can just tell Tom you had to work late."

Incredulous, Alissia's jaw dropped. Anger drenched her. "You must be even more stupid than everyone says!"

Richard looked like he had been punched in the gut. Alissia felt sick. Like she had kicked a puppy. *How could I say that?* She knew the man's inadequacies. Ineffectual, he flopped and splashed around at his job. He postured because of incompetence.

"Richard..."

He turned away.

Alissia stepped around in front of him. "Richard, that was uncalled for. I apologize. It does not reflect on you. It reflects on me. I am the one who is stupid. Please forgive me." *What am I turning into, engaging at his level?* She was shocked that she had again lost self-control.

Richard started to leave the room.

"Richard, please." She put herself between him and the door. She knew it wasn't true, but said, "I'm sure your invitation was meant as a compliment and I will take it that way. Richard?"

With a nod, he relented. He exited without coffee. The break-room seemed to have become perilous. On another occasion, not long after, as he stirred sugar into his coffee, a well-meaning associate began small talk with Alissia about her coming wedding.

"Where will you and Tom live?" he inquired.

The innocuous question triggered her adrenaline. She forced a smile and steered conversation away from the event.

Alissia had assembled with care the pieces of her professional life. She almost belonged. Marriage would help integrate her into the life she envisioned, she thought, but she didn't know how to manage her growing qualms about formal commitment. Tom was smart. She respected his integrity. She relied on his stability and she was physically attracted to him. She wanted happiness for Tom as well as for herself. Why did she feel such apprehension? She wondered what was wrong with her.

That evening, at her apartment, Alissia went back to rummaging through the Aruba box. She picked up her grandmother's notebook and read in it here and there. It conveniently collected together in one place a series of disparate observations and comments made over years. References to some incidents and people were familiar. These shards of information from past generations could be pieced together to tell a story, but right now just shuffling through photos felt easier. Alissia turned back to a stack she had set to one side. Examining the pictures, she pulled out the best memories of her childhood, the idyll she used as a shield.

The phone rang. It was a wrong number, but it jarred her back to the present. *I have to deal with my loss of self-control, the outbursts. And I must do the right thing--I need to fully commit and to marry.* Before she could quash it, a fleeting thought ballooned. *Is marriage the right thing--or is it just what is expected?* She thrust the misgiving aside and made herself sit up straight to focus on what she needed to do. She knew that her antics as a child contributed in many ways to her who she was and, in addition, recalling them brought her pleasure, but nonetheless, she told herself, such frolics were trivial in the face of the weighty and serious matters she must make herself face. What importance did childhood escapades have relative to life lived in the context of the megalithic oil industry and the aftermath of a world war? She felt as if she were trying to mesh together two disparate worlds. The whole tried to weave some intricate pattern that eluded her.

CHAPTER 10
CAPERS OR CRUX

Alissia's engagement was a commitment and she honored commitments. How should she deal with this marriage that she needed? Could she just smother misgivings? Bury them? Normally decisive, she was not accustomed to confusion. It was Sunday morning and she sat at the table of piled photos. She considered her options. She could let her problems run their course to see if they would fade away, but that would be tantamount to doing nothing and time was running out. She asked herself if it would be better for Tom if she broke off the engagement. Finally, she dared to ask herself, *would it be better for me?* She moved on quickly from the troubling thought. It did not fit the program she had mapped out.

She turned back to the photographs, picking up a few to help her slide more easily into a past that she had not yet been able to bring into sharp focus. She felt like she was wasting her time when she could be out running or working--doing something real and productive. She tried to concentrate, but that just triggered further questions. *Was Tom too conventional? Was he like her father?* She did not want the answers. She recognized that Tom had some expectations she did not meet. Maybe she was not willing to meet them.

The life she had built was ordered and smooth, but constantly trying to hold it together forced her to snuff out the sparks of wanderlust that reignited her desire for adventure. She considered the part of herself that she was sacrificing and slogged through regret and sadness. Was the price she had to pay too high? That was the real question. She suspected that her control over her life was an illusion, that she still played by the rules of others.

Reality may not be what it seems, she thought. *Not then, not now.* Then she ventured further, to the very edge. What would happen if, totally irresponsible, totally free, she just jumped ship?

A key turned in the apartment's front door, interrupting Alissia's stream of thought. Tom let himself in. She had just returned from a five-mile run and still had on her running shoes. Her jacket hung on the back of her chair. She sat, pleasantly spent, hands folded in her lap, contemplating notes and photographs strewn across the table. She saw Tom's appraising look. He walked over and stood behind her, looking down. It was clear that she had been out running and obvious that she had not worked out any decision. Steady, indulgent Tom inflated with anger.

"Are you still at this? I've had it with your procrastination. We've got ten days left to make the deposit. What's your conclusion from this mess?" He waved his hand over the table.

This could not be good for Tom. Alissia did not want to lose this man and she knew she had to act. The photos wakened memories, raised questions, but she could not procrastinate any longer by rummaging through reminders printed on paper when the answers she sought from the past lay on the island itself. *I have to go back. But that's insane. Work is more demanding than ever right now.* If she went now, she would have to take time off without notice. MedTech would be furious. She might lose her job, especially after her recent scattered attention. And she feared digging into what happened in Aruba. But she could go. She felt short of breath.

Thoughts of grappling with evil and guilt crept up over her skull and her scalp froze. She felt powerless to move but made her decision. She looked up. Her pulse raced.

"Tom, I will sort this out. I'll just go back. I must be crazy. I'll leave tomorrow. I'll find my answers. I will fly to Aruba." She stood up and embraced Tom. She kissed him on the face and on the mouth. Emotion filled her chest. Belly to belly, slowly, in short steps she shuffled him backward, unresisting, toward her bedroom.

II

Oil & Water

As we all know, memory is selective. Individuals, like tribes and nations, continually revise their own pasts to conform with current self-images.

–Robert D. Kaplan

CHAPTER 11
RETURN TO PARADISE

The plane flew high over the Caribbean. Purple bands of anxiety funneled up into the cerulean skies of her anticipation. For comfort, Alissia looked out over the water. To see the sea spread to the horizon where it joined the sky to travel on to infinity brought her a sense of peace.

The recent office conversation she had overheard nagged at her, again provoking doubt. *How did such important enterprise end up in Aruba?* she wondered. *Why did all of my family come to such a place? Did we really live in the middle of nothing, just a nowhere desert of cactus and donkeys?* Such questions had never occurred to her. Before leaving for the island she had tried to shore up some of the truths she had always taken for granted. She had searched further through the box; she visited a library.

Looking through the plane window at the sea, all that water, the phrase "scarcely a drop to drink" came to mind. Alissia knew that the three ABC islands were arid, their soil infertile. In fact, when first discovered, written records classed them all as equally useless. Alissia ranked them for herself by size. Curaçao came first, with 176 square miles, Bonaire next with 113. Trailing third came Aruba, with its scant 77. Her clan lived on the runt of what had been called a worthless bunch. She thought of the contradiction between cliché and reality. Her tropical paradise was not what people pictured when they heard the word "tropical." She smiled. No one would ever have to fight their way through any riotous vegetation in Aruba's dry landscape. She thought of the island's people, then pulled out Grandma G's notebook to find the observation she wanted.

> July 21, 1930. It's Monday. Gus worked the graveyard shift, midnight to 8:00 this morning. He's still sleeping. I'm learning about the history of this place. I guess early times here were pretty simple. Even more than now. The first people here were Caquetío Indians from Maracaibo. In Aruba they call them Arawaks because they are part of that group. The Arawaks were more peace-loving than the warring Caribs (that's where the Caribbean gets its name). Of the three ABCs, Arawaks influenced Aruba the most because it's the easiest to reach by canoe. You can see Arawak in Aruban faces, sculptured, their skin a warm color. Arubans are not just Arawak, though. For centuries sailing vessels have stopped here and lots of genes got stirred into the pot. With great enthusiasm, I'm sure. Dutch, Spanish, African, French, and who knows what. Arubans are a handsome mix.

Alissia returned the notebook to her bag to watch the island take form in the distance. Its main axis lay northwest-southeast. She remembered her father saying that the approach by sea was hazardous. The northerly, windward coast was rough and dangerous, with no place for a boat to land. The lee coast had a barrier of coral reefs that was almost unbroken. The reefs shielded some good spots to anchor, but the reefs presented their own hazards. Thinking of life here, she reached into her pocket and rolled two marbles around in her hand. On a last-minute whim, she had brought these silly keepsakes with her.

The angle of flight changed. Now, in the distance, Alissia could see from leeward to windward coast. Few distinctive features marked the landscape. With sparse vegetation, Aruba looked wan from the air. The plane flew over the concession area of Lago Oil & Transport Company at the south end of the island where bungalows dotted a small grid of streets. This was the tiny Colony where three generations of her family had lived, the place where as a child she ran free. To one side sat a few pale buildings on a small rise that had been christened Hospital Hill. They crossed over giant white mushrooms that rolled by beneath the plane until out of sight, the spheroid structures of the petroleum tank farm. Then, between the Colony and the town of Sint Nicolaas, the stacks of the refinery slid by. Alissia's brow furrowed. *I know this place so well.* She ran her fingers through her hair. *But how did it all start?* It didn't all paddle here by canoe from Venezuela. What part did history and geography play? How did "nowhere" fit this tiny island's place in the world, she asked herself. She needed to understand the context and summoned up what she knew.

The Spaniards settled here in 1527, using the whole island as a free-range *rancho* for horses. It was said that this practice left a particular legacy. Horses are the mammals most susceptible to tetanus. When infected they excrete bacterial spores in their manure and such spores were mixed widely into Aruba's soil. As a result, tetanus became endemic to the island and this lasted well into the era of oil.

After the Spaniards came the Dutch in the early 1600s. Alissia's birth certificate stated, in Dutch, that she was born in what was then called Aruba, Dutch West Indies. She thought of a notebook comment about the indigenous Arawak people. The Dutch deported most of them, but when gold was discovered in Aruba they brought some back to work as slaves in the mines. Her mother's heavy wedding ring was cast from Aruba's pink-hued gold. Alissia had it made into the earrings she always wore. She raised a hand to finger a familiar circle. By the 1600s, Arawaks had been eradicated almost everywhere. However, since *indios* were used in Aruba's mines into more recent times, the last known full-blooded Arawak died on this island in 1862.

As the plane neared the airport, Alissia turned her attention back to the flight. She could see Oranjestad. Tidy white houses stood in rows along the waterfront, as if waiting to greet arriving ships, a big change from the deserted rocky beaches Standard Oil found when they sought a storage site near Venezuela's Lake Maracaibo. The plane lined up with the single runway. There was only one runway because here the wind always blew in the same direction.

CHAPTER 12

EDEN

Just seventeen miles from the Venezuelan coast, Alissia's family had put down deep roots. A small island contained her clan's entire world for three generations. Over time, Alissia thought, what an assortment of Colony residents experienced individually seemed to have gathered into a sort of collective memory, a kaleidoscope that formed and reformed, sorting and resorting bits of information from what people knew, what they subsequently read, and what they later heard at gatherings of family and friends. The image that each person had of their microcosm might alter with the capture of another's viewpoint--or just in looking back from a different place and time. With passing years, it became harder for Alissia to remember which memories and what information came from where.

After discovery by the Spaniards, for centuries Aruba had just lolled along. Despite a Spartan existence, inhabitants drifted through life graced by sun, sand and sea, but a big change ushered in the epoch that Alissia later knew. It began in the late 1920s when Lago Oil & Transport Company burst into the island's tranquil bubble to build a refinery that soon became the largest such operation in the world. Jobs and money and an international pell-mell of people poured in. Thrust together on a Caribbean speck of land, these elements compressed into an incendiary amalgam. The production of petroleum products went on to provoke explosions, fire, and disaster from an improbable source and the role that the island played in World War II was little known to outsiders. What happened to Alissia's family scarred them all. Alissia had processed stories of family loss from the perspective of a child and the illogic of that understanding became her reality. She still lived it in the dilemma of the present.

Then, as now, the fresh smell of the sea spread everywhere and the cooling, ubiquitous wind saw it all. It was during the Lago era, from the 1920s to the 1950s, that personal and hidden calamities befell some in the Colony. On the surface, everyone seemed to live a languid and happy existence, but there was another side to their Paradise.

CHAPTER 13
RE-ENTRY

The plane rolled to a stop on the runway of the Oranjestad airport. Alissia sat erect. It was time to salvage her life. As she began the descent from the aircraft, she felt as if she were tumbling down a deep well into the past. Reaching the bottom, with sandaled feet she stepped back into her island world. Familiar sounds and sights and smells cocooned her; garrulous *chuchubi* birds cavorted among purple and pink bougainvillea flowers. She plucked three satin-petaled gardenias from an airport hedge and took them with her. She settled into her rental car where the lush, creamy blossoms drenched her with their heady perfume. She breathed their fragrance in deeply as she reminded herself, *I have five days here, five days to unravel secrets of decades.*

The quest began. She put the car in gear and commenced the drive to the Lago Colony at the other end of the island. She passed by a house near the side of the road. A low wall of piled rocks squatted in front. Around the sides and the back of the yard, cacti planted in a row linked arms to press their tall, thick trunks together tightly. The spiny plants reached up ten or eleven feet to form an impenetrable living barrier--not that there were any great dangers to ward off in this place. In front of the house, a short wooden gate clung askew to the waist-high wall. A tall Flamboyant tree in the front yard pushed abundant clumps of bright orange blossoms toward blue sky. Pink oleander with pointy leaves hugged the house and bushes of Pride of Barbados riotously waved at her with complex and sexy red-yellow-orange petals and pistils. In the deep shade of the eaves Alissia discerned the shape of a woman lazing against the wall, one hand lifted to shade her eyes as she looked out into bright sunlight. The woman waved and Alissia waved back.

Alissia knew this route well. She had traveled it many times as a child. She gazed out the car window at the monochrome countryside called the *cunucu.* The rough road was infamous for causing flat tires and it had been improved little. Across the expanse of the *cucunu,* thorny scrub and lonely cacti dotted the hilly interior; sparse vegetation huddled in refuge on the lee side of a few low hills. To survive the arid environment, the leaves of xerophytes sprouted hairs to reflect burning sun and deflect the wind. Across the landscape, their silvery sheen threw back bright light. There was little soil cover anywhere because of wind, dry climate, and lack of vegetation—a self-perpetuating cycle. She knew the wind-beaten east coast of the island was even more barren. She passed by Mt. Hooiberg, the island's best-known landmark, a lonely bump on the landscape, then her smile broadened at a common sight. A small goat, sure of foot, balanced in the wind-swept branches of a stubby divi-divi tree where it pulled at the tree's tough leaves, pausing to survey its domain. She passed a man grasping the bridle of a horse, reminded of the deadly tetanus spores harbored in the Aruba environment.

As she drove, Alissia considered the disparaging comments of her office colleagues. Their remarks had cracked fissures of doubt into her vivid memories of this place. Now, scanning the stark interior landscape of the island, she admitted that she did not really see its harshness because she filtered reality through the lens of subjective experience and memory. She tried to observe with the eyes of an outsider, seeking a more objective focus. It seemed clear that, if one thought about it, unalterable factors of geography and climate did play an important part in how the history of this place evolved. Some were desirable, others not. For the first time, she perceived the barren cunucu as uninviting and the realization made her start. *Have I been deluding myself?* She flinched at the question. *Is my paradise something I made up? A fairy tale? Was it how I coped?* She had never before considered any negatives to the *cunucu.* It had always felt like a familiar old friend. She pulled over as far as she could to the side of the narrow road and stopped. The car blocked half of the right lane, but it didn't matter because there was little traffic on this lonely route. She drank from the bottle of water she had brought with her. *If a person had no connection here, their perception would be different from mine,* she thought. *This is a parched, harsh landscape.* For a few minutes she did nothing. Then it occurred to her that the limitations of this place did not perforce cancel out all of the positives she had lived. The thought brought her solace, but broadened her task. She had to face not only her personal torments on this trek, she also had to comprehend how experiences so real to her meshed with unalterable facts. She was missing pieces to the puzzle to put together the full picture. She pulled back onto the road and drove on, thinking of the notebook.

> July 26, 1930. Lago is hiring men from all over the world to work. We hear all kinds of languages and accents. Our latest "foreigner" is a man everyone calls Tex. Gus says he knows a lot. From what I've seen of him, he has quite a sense of humor--and quite an accent, too. I wonder how some people can understand him. He came to the house and he and Gus were talking about the oil boom here. The world started getting really hungry for oil in the early 1900s, he

> said. That's not so long ago. Then there was the big discovery of oil at Lake Maracaibo. People say Aruba was always a humble, sleepy place. Well, all the oil activity is sure waking it up! The refinery will be a big operation. I wonder what the future will bring to such a little place that will refine so much oil. There is a lot going on in this very small area next to Sint Nicolaas.

Alissia gazed out over the *cucunu.* A few lonely, solitary houses dotted this interior landscape. Arubans had always favored the sea. By preference they built their dwellings along the protected, downwind side of the island, near the natural anchorages provided by the reef. On the lee shore plant life was densest where the *rooi,* the dry riverbeds, widened at their mouth, their *boca.* The *boca* filled with brackish water where mangroves flourished and sea birds flocked.

As the interior road veered to more closely parallel the coast, Alissia skirted the little town of Sint Nicolaas. *What will I find in the Colony? And who?* she wondered. *How will things have changed?* The major exodus from the Colony finished in the early 1950s. Was anyone she knew still there? Or anyone who knew her family? It would be wonderful to find Dr. Ritsema and his wife, Rika, her mother's good friend. She really wanted to see Rika. And could she find Tex? She remembered him well. He was entertaining—and competent, her father always said. And what about her playmate. What about Eddie?

Alissia smiled, but with the thought of Eddie came the memory of Eddie's father. Her face closed. Although she wanted news of her constant childhood companion, at the thought of his father her shoulders pulled up to her ears in defense. She forced them back down but then stiffened as the unbidden and foreboding presence of Máximo invaded her thoughts. Something told her that Máximo was the key to the very darkest of all the secrets. But there was worse. There was Red. If Red were here, on her knees she would beg that wonderful man's forgiveness--but if Red were here, Alissia knew she wouldn't *need* to be forgiven.

Alissia passed the refinery. She drew close to the Colony and stiffened with apprehension. All of the shadowy forms in her mind that she had been suppressing loomed back up. She felt their menace. She willed her taut shoulders to relax and forced her fists to loosen their clench on the steering wheel. Then, steadying the wheel with one hand, she contorted to reach up behind her back with the other hand to finger a shoulder blade. She regained composure. She took a deep breath and held it as she entered the Colony enclave through the open gate. She was back. But first, to truly re-immerse herself in this world, to quell the feelings that unsettled her, Alissia had to go to the sea.

CHAPTER 14
LAGOONS AND TINFOIL

Supine at Baby Lagoon, Alissia lazed on the fine, rosy sand of Pink Beach. The trade wind caressed her skin. No other human being was in sight. Wavelets lapped in gentle rhythm as the sun warmed her body while, overhead, flying and free, gulls called out their cacophonous complaints. For a time, she lay stretched out like the trunk of a coconut tree. Finally stirring, she rolled over and then again over into the warm water of the lagoon, returning to the familiar briny water from whence, some infinity ago, she came. Immersed in the water all her tension faded. Nowhere else could she have been a child in this specific wonderworld. Memory twined bright-colored strands of kids' capers into the rope of the serious matters she had come to explore. Who would have thought that in such a protected place her whims as a child would have led her to observe what she now needed to understand, that caprice could have snarled her in damnatory situations for which she would have to pay a price? The wind sighed sober thoughts, rousing her from her selective reverie and the embrace of warm water. She sat up. *It's time to visit the Colony*, she thought. *It's time for me to be serious.* She had mixed feelings. Although she hoped that the Colony streets and bungalows would stimulate recall of details long blocked from memory, apprehension chilled her.

Alissia left the comforting embrace of the lagoon but did not stop at any of the bungalows. Instead, she bypassed them and drove directly to the far side of the Colony to the east gate of the refinery. There she sat in the car and inhaled the plant's familiar, chemical smell. The pungent odor penetrated to the base of her brain and swept her back in time. It reminded her of what she knew.

She pictured the steady trade wind billowing out ships' sails, driving the vessels onward. Discovery of Aruba in 1499 by the Spanish ripped it out of the Stone Age through which it had floated for untold eons. It was not until 1928, when Lago began construction of the refinery, that the sudden injection of American capital into Aruba's small world fueled an explosion of real growth. The advent of oil generated fast, significant change. It brought an abrupt influx of people in the 1930s and '40s, first for construction, then for refining. The arrival of so many newcomers at once was too much for sparse local resources. Lago, "The Company" as it was called, built a community of bungalows adjacent to the refinery for housing.

For a while, Alissia just sat by the gate, suspended in memory. Through the car's open windows, the insistent breeze blew over her. An image of Tex came to her. He had worked in the refinery when her father was still a boy. Later, Alissia's father followed Tex and his own father to work at the plant. At some point, it became customary for men who had just finished the eight-to-four day-shift to regularly gather at the Saxton bungalow. They invited two new men whom Lago had just hired. There was a welcome bonus to this—newcomers gave the group a good pretext to retell the stories they never seemed to tire of recounting. The men would all hang out together in the afternoon shade of the back patio, talking, laughing, drinking Heineken or Coke. Whenever Tex told one of his many stories, he commanded the group's attention. *His stories commanded mine, too,* she reflected. *I learned very early how to hide to eavesdrop on conversations.* She recalled one afternoon and smiled.

Alissia had snuck close enough to hear the men who had gathered that day. Hot and sticky, she hunched down in bushes of pink hibiscus and red starflower plants in the lee of the bungalow where the fierce rays of the afternoon sun beat down and the wind barely moved leaves. Sweat beads formed on her back and tickled as they slid down to her waist.

"We had more guys than bungalows," Tex drawled. "Then the wives and families started coming. When Mexico nationalized oil in '38, Standard Oil had some good guys in Veracruz they had to find work for. They sent us a bunch. That made the housing shortage we had then even worse." He shook his head. "Lago was building bungalows fast as they could crank 'em out. Just built 'em on top of that grey coral with a scraggy cactus sticking up here and there. At one point, they crammed sixteen guys into a single bungalow. They worked different shifts so the men would just sleep in any empty bed. The Company couldn't build bungalows fast enough, so they started putting people in what they called 'vacation houses.'"

Alissia's mother, who had come out with more cold beer and Cokes, exclaimed, incredulous, "Vacation houses! Here?"

Tex laughed. "Yup. Fancy name. Means the occupants were on vacation. I finally married my Texas gal and got her here. Would you believe? We lived in five different houses in a row while people were on vacation. Then, no house. I had built me a little boat shed on Roger's Beach and we snuck down there to live. Didn't have nuthin."

"You had to camp on Roger's Beach?" exclaimed Stass. "What did people say?"

"Everybody kinda looked the other way. We hauled jugs of drinking water and cooked over a fire. Never knew a guy could brush his teeth, take a bath and wash clothes in just salt water. Didn't hurt us none." Tex looked at Stass. "Know what the greatest invention was those days?"

Her dad replied no. He made a winding motion with one hand for Tex to elaborate.

"Tinfoil. We just wrapped stuff in it and tossed it on the fire. Food was great and no dishwashing." He thought a moment. "At first, I was feeling kinda sorry for myself, like people had abandoned us. But, truth is, I never felt so free. A guy don't need much." Tex paused. "We used to walk naked under the stars. We slept skin pressed to warm skin. We was almost sorry when we got us a bungalow." He stopped an instant, then continued. "I lost Betty to lockjaw. She cut herself bad trying to wrestle a coconut with a machete." He shrugged, as if to shake off the memory.

The memory of Tex's description of living on the beach rekindled Alissia's euphoria in the life of physical freedom she had lived here and she wallowed, relaxed, drifting in thoughts of it. She had frisked and probed like a wild goat. Her mission in life then was to circumvent constraint and explore her surroundings, unfettered, always with bare feet. That and to escape into her world of books. She tended to chores; she was respectful; she became crafty at dodging adult attention. She had learned well how to guard her freedom.

But tension began to creep into her luminous musings and she felt her neck tighten. There were two sides to life here. She thought back to Sunday afternoon gatherings, sometimes at her family's bungalow, sometimes across the street at Miss Cynthia's—she always called Eddie's mother Miss Cynthia. She and Eddie would hang out while their parents and sometimes other adults lazed and talked to the tinkle of ice in glasses and *aaahs* of satisfaction at a draught of cold beer. With the sensitive antennae of children, she and Eddie could always detect a mood change. It stopped them stone still. They listened to voices become low and dense whenever someone used the word "attack" or "German" or "war." There had been explosions and fire and death by the refinery, the adults said. She and Eddie always would stop what they were doing and look knowingly at each other when they heard the key word "sonuvabitch." It signaled the shift to a sudden anger that overpowered the adults' sadness.

"There had to be a spy," they heard, and the two children would look at each other with wide eyes. "I think they're still looking for him," Eddie would whisper. The contagious anguish of those tense adult conversations still tied the muscles of Alissia's back into knots. Somehow it all fueled her current loss of control—her own explosions.

CHAPTER 15
FAMINE TO FUEL

Alissia still sat at the refinery gate, pensive. *How do I unravel the reality of this insular world? It's the basis of my being, part of who I am. If I don't know who I really am, how can I know what I really want--or what I need? Where am I going? The detailed plan I have drawn up for my life is useless if I don't know where I should be going.*

The past held both comforting and distressing answers. She examined her perceptions of the island itself. What motivated men and families to move here, to a place so obscure and foreign? Information about the island was even more difficult to come by in those days than it was now. Obviously, people came for work. But how did they perceive their life here? Were there facets of paradise for them? Or did they smack their foreheads in dismay and say they were lost in a desert of cactus and goats? If she could understand what the island meant to some of them, maybe it would help answer her own questions.

Thinking back to people she had known here, Máximo, Red and Tex stood out. *Tex's easy drawl and laid-back manner might have fooled a person who didn't know him,* she thought. Her father always said "that guy really knows his stuff." Once she heard him ask Tex to tell the newcomers what brought him to Aruba.

"I was working in Maracaibo, over in Venezuela, when I saw that ad. It said Lago Oil & Transport was looking for workers for Aruba with an eighteen-month contract. That was 1929. They was even offering 30 days paid vacation plus 10 days travel. Paid vacation. Can you imagine? I hopped me the first fishing boat to Aruba I could find. Seventeen miles ain't far. Just walked in and told Lago, 'I'm reporting for work.' They was kinda surprised when I showed up like that, but they hired me on the spot. I had that Maracaibo experience and I could start pronto. I think they woulda hired me if I had two heads, long as I had two hands. They was begging for men to move to a place no one ever heard of."

Stass reflected a moment. "My family came the same year," he said. "I was ten. Then Nessa's parents brought their two kids about year later, when Nessa was six. I think Gil Williams's family got here the same time as Nessa." He rubbed his chin. "Tex, what was Lago paying then, do you remember?"

"$185 U.S. dollars a month. And get this. I got free laundry and medical. Pretty sweet for them days."

It had apparently all started when Lago Oil & Transport Company sent Captain Robert Roberts out to find a good location to store Maracaibo oil for shipment. The story was that, when Roberts finally saw Sint Nicolaas bay in Aruba, he shouted, "This is it! And I love that wind." The company soon realized that it made sense to refine crude in the same place they stored it, so in 1929, on an insignificant island near the mouth of Venezuela's Lake Maracaibo, on the east side of rough-and-tumble Sint Nicolaas, Lago began work with a spurt of activity that startled local man and beast. Abrupt change was thrust on sleepy Aruba.

The trade wind brought consistent relief to what would otherwise have been an uncomfortably hot climate, but it could not relieve Aruba's historic, recurrent famines that twisted hollow bellies into knots and shrank chests into ribbed washboards. Then came oil. When Lago brought in an international potpourri of people to work in a place not to be found on most maps, the company also hired and trained Aruban workers. Into harsh island reality the refinery injected a gush of welcome money. Money could purchase food from the boats that came to Oranjestad. Lago created a spate of jobs during the Depression when men were desperate for work everywhere. At the operation's peak, little Sint Nicolaas harbor came to rank among the world's highest in shipping tonnage. Lago refinery production grew to be the largest in the world. Heady times had arrived. But, as Alissia knew, time and circumstance kept pouring volatile factors into a simmering cauldron, a dangerous mix that finally boiled up and over. It spilled through distance and time into the present.

CHAPTER 16
PUSH FOR PRODUCTION

Sitting in the car by the refinery gate, Alissia read in the notebook.

September 12, 1930. Lago still needs more labor. Gus says they are hiring unskilled Arubans. They teach basic jobs to some. Others just fetch and carry. The Arubans usually walk in from wherever they live and camp around Sint Nicolaas near the refinery. They have to come a long way on foot, so most only go home on their day off. Each man has a hammock and a bag of corn meal. They fish every day on off hours and eat together in the evening. They always fix the same thing: *pisca y funchi.* That's fried fish with a stiff cornmeal mush. It's the staple diet here.

The only thing one man does is carry around drinking water to men working in the refinery. He gets 1½ Netherland Antilles Florins per week. And every evening at sunset, I see a man ride a burro to the lighthouse at Ceru Colorado. He climbs up and lights the beacon. Gus says the beacon is fueled by kerosene. He also says that the man's burro is a luxury. I wonder where he keeps the animal.

At the thought of the lighthouse, tranquility enfolded Alissia. At night its beacon rotated 360°, around every point of the compass. When her dad was working, her mom would loosely schedule the evening meal and, on those evenings, Alissia would slip out of the bungalow at dusk and climb to her perch in the Seagrape tree. Darkness would thicken and she would lean back, shifting around to press the length of her spine against the tree's trunk. The beacon turned steadily around and around, projecting a shaft of light that passed over the bungalows, swiping across roofs at regular intervals during all the night hours. *I liked seeing that narrow river of light. It seemed to signal to us that all was in good order in the Colony, all was well.* The reliability of the ritual had always comforted her, a trustworthy and steady counterpoint to erratic bursts of dissonant mood in the Saxton household.

Alissia now needed to deal with the eruptions of emotion that threatened to destroy her life. She felt safe in the small, tranquil memory niche of the beacon and it occurred to her that she might be able to shine it on her current nightmares to disperse them. And maybe, when destructive turmoil engulfed her, she could picture and follow that beam of light to a tranquil, safe place in her head.

The afternoon back-patio ritual at the Saxton bungalow had also reassured her with its constancy. But, best of all, it was a rich source of unedited information to which she would not otherwise have been privy. She laid down the notebook and recalled a particular day. The usual covey of men discussed labor while Alissia, also as usual, cached herself nearby out of sight.

To keep Tex's stories flowing, the men threw in questions. Tex elaborated. "The Company was needing a lot of labor in the '30s, so this guy in personnel got a bright idea. He went to scout the Guajira peninsula because it's so close--right on the west side of Maracaibo. He found him some Wayuu Indians and brought back fifteen men and three women. The minute them *indios* got off the boat they scattered every which-way like *cucarachas.* The guy sure was mad. Took a week to round 'em all up, so the Company had them all sleep near the refinery to keep track of them. The women cooked food over an outside fire." To report to work, Tex said, the men walked in single file. "Oldest guy first. They always walked oldest to youngest."

The *indios* only spoke Waiyuunaiki except for the elder, who spoke some Spanish. "Personnel told their supervisor to talk to 'em in Spanish," said Tex. "I heard him. He started with, 'Hand me el wrencho to use on this here valvo.' Hell, that ain't even Texas Spanish. Didn't work, neither." Tex explained that Personnel got a real interpreter. The supervisor spoke in English, the interpreter translated into Spanish, and the elder re-translated into Waiyuunaiki. "But, problem was," said Tex, "they didn't have words for stuff they never seen." He shook his head. "They didn't know what a wheelbarrow was. And excepting for a hammer, we had to teach them how to use tools. But they was one big problem right away. The *indios* thought they could come to work when they felt like it. I figured there was one way to get'em to show up when they were sposed to. I told the supervisor to give two Lucky Strike cigarettes to each guy who came on time. Worked like magic." He grinned, then sobered. "Man, we never knew the hell all our hard work in the refinery was going to bring down on us." Tex seemed to lose his story in some dark place, but then came back.

"The Company needed to put up poles for power lines. Taught the *indios* to use post-hole diggers. They fell in love." He laughed. "Supervisor couldn't get'em to quit at the end of the day. He'd holler 'Stop, stop!' Then he'd wave his arms and shoo them away. 'Go on. Go. Git.'" In two weeks, the job was completed, but the Wayuu still wanted to set poles. "They wanted to put 'em up free-standin in any direction. Not even in a line," said Tex.

One day the *indios* converged on the supervisor and the elder informed him that it was time to go.

The Lago supervisor was confused. It was mid-morning. "Go? Go where?" he asked the elder *indio*. "To Sint Nicolaas?"

"No. To Colombia."

"Colombia!" The man smacked his forehead. "Why?"

"We go now."

The small band pressed forward and chorused unintelligible comments that they reinforced with gestures and intonation that made their urgency clear. It was planting time, said the elder. No more work here. At home the rains would start. They needed to leave immediately.

"They all kept hollering," said Tex. He waved his arms around. "Pronto, pronto!" he said, imitating the Waiyuunaikis' excitement. "Lago shipped them back in a big hurry. The Company sure crossed that place for workers off their list."

He continued. "Lago completed construction and lost no time putting the refinery on stream. The Company pressed hard for production and everyone cheered the first cargo of gasoline that was shipped. It went south to Rio de Janeiro. By 1934 the Company was shipping as far as the Suez Canal and Dakar."

Alissia well remembered the refinery men's focus on keeping fuel production up. They worked hard and they made sure that all the labor around them did the same. Sometimes, when he was home for dinner, her father commented on work at the table.

One particular evening, Stass was unusually quiet. Alissia and her mother had started on their dessert of fried plantain with sugar as her father forked into the last serving of lemon meringue pie. He seemed to reflect. Then, with no preamble, he slapped his hand down on the table so hard that the plates and glasses jumped. "Our guys didn't know what they'd get for busting their behinds to supply fuel to the Allies." Stass's face closed. "We, ah..."

He cleared his throat. "We didn't know—" His voice was low and thick. "We didn't know that war would cost us so damned many men!" Alissia put down her fork and sat very still. She couldn't tell whether her dad was angry or sad. She did not dare ask.

In retrospect, it seemed to Alissia that just working harder and harder to resolve a situation could be either a cure or a kill. It was what she was doing now. *Maybe there's another way to fix things.*

CHAPTER 17
WATER

Alissia held her head with both hands, staring at the refinery gate. She slumped. *How do I deal with this? It's always there.* She clenched her teeth. After a while she pulled herself up straight and drew in a long, slow breath, making the intake last so long she felt she would burst. Then, releasing it slowly in a thin, long whisper, a bizarre realization struck her. *It was learned. I learned to live the catastrophe from my family. It's crazy. I find myself believing I was actually there, but it happened just before I was born.* She shook her head. *And there are the other things. What I actually did live. I have to face them all. I can't just keep running, running in any direction to escape.* She sat very still. Then she squared her shoulders. *I'm making progress, she told herself. I came back and now it's time to make myself go to the bungalows. First, though--first, I'll go to Big Lagoon.*

Alissia stood on the cliff that looked out over Big Lagoon and stretched her arms up toward the clear, blue sky. The scene exalted her. She reveled in its vista of untamed beauty. Exotic driftwood shapes and shells always washed up on the little beach, an ever-changing sculpture garden. The free-soaring gulls cried out raucous improvisations to the measured beat of small lapping waves. The wind blew her hair out in a horizontal stream like it had shaped the branches of the one-sided divi-divi trees. She remembered trotting off from the bungalow in bare feet, carrying a towel under one arm. Here was where she graduated from dog-paddler to strong swimmer. It meant she would be allowed to go off swimming by herself--she had started her struggle early. Even as a little kid, she was always finagling, always trying to justify more freedom. *In addition, the lagoons were a regular fix for me when I couldn't handle the tension in our house. And if that didn't work, I could fly in my head. Flying was always a sure remedy.*

Alissia walked closer to the edge of the short, grey cliff that bordered the lagoon and looked down at two small docks, her gaze then traveling over the lagoon and out to the sea. Then she began to thread her way from foothold to foothold down the cliff, descending to the narrow strip of sand at its foot. A forgotten shirt lay there. Someone would eventually reclaim it, she supposed. She looked around and, seeing no one, she slipped off her clothes and waded into the water in her scanty underwear. She took off in a strong overhand crawl and swam out between the T-dock and the diving dock. She targeted an anchored raft inside the reef where it sheltered from the open sea. She raised her head a few times to correct direction. When she reached the raft, she pulled herself up onto its weathered wooden deck, some twenty feet square.

Arms around bent knees, Alissia sat and looked back over the lagoon toward the beach. A familiar, rhythmic rocking of the platform cradled her and she listened to the soft sound of water pulsing against the raft's side. She inhaled and exhaled several times, long, slow breaths, consciously sending thoughts into open space and drawing in the smell of salt water. Solitude, sky, sea, and sound suspended her sense of time. She thought of her mother, Nessa, and how much she missed her. She wished she had known her Uncle Ruddy, named Rudyard after Grandma G's favorite writer, Rudyard Kipling, Alissia's mother had told her. Unbidden, others she had known came parading back. Red first brought nostalgia, then acute pain. Then visions of Máximo and Gil muscled in and she stood up abruptly.

She dove into the water. With strong, fast strokes she swam several laps to the beach and back. She finally ended at the diving dock, her chest puffing with the exertion. She pulled her clothes back on over her wet undergarments and climbed wooden rungs up ten feet to her familiar aerie on a small diving platform where she stretched out full length. Face down, she lay still. She cradled her head on folded arms to draw in just that specific moment with every one of her senses. The shadow of a traveling cloud blew over her. It blocked the warmth of the sun and filled the moment's diaphanous brightness with dark thoughts that fed self-doubt. Tom, her problems at work. With a brusque movement of both shoulders, she shook off the pall. She looked across the turquoise of the lagoon to the saturated blue of the sea for comfort. On this return to her island, she had been indulging herself in only the beauty of the place and pleasing memories. She had to remember her mission because her time here was short. Lago had brought in great, abrupt change; she and her family had been part of that new era. Questions flowed into her head and she voiced them to the faithful wind as if seeking answers. The wind ruffled her hair and seemed to murmur its response. Maybe she had known, or had heard and forgotten, the fragments of information that vied for her attention.

In the nineteenth century Aruba's population was listed as 1700 people, increasing to some 9,600 by the early 1900s. By the 1930s, the Lago refinery had over 1700 men on its payroll and various contractors employed some 500 more. The Lago Colony was full, Sint Nicolaas exploded with refinery workers and island population hit 17,000. All sought to better their lives. So many people pouring in overwhelmed resources around the refinery and the island's limited water supply, always of concern, suffered a critical shortage. Water that locals categorized as potable was, at best, suspect in quality. Lago urgently needed to provide "fresh" water to all the bungalows the Company constructed to house employees and their families.

For as long as she could remember, Alissia had heard people discuss Aruba's water. They said that water in Aruba was as precious as oil and both were the frequent subjects of serious conversation. Alissia's grandmother took early note of the importance of water.

September 1, 1930. Fresh water is a big concern here. It either rains little or less. The whole place is always thirsty. 1912 and 1913—two years in a row—and then 1915 and 1917, were terrible drought years I am told. They say that the droughts always caused malnutrition here. Arubans couldn't grow even their usual poor crops then. Malnutrition is bad enough, but potable water is an even bigger problem, even now. A lot of the locals' drinking water comes from *tankis.* The *tankis* are shallow ponds where water pools if it rains. At best, it's stagnant, and both people and animals use them. Gus took me to see some and the smell made me gag. He says that at the bottom they have two feet of mud mixed with manure. During the driest seasons, *tankis* spread intestinal diseases. Arubans can get drinking water from wells, but there aren't very many wells and they are widely scattered. Besides, the water in the wells is not really fresh. It's brackish.

The young doctor I met, Dr. Ritsema, told me that, for centuries, famine during the worst droughts has caused scurvy on the island. I never knew scurvy was so awful. He said the body tissues are starving and try to feed on the person's ruptured blood vessels. Death is painful and horrible.

I'm lucky I lived here during the era of oil, not famine, thought Alissia. *And lucky I survived the drinking water.*

To build the refinery and adjacent housing, Lago had negotiated with the Dutch for what was called the Concession Area where the Company was responsible for providing everything needed. To provide water for housing—to each Colony bungalow--Lago ran an organized system of pipes above ground. Not a drop of potable water could be wasted, so narrow designated pipes ran drinking water to kitchen sinks only. The bulk of the pipe system carried brackish water for all other household use. Even brackish water had to be used sparingly.

Sitting at the top of the diving tower, Alissia considered the Colony's water supply. She loved the system of horizontal pipes that Lago put in between the rows of bungalows. For her, they had served a special purpose. She adopted the largest fat pipes as her personal travel route around the Colony. Barefooted as always, off-street and unobtrusive, she walked and ran along them, just above razor-edged coral and patches of needle-sharp cactus and burrs. She usually traveled the pipes alone, but often she ran them with Eddie. She knew that although Lago supplied water to the Colony, the Company did not supply water to Sint Nicolaas. She had once heard Tex say that Sint Nicolaas was outside the Lago Concession Area; water there was the sole purview of the Dutch.

Everyone who knew Tex knew that he took as much interest in water as he did oil. Maybe that was because he came from dry West Texas. To supply sufficient water to the Colony and to the refinery for operation, Lago could not take water from the precious wells of Arubans, nor were the filthy local *tankis* that swarmed with intestinal parasites a viable source. The Company could not rely on rain, either. Although squalls sometimes hit the island, they came infrequently, bringing only brief showers. As the refinery and Colony grew, Lago had to quickly find an adequate source for fresh water. Tex latched on to the experts brought to the island to consult.

"I'm stickin to them close as a tick on a hound dog," he said. "There's what's called a Kleinschmidt compression still. But the Dutch went for distillation of sea water. Distillation is the oldest and most common method of desalination in the world. And we sure got plenty of sea water."

He had once explained that, in 1928, the Dutch set up a land-based desalination plant in Curaçao with good results. In 1932, they built a similar plant in Aruba near Savaneta and Aruba then boasted one of the largest and most significant desalination plant operations in the world. When fresh water was piped seven miles from the desalination plant to nearby Sint Nicolaas (where only brackish water had ever been available), many residents there tasted fresh, sweet water for the first time in their lives. But the Dutch desalination plant did not supply the Colony. Alissia would find it hard to believe the solution that Lago finally adopted if she herself didn't knew it to be true.

Lago decided the desalination process was too expensive. Seeking an alternative, someone in the Company came up with an idea. The Company could bring in water on the tanker ships that went to unload oil on the East coast of the United States. "After all, they come back empty. Might as well use them, since they're coming back here anyway," someone said. The ships' oil tanks were purportedly steamed out before being filled to bring "fresh" water on their return trip. On examination, Tex saw that the tanks used to carry water on the S/S Crampton Anderson had been painted inside with what looked like red lead paint. He figured that's probably what it was. Steamed out or not, the tanker ships circulated perpetually in an environment of petroleum and its products. It would be impossible to rid the ships of all residue of oil and fuel.

Tex pressed his concerns about the quality of water to the Company. The matter would be "looked into" was the grave reply. Someone, somewhere, was supposed to examine the potability of the "tanker" water sometime, but all attention remained focused on refining.

Reminiscing about her childhood here in the 1940s, Alissia recalled how they all used to eye basins of "imported" water, purportedly fresh, that happened to be left sitting around in bungalows. Adults would point out the pretty, iridescent rainbow sheen that coated the water's surface--floating whorls of toxic heavy metals. Alissia shook her head. *That was what we all drank. It's a miracle I'm still alive.*

She remembered well the specific hierarchy for water piped to the bungalows. Salt water flushed toilets. Brackish water, the next step up, served for showers and cleaning. At the top of the ladder was the precious, imported, so-called fresh water for the domain of the kitchen, reserved for drinking and cooking only. For special occasions, Alissia's mother would bootleg a pitcher of the precious, potable, non-brackish water from kitchen to shower. There, after washing her hair, Nessa would indulge in a final rinse with the Grand Reserve liquid to restore softness and sheen to her tresses. Eddie's mom, Miss Cynthia, who lived across the street, did the same. Even so, her mother always said that rain water was best. When there was an afternoon squall, her mother and Miss Cynthia would scurry around outside with buckets and basins to capture the rain water that they saved to rinse their hair.

In addition to its use for showers and cleaning, the brackish water that was piped to the bungalows was also used to water outdoor plants and scraggy lawns. Alissia saw herself waving a hose to spew brackish water over the spindly St. Augustine grass in the yard of their bungalow, one of her chores. The tough runners of grass seemed to tolerate the semi-salty water fairly well, as did the hardy, flowering Caribbean plants that her mother planted in flower beds. Coconut and banana trees didn't seem to mind brackish water at all. However, Colony residents who suffered from prickly heat did not fare as well. They complained that bathing in brackish water exacerbated the itchy heat rash and it drove them crazy. *Brackish never bothered me,* thought Alissia. *When we were out running around on our many forays, when we were thirsty, Eddie and I used to drink the stuff from any garden hose we could find in any yard. We certainly couldn't be bothered to go back to our bungalows to get a drink of water in the kitchen.*

When Tex had pursued interest in the Colony's water supply, he found that the main source for the brackish water used in the Colony was the Mangel Cora well located in a system of caves and tunnels that ran under the bungalows from Baby Lagoon to the Ceru Colorado lighthouse, an off-limits labyrinth which often proved too tempting to some. In the 1930s, Colony residents were accustomed to the sight and sound of windmills that turned and creaked as they pumped water from Mangel Cora. But despite real concern over drinking water transported by oil tankers versus brackish water, with a straight face Tex would insist to his back-patio buddies that "brackish is OK because a scotch and water made with brackish water tastes better anyways. Has more character."

Stass's classic response was that, given the amount of scotch Tex poured himself, the brackish water he put in his drinks was inconsequential. This conclusion always drew general approval and laughter from the group. "Tex, if you ever do notice the brackish water, you won't give a darn after that first stiff drink."

Thinking of water, Alissia's thoughts streamed back into the Mangel Cora labyrinth of caves that ran under the Colony. The complex, dark maze of tunnels and deep holes was strictly off-limits to Alissia and Eddie. She well recalled the underground morass of twists and turns and a little shudder ran down her spine.

Alissia brought her thoughts back to her present task. She looked up. Towering cumulonimbus clouds had formed, a good omen in this arid place. February to May was the driest period; the misnamed rainy season came from October to January. Rain in Aruba usually fell late at night and fled before dawn. A daytime shower would be a welcome event. *But at least Aruba doesn't get hurricanes,* she thought. *The more common effect of those raging storms is to becalm the placid island. They suck up the trade winds to add to their traveling fury. The surface of the lagoons turns to glass.* She thought she smelled a squall building in the air and her thoughts turned back to her quest here. She still had crucial answers to wrest from this place. The clouds loosed a few fat, scattered drops. Large and warm, a handful splashed on her face and arms--just enough to make her wish for more.

She climbed down from the tower and clambered up the cliff to the street. She walked along the asphalt pavement of the One Hundred Row that bordered Big Lagoon and saw herself on her way to play. In bare feet, above sharp coral, happy in her freedom to roam, a small girl ran the pipelines that still crisscrossed the Colony. More often than not, rather than heading off along those pipes just to play, she knew that the busy, nosy little kid she pictured had set off on missions to pry into affairs that people thought they had kept quite private. Uncomfortable questions about things she witnessed on these forays nagged at her, and then thoughts of her job and Tom began to fill her head.

She felt raindrops plop on her skin as they began to fall. Rain. Fresh water, always important in Aruba.

CHAPTER 18
A BIG PROBLEM

That night, Stass appeared more fatigued than usual. At the dinner table, he began to rant about the fiasco of the day at the refinery.

Red had come to him at a dead run. "We have a big problem!" Face scarlet and breathing hard, Red mopped sweat out of his eyes.

Stass jerked to full attention. "What happened?"

"The water from the faucet in Number 3 Lab is running blue."

"Kee-rist." Stass shook his head. "We don't have time for this with the volume of oil we're processing. We gotta get those lines purged. Put Gil on it."

"I guess he can handle it. He only has to turn faucets and watch water run," replied Red.

Stass nodded. "I'll ask Tex what happened. He'll know or find out who's responsible. He's a damn bloodhound."

Everyone knew that Tex took special interest in the subject of fresh water. He once declared, "I was born in a drought in the middle of a dusty oil patch in West Texas. Must be half mustang and half buzzard."

Red delivered the best response: "I can see ye take after the buzzard."

Faced with the contamination problem, Tex seized the bit and galloped with it. The blue signaled that the caustic soda—lye—used in refining petroleum had been mixed in with the plant's precious potable water. A few days before, 50,000 gallons of drinking water had been unloaded from one of the tankers that brought fresh water coming in and took fuel going out. Someone had left a valve open that everyone knew had to be closed. It didn't take Tex long to track down the culprit: Gil Williams. Tex found Stass and took him aside. "He screws up everything he touches. Anything to do with work, that is," Tex said quietly.

Stass shook his head. "I know. He's been working here since high school, same as me. He should know better. And now we've got him monitoring the flushing for the problem he caused. Shit. I'll tell Red to keep close watch."

"I will handle it," Red snapped. "He probably turned the bloody valve on instead of making sure it was off." The easy-going Scot could flip from sociable *chuchubi* into sharp-eyed raptor in an instant.

"We need to take care of this mess," Stass said. "Let's try not to show him up to everyone like the total idiot he can be."

Red honed in on Gil like a Shoco owl on prey. He would not let Gil cause them all more trouble, at least not with this mess.

When Red approached Gil, the man visibly started, then turned away. Red reined in his temper. Gil knew when he had screwed things up. It would not help to further shame him.

"Keep a close watch for us, will ye, Gil? It's important. Keep me posted on how ye think it's clearing."

Gil nodded, but did not speak.

Before dinner that evening, eyes round and mouth hanging open, Alissia watched Gil Williams savage the hibiscus in his garden. He slashed at them savagely with a long stick, attacking and shredding the pretty, defenseless blooms. It was one more upsetting image of Gil that at times, without warning, would creep into Alissia's conscious thought.

It had taken three days for the contaminated drinking water in the refinery to lose its blue tinge and to run clear. At the dinner table that evening, Stass had talked about the water mix-up.

"What a damn waste," he said, "but at least we didn't lose anybody to that jackass mistake. It could have killed people. Good thing Red caught it right away. We've got some darned sharp guys." Alissia watched him nod his approval. There was a lull and he seemed to relax.

"Dad, guess what," said Alissia.

Stass looked up, surprised at the interjection. "What?" he said.

"In school today, I was first in the spelling contest," she announced. She waited.

Stass considered her, then responded. "How many were in the class? One?" He left the table.

That night, instead of falling into her usual, instant sleep, Alissia lay awake. She ached with the unsated need to feel good enough, to feel wanted. The tropical night embraced her with tenderness and she listened with quiet melancholy to the soughing of the wind. Through the window's louvers, dark palm fronds waved their consolation and the moon cast long and shivering shadows outside under the divi-divi trees. Huddled on a branch in a nearby flamboyant tree, a *chuchubi* bird briefly burbled its own dreams of gratification, then quieted. Alissia, too, finally slept.

CHAPTER 19
FLOWER BY FLOWER

Alissia's family had left the island in 1952. Now, she returned to this place flower by flower, scent by scent and sound by sound. Skimming through memories, she explored what she knew of the 1940s, but she did not probe too deep or into corners where the shadows lurked at the edge of bright sunlight.

She drove slowly along the asphalt streets of the Colony. There was no visible activity. Bungalows sat in tidy rows at roomy intervals, but most of them looked abandoned. A thought struck her. *To outsiders, this housing must have a peculiar look.* The utilitarian, boxy structures squatted up on stubby, cement oil pots that supported them, as if the dwellings were trying to shrink up and away from the sharp, inhospitable coral surrounding them. At the top, each square pot had a shallow moat filled with black crude oil, a practical attempt to keep out scorpions, centipedes and assorted insects. The Colony's functional bungalows were a luxury, with electricity and running water. She thought of some of the houses around Sint Nicolaas—sticks, mud, thatched roof and dirt floor with kerosene for lamps. A number of refinery workers had lived in such rudimentary structures while waiting for bungalows being built in the Colony. Alissia remembers her father talking about women who shrieked at the sight of every cockroach and pest. He said that some sprayed themselves with Flit as an insect repellent, using the manual pump in the long metal arm of the yellow can. Her father would shake his head. "That's nuts. That stuff has DDT in it." At the thought of the DDT, Alissia grimaced. Her family always used Flit around their bungalow, but they never sprayed the insecticide on themselves.

She drove on, surveying the bungalows. Blocks of cement steps stood free at their front and back doors, stacks that did not touch the houses. To enter, one had to step across a two-inch open gap. Occupants always trimmed plants around the house to make sure that none touched it, thus removing paths for small pests to crawl up and in. Sometimes Alissia's mother gave her scissors and a chore. She was to go all the way around the bungalow and clip off any stray leaf or twig of a plant brazen enough to touch its side.

She slowed further to look at the place where her grandparents had lived. Their bungalow perched on the low cliff that overlooked Big Lagoon. Its appearance hadn't changed much. People always referred to the dwellings by number; streets were named by hundred row. Grandma G had lived in Bungalow 106 on the One Hundred Row.

Alissia continued slowly down the simple street—no sidewalks here. Some bungalows had low concrete walls which enclosed ever-hopeful gardens. Coaxed flowers dotted low beds with bright color and determined runners of coarse grass wove brave traces of green through gritty sand mixed with token dirt. Other yards just lay open, an invitation to wander in and out in any direction. Along the side of the street, the small blossoms of a few hardy snapdragons flashed bright smiles of color.

The bungalows were functional and pleasant, each with a detached single-car garage. They all faced downwind, looking out toward the sea and Venezuela, with no regard to whether the street lay to the front or the back of the dwelling. Screens covered glassless windows; wooden louvers inside could be closed to shield from rain and wind. Except for the number of bedrooms and bathrooms, the layout of the bungalows did not vary much.

Alissia stopped the car to consider a bungalow at random. It sat raised some eighteen inches off the ground and, as always, the trade wind blew underneath. *The wind must cool them some,* she thought. *No bungalow ever had air-conditioning.* She knew that women had always liked the oil pots for keeping out pests. She grinned. *But kids liked them best.* She remembers poking sticks or whatever came to hand into the black, viscous stuff and, with Eddie, making infamous messes. Their dabblings were most unwelcome. Sitting there, considering housing, it occurred to her that she had better find a place to stay. She would rather be in the Colony than have to drive every night to a hotel somewhere in the direction of Oranjestad. *Can I find anyone I know still here?* she wondered.

Putting the car in low gear, she moved on to where she saw a man walking with an armful of gardening tools. She stopped to speak with him through the open window.

"Hello. If you wouldn't mind, I have a question, please."

"Sure."

"Do you know if a man everyone called Tex still lives here? "

"Well, he still lives here, but he's on a trip to Venezuela right now. Don't know when he's due back."

"What about the Ritsemas?" she asked. "Dr. Ritsema."

"Oh, I used to help them with work in their yard. The doc is no longer living and his wife moved to Sint Nicolaas. She could still be teaching school there."

"Do you know where Rika—Hendrika--lives?"

"No. Your best bet is to just go ask around. If she's still there, you probably can find her."

"I'll do that. Thanks for your help."

CHAPTER 20

BUNGALOWS

Alissia wanted to see a few more places in the Colony and then she would head to Sint Nicolaas. She turned onto the 300 Row and when she came to Bungalow 362 a spurt of adrenaline stole her breath. She got out of the car and stood in the street. This was the bungalow where she had lived. She had fond memories of her solitary morning explorations and other childhood adventures. She turned to look at the bungalow across the street, her playmate's house. Eddie Williams. *But that was also where Gil Williams lived.* The smile on her face crumpled into a scowl and she dug her fingernails into her palms. Mixed feelings brawled with each other, disrupting her thoughts.

She turned back to her bungalow, which spilled over with recollections. It seemed that no one lived there now. The Saxtons always entered their bungalow through the back, from the street. She opened the tall wood gate and entered the large, covered back patio with high walls. Here is where her Dad and the refinery men gathered. Next to the patio, on the left, sat an outdoor laundry sink with a concrete washboard. She walked through the patio to the back of the bungalow and ascended the few steps to the back door. It wasn't locked. Kicking off her sandals, she entered the kitchen, large enough for a table. On bare feet she walked across the linoleum and crossed onto the polished wooden floors that extended through the house. Standing in the living room, images of the house as it was when she lived there played through her mind. In the living-room stood the Chinese bookcase, intricate figures and stories carved into its dark wood frame. The books on its shelves also told tales. On top of the bookcase, at eye level, she visualized her mother's colorful tea-sets. She went on to walk through the bedrooms with their big, walk-in closets and then through the bathrooms with showers constructed of cement over which tile was laid. She returned to the living area. She had always loved the large central dining-living space that extended across the bungalow from back to front, opening onto a big screened porch with just enough elevation to see out to the blue Caribbean.

Saving the best for last, she went out to the backyard to visit her favorite Seagrape tree. She looked up to contemplate her niche--her special, safe perch--high in its branches. *That's where I so often took refuge.* She thought a moment. *I still seek refuge— sometimes outside running, but especially when, in my head, I fly away from all problems and worries. I can escape.* She stood looking at the tree. It felt like a faithful friend. After a few moments, she proceeded to the very back of the yard to peer over the waist-high cement wall. She smiled and nodded a greeting at the familiar network of pipes that lay outside.

Alissia returned to the car. There was still the other place, nearby. *I need to face what happened. Maybe going there will help me deal with the trauma and my guilt.* She sighed. *I only have a short time left here.* With dread she left the Saxton bungalow and forced herself to drive. A few blocks away—the Colony was a small place—she again stopped, this time in front of Red's bungalow. It was here. She could not bear the sight. She had failed him. Grief strangled her. Dark memories roiled up and splashed large tears down her cheeks.

CHAPTER 21
CONNECTION

It was time to look for Rika and then she would need to find a place to stay. Alissia drove the short distance to Sint Nicolaas. The first person she asked was able to give her directions and she easily found the small and modest house. She knocked and a woman opened the door.

"Hello. *Mevrouw* Ritsema? I think I recognize you. I apologize for coming unannounced. I don't know if you remember me. My name is Alissia Saxton."

"*Mijn God*! Little Alissia. Of course. Of course, I remember. I could never forget the Saxtons." She stepped out, wrapped Alissia in a fond embrace, then held her out at arm's length by the shoulders. "How you have grown! And not *Mevrouw*, please. *Mevrouw* is too formal. Call me Rika, as when you were small." She gestured with her hand toward the open door. "*Kom binnen, kom binnen.*" She led Alissia inside. "What a wonderful surprise for to see you."

"It is wonderful for me, too," Alissia responded.

Alissia had many questions. She and Rika talked for hours. Then Alissia just sat silent.

Rika waited.

"Oh, Rika. I made myself do everything right but everything is going wrong. Like when I was a kid with my father. I could never do anything right enough then, either. What am I going to do?"

"You tell me Tom a good man is, that you have the kind of work always you wanted. Only you can say how important these things are for you."

Alissia sighed. "It seems like all my effort isn't enough. Nothing is ever enough. How high a price do I have to pay to find peace?" Alissia stood up and walked around the table a few times.

Rika listened and made no comment. She let Alissia talk.

Alissia continued. "I was too willful." She clasped her hands behind her back and stretched. Then she said it. "I was… I was a coward." She cleared her throat and said in a low voice, "I made terrible things happen." She sat back down.

Rika poured Alissia another cup of tea and waited.

"You know what I really want, Rika?"

"What is that?"

"I don't want to have to be perfect to be liked." She hesitated, then said it. "I don't want to have to earn love." She paused and then it gushed out. "I want to be totally irresponsible. I want to be carefree, like when I would slip away to just wander around outside as a kid. I want to quit my job, leave the city where I live and take off by myself. I want to escape to some beautiful warm place."

"You have that choice."

"The thought is so tempting it terrifies me." Alissia placed both hands on the table. She clenched them into fists. "It's obvious I'm not thinking straight. I came here for answers. If I don't deal with the issues that are ruining my life, I will take my problems with me wherever I go."

The two women both just sat for a while.

Then Rika floated words on the silence. "Alissia, from what you say, you have two sets of memories. I think this is confusing, yes?"

Alissia responded in a dejected tone. "Yes. Some are terrible." Then her face melted into a smile. "But others are absolutely wonderful."

"Of good memories we shall speak. Like three together at your bungalow—you, me, and your mother. Things have changed now. Your parents are gone. My Pieter is also gone. So now we shall be two together."

"Yes, two together, *Mevrouw...*" Alissia corrected herself. "Rika. Rika, I used to like it when you came for tea." She smiled. "My mother always said she had to make strong tea for you, and only the best, like the Dutch." She shifted in her chair, then glanced at her watch. "Oh, I didn't realize it was so late. It has been wonderful talking with you, but I have to go. I need to find a hotel."

"No, no. Here you must stay. I have an extra bedroom."

"I don't want to impose..."

"It is not imposition, it is pleasure," Rika quickly answered. "I welcome your company in this empty house." She paused. "*Lief*, we will talk more about these things that so trouble you."

Alissia smiled at the term of endearment. She remembered it well. *Lief.* Like a leaf on a tree. Rika was comfortable, familiar.

Rika continued. "You want to spend time in the Colony to find answers, to understand certain things. And maybe there are some things you don't want to think about, I don't know. But here you will be close. You will lose no time to drive."

"It's really good for me to be with you. I'd love to stay." Alissia's voice broke. Quietly she said, "My life is falling apart."

"Then settled it is. Bring in your things," said Rika. Then she stopped and held up a hand. "Alissia. *Lief?*" She made sure she had Alissia's attention. "I know there are things you don't want to discuss, but it will help for understanding your family if you know what your mother went through. Nessa had problems of her own. And the people you ask about—Red, Máximo. I will tell you what I know. Some things we only knew in later years, after you were gone. *Lief*, the stories are not simple. Time we must have for that. It is good you will stay with me."

That night Alissia lay in bed and thought of her mother. She had heard her father say ugly things to her and she had felt terrible when she witnessed her mother's pain. She also knew that there were some things that Nessa didn't talk about. And what about Red and Máximo? Two people could not have been more different. She had unsettling memories about them of her own that she had never understood.

CHAPTER 22

BLACK GOLD

Another splendid dawn announced the second of Alissia's five days. After breakfast, she left Rika's to prowl around the streets of the Colony. Here and there she stopped to sit and observe and think. A typical Saturday at the Saxton bungalow came to mind; those Saturdays were a source of a lot of information not intended for her ears. It must have been around 1949 and she would have been seven years old at the time. It was late afternoon. She and Eddie had gone to cavort and swim in the lagoon and afterward, at home, instead of snooping as usual, she lazed on the floor of the bungalow's screened porch, reading. A burst of laughter erupted from the murmur of men's voices on the back patio, interrupting her focus. She jumped up and ran to look through the screen door of the kitchen. Men who had just finished their shift were talking about The Wagon.

Tex was well-known early on in Aruba for what everyone affectionately called The Wagon. It was a vehicle that had been cobbled together on a chassis using front and back end parts from two different wrecked Fords, plus an assortment of pieces cannibalized from other defunct automobiles. It had no windshield and no body, boasted a motor which usually started, a steering wheel that worked, and brakes. On the back of the vehicle wooden planks had been nailed together to form a platform. It was a sight to remember.

When sniggering at some new joke about The Wagon subsided, conversation about oil resumed. Oil, war, and sensual life in paradise--inexhaustible topics which saturated the region and life in the Colony.

"Tex, how did you end up in Aruba, anyway?" asked Stass.

"I was plenty young when I came to this part of the world. Came to work in drilling fields of Maracaibo. It was the birth of a new era—the 1920s. Saw some pretty spectacular stuff."

Red interrupted with a laugh. "Not much around here as spectacular as The Wagon."

"Settle down, guys," said Stass. "Tex, tell the new guys how it all got started."

"Well, Royal Dutch Shell was an English-Dutch merger formed to compete with Standard Oil. Royal Dutch started exploring in Maracaibo early and the big boys followed them in like buzzards. It was the early 1900s. Drilling took off like crazy. They was discovery after discovery."

"Everybody wanted oil then," said Stass. "By the twenties, cars were king in the U.S. Some say it was gas-powered vehicles that won us World War I."

"The twenties kicked off the era of Black Gold," commented Red Burns.

"Yup. World was starving for fuel," agreed Tex. "Maracaibo had one of the biggest supplies of crude ever found."

Máximo Hirsch, always well-informed, spoke. "By the 1930s Venezuelan oil was so cheap that even Mexico imported it."

"Tex." Red gestured for attention. "Did ye see the famous blow-out?"

"Sure did. Happened in '22, when I just started working there. Jay-zoos Murphy! Was that a sight. You shoulda seen that mother.

Venezuelan guys was hollering *madre de dios* all over the place. Saw one fellow drop to his knees." He thought a moment. "That was Barroso No. 2. That well was 1,500 feet deep. It gushed black crude to the sky. Lasted for nine days, would ya believe? We thought it would never stop. Tore the oil derrick clean apart. Never saw nothing like it."

Máximo interjected. "By the time the blow-out was capped it had spewed almost a million barrels of oil over the countryside."

"I'm just surprised there weren't more big blow-outs," said Stass. "Maracaibo had wells everywhere."

"To compete in Maracaibo, Standard Oil bought Lago Oil & Transport," continued Tex. "Standard wanted to refine its own crude. That's how Aruba got in the picture."

Máximo Hirsch knew the area well. "The lake is big, about 130 miles by 60."

"I dinnae know that!" exclaimed Red. "We would lose Aruba in it."

"The geography is important," Máximo explained. There are miles of plains with heavy vegetation and high mountains on three sides. The basin only opens to the north, on the Caribbean, so the only way to get oil out is by sea. And that, *caballeros,* is why we all now live and work in Aruba, by the mouth of the lake." He bowed.

Stass avoided asking Máximo a question unless it was necessary and had to do with work. He was always conscious that the Colombian had a formal engineering degree, while Stass had only finished the local high school. An erratic gust of wind rattled the patio roof, making a racket. The men glanced up. Stass pulled his shoulders back and told himself, *I know that refinery better than any engineer Lago can bring in from outside. I grew up with it. I lived it.* He asked his question. "Máximo, speaking of the lake, you head up maintenance for the Mosquito Fleet. Do you know how the Mosquito Fleet got started?" In fact, Máximo intimidated most of the men by personality, education, and social polish, but they respected his many skills and competence. Everyone listened as, with apparent goodwill, he responded to Stass's request.

"Lake Maracaibo is deep enough for ocean-going oil tankers, but they have deep drafts. They can't cross the shallow sand banks at the lake's mouth. Those banks shift around, and this makes them even more treacherous. Venezuela won't dredge access because they don't want entry to the lake to be easy. They fear uninvited ocean tankers of oil-hungry foreigners. Probably with good reason."

"How deep are the sand banks?" asked Stass.

"Maximum draft to cross is eleven feet eight inches. But only within one-and-a-half hours of high tide. Which brings us back to the Mosquito Fleet. Lago had to order specially built lake tankers from the Harland & Wolff Shipyard in Belfast, Ireland," said Máximo.

"That's a fine shipyard," said Red Burns. The men nodded.

"The Mosquito Fleet tankers can carry full loads with shallow draft," Máximo continued. "They have twin screws and quick-turning engines to maneuver through the shifting maze. However, this solution created a new problem. The Mosquito Fleet cannot be used for shipment of oil to destination. Their draft is so shallow they're unstable on the open ocean. And once the Mosquito tankers get out of the lake, transfer of oil from one ship to another offshore is always a precarious operation best avoided."

"Sounds like Lago couldn't win for losing," said Tex.

"What's the point?" asked Stass.

"The point is that Lago needed storage near Maracaibo to hold crude for transhipment," replied Máximo. "The Company considered several sites. Aruba is close, it has the natural Sint Nicolaas harbor, and next to the harbor was a good place for an oil tank farm. Besides," Máximo said, "to invest your money, would you prefer the insecurity of Venezuela or the reliable, stable Dutch?" With mock seriousness, he held out both hands, palms up, as if one would even weigh the two options. The men laughed.

Tex laughed. "Hell. I been both places. Where do you think I work now? I'm not nuts. Venezuela's *still* worse than the Wild West ever thought of being."

Máximo nodded. "Maracaibo oil was tempting, but conditions scared off all but the most intrepid. In the early 1900s, under Cipriano Castro, Venezuela was in chaos. The man was totally decadent. Then came Juan Vicente Gómez, an uneducated tyrant, but disciplined. He calmed things down and paid off external debts. The Venezuelans paid a high price for a little stability, but foreign governments and oil companies liked Gómez. The oil companies stayed even when he put heavy taxes on oil in the '20s." Máximo motioned toward Tex. "You were there then."

"Yup. You didn't want to cross Gómez, for sure. But no one could keep order in Maracaibo. Guys drank, gambled, picked fights. Prostitutes was raking in money and corrupt officials was raking it in, too. People did what they wanted. It was mighty hard to duck trouble."

"Gómez was in power for twenty-seven years." said Máximo. "Until 1935. That's not so long ago."

Tex agreed, then added, "I know they was a few officers in the Mosquito Fleet that did OK then. They set themselves up a little side business as smugglers."

Stass looked puzzled. "What did they smuggle to Aruba from Venezuela?"

"Naw. Ya got it backwards," said Tex. "Smuggling went the other way. Cigarettes, liquor--and pajamas, would ya believe."

Gil, who had not said much, exclaimed, "Pajamas!" He shook his head. "Pajamas?"

"Yup. They was a hot item for a hot place. Venezuelan men used to strut around the streets of Maracaibo wearing 'em. Proud as banty roosters. Never had duds so cool and comfortable." Tex went on. "The Mosquito Fleet guys bought scotch duty-free in Aruba, two dollars U.S. for a bottle. They'd grease a few palms, then sell it in Maracaibo for forty. Said ya had to be crazy to pass up that kind of deal."

"Is that still going on?" Gil asked.

"Not anymore. Times change."

"Well, chaos in Venezuela hasn't changed," said Máximo. "When people wake up in the morning they must ask themselves, 'Who do I run from today?' It's not surprising some always run to Aruba when things heat up and go back when they cool down. And some just stay here. It's not surprising, either, that Lago built its oil storage and a refinery just outside of Venezuela's reach."

"There's a song that's Venezuela's unofficial anthem," said Stass. "The *Alma Llanera.* Some of the big tenors sing it." Stass had had more beer than usual and was a little unsteady. Heads jerked toward him in surprise when, in fractured Spanish and a clear tenor voice, he launched into song. Alissia liked to hear her father sing. He was always in a good mood when he sang. That was when he was uncritical and she felt safe being visible.

Stass mimed great emotion. With wide gestures, he hammed up his delivery for the men. Afterwards, he recited a translation he had memorized.

I was born on the banks of the pulsing Arauca River,
I am a brother of the foam,
Of the herons and of the roses
And of the sun.

The reveille of the breeze has lulled me in the palm grove
and that is why I have a soul
like the perfect soul
of crystal.

"How unfortunate that Venezuelans have not benefited from that perfect soul in their leaders," quipped Máximo with a tight smile.

Recalling that past conversation reinforced for Alissia that it was a composite of a particular place and a particular time that created the special world in which she had lived. She had needed to come back here. The, before she left the Colony to return to Rika's for the night, she drove to a familiar overlook to spend a moment. She got out of the car and walked over to sit at the edge of the low cliff. Overhead, with the freedom of flight, gulls circled and cried out as they rode the wind. Enjoying the strong breeze, she sat and gazed down at the Sint Nicolaas harbor. This was where people in the Colony came to watch Lago's fleet of twenty-one manoeuvrable little lake tankers. Alissia had always liked that they had been dubbed the Mosquito Fleet. It sounded affectionate--an ironic, endearing understatement for the specialized ships. Everyone recognized their indispensable role in transporting crude oil from Maracaibo, and the familiarity of the swarm of little tankers always in some way felt reassuring. People could never have presaged, she thought, what they would witness from this very same spot. Afterward, they would never again be able to come here for a feeling of well-being. The terrible night had precipitated a long and lasting chain of emotional consequences in the Lago Colony, and they still fed the turmoil in Alissia's present.

On the horizon, the mango sun began its slide into the sea. The evening sky darkened. By the time Alissia returned to Sint Nicolaas from her rounds through the Colony to Rika's in San Nicolaas, night had spread its mantle over the island. After dinner, Alissia and Rika talked until well after midnight. Rika spoke with fondness of the ebullient and good-natured Scot, Red. Rika also made comments about Máximo. Hearing his name somehow unsettled Alissia. Did she really want to understand the man?

CHAPTER 23
TWAS BRILLIG

As the sun faded from Alissia's second day, she and Rika ate a light dinner together in the kitchen.

"I want to visit Baby Lagoon tonight," Alissia said to Rika. "I'm sure you remember some of my mother's crazy ideas."

"Indeed." Rika laughed. "You were lucky. Many of us were also enough lucky to enjoy Nessa's ideas.

"Well, I'm still lucky. There will be a full moon, so tonight will be perfect. I have wonderful memories of one night in particular when my mother took us there." She stood and walked around behind Rika's chair. Bending forward, she put her cheek against Rika's and hugged her. "Rika, thank you for everything. For your hospitality. For listening to me. For your good counsel."

"You are most welcome, *lief*."

"I'll also drive over to the north shore. It's so wild there. Don't wait up for me and don't worry. I'll be back late."

At Baby Lagoon, Alissia sat on the sand, arms around her shins, head on her knees. Lost in reverie and as the trade wind blew, she dozed off in the moonlight. After a length of time that she could not determine, she roused herself with a start. She left the lagoon to drive to the other side of the island.

On the north, windward shore, she got out and, drenched in silver light, for a time she walked along the beach. She stopped and looked out at the sea. Moon-rays danced on white foam, boiling on wild water in the astounding brightness. Wind and salty spray ran circles around her as large waves crashed on the shore in irregular, driving thuds that vibrated through the soles of her feet up into her chest. The beauty of the night and place was heady, exhilarating, but she knew that Aruba's unprotected windward shore could be a dangerous place. Here, surrounded by savage beauty, exposed, outside the more shielded bounds of life on the lee side of the island, she had been preyed upon. She had been young and defenseless then. But no more.

Saturating her senses in the dynamic splendor of this place, Alissia walked for an unmeasured length of time. When she began to feel weary, she drove back to Rika's.

Lying in bed, Alissia shifted around to get comfortable, then put her hands up on the pillow to cradle the back of her head. Tom, her job performance, mockery at the office--all vied for her attention. *I need to turn it all off. I really need sleep.* She made herself refocus. She listened to the soft sibilance of the wind as it blew through the window screen into the room. She felt it caress her skin. After a while she turned her concentration to her conversation with Rika. Red and Máximo. Her mother, Nessa. Listening to Rika had helped Alissia understand that all three had greatly impacted her life. Finally, she rolled over onto her side. As her thoughts drifted to her mother, sleep blanketed her and she sank into a dream of times past.

It had been summertime. Since the weather did not vary much from one month to the next, such reference to season in Aruba referred only to the vacation at the end of the school year. The timing was ideal for several reasons. Alissia's father and Gil Williams were both working the graveyard shift at the refinery, school was out, the moon would be full. It was perfect for one of Nessa's midnight picnics.

"Time for bed," Nessa and Cynthia announced to the children. "Get some sleep. We'll wake you up when it's time." At 11:30 they roused and loaded them into Nessa's car. They drove the few blocks to the lagoon where the kids spilled out. Nessa and Cynthia spread out two sheets on the sand, then deposited the picnic basket and towels on top.

The moon was so bright that one could read a book by its light. Alissia danced and twirled with her moon shadow along the beach. She chanted to herself, "Twas brillig, oh yes. It was." She dipped. "The slithy toes. Yes, yes. Did gyre and gymbol in the wave." She spun. "All mimsy were the Seagrape groves, and the mome grapes outgave." She *was* in Wonderland. Then she put on her swimming mask and everyone splashed into the lagoon. Alissia lay face down in the shallow water and propelled herself along using her hands on the sandy bottom. Magnified by the water, a copse of algae and seaweed undulated, waving at her with gloomy gestures. Unidentifiable shadows slunk through her peripheral vision. Everything looked so different in the water-diffused light of the night. The eerie underwater world seemed to menace the bright and reassuring moonlight as if to presage dark torment that would threaten the safe, public world she would later construct for herself with such care.

She jumped up from the water and took off her mask, tossing it up on the beach to cavort around in the lagoon. The night was a feast for the senses. The trade wind whistled and stroked her face and arms. She laid back to float, arms stretched out, buoyant in the warm water that tasted salty on her lips. She inhaled the scent of the sea deep into the core of her being. The bright beach and luminous night sky filled her eyes and she seemed to see herself fly up into it, totally free.

She got out of the water and again stood on the beach. After a while, even though it was warm, the water and the trade wind made skinny little-kid bodies shiver. Goose bumps dappled their skin in the moonlight. Everyone trooped over to sit on the sheets and each wrapped up in the comfort of a big towel. Nessa, Cynthia and the children gathered close and sat cross-legged to eat and drink. Alissia warmed up and her shivers subsided. As excitement waned, her head drooped. She lay down, lulled into sleep by the pulse of warm water that played its gentle beat on the beach of this sheltered coast.

In the morning, Alissia awoke still feeling the presence of her mother. Rika had told Alissia that she needed to understand her mother, Nessa.

III

Nessa

CHAPTER 24
THE NEXUS

Nessa Allison Saxton's nonconformist gathering in 1948 was not the sole link in a chain of consequential events. The garden party had raised eyebrows and waggled tongues from one end of Aruba to the other, but the most interesting intrigues of the evening slipped by unseen by most.

Alissia's mother played and danced to her own lively tune. For this special occasion, Nessa did exactly what she wanted and her husband, Eustace "Stass" Alban Saxton, dubious, indulged her flaunting of custom. Nessa invited people she enjoyed and people whom she wanted to know or know better, notwithstanding anyone's social standing, nationality or race. So the event was, in every sense of the word, full of color. Although the island's diverse population co-existed with few overt clashes, the unusual social occasion deviated from the usual gatherings of families who were of Anglo-Saxon and European heritage--that is to say "white"—whose men worked in the Lago Refinery.

The party was held outside at the neat, square bungalow in the Lago Colony. Nessa was a handsome woman in her mid-twenties. She had twisted up her long brown hair and wore a green-and-white dress that complemented her hazel eyes. Hands on hips, she gazed with satisfaction at the flowers of her garden: magenta bougainvillea, showy pink hibiscus, creamy frangipani and diminutive red starflower blossoms. Unbidden, an aching thought of Ruddy, her beloved brother, slipped in. She made herself return her attention to the party.

Alissia stood beside her mother. Nessa had named Alissia after the constant, blowing trade winds, the *vientos alisios*, and after the island, both of which would strongly shape her. As was customary, Alissia Aruba Saxton had been vaccinated against smallpox on the sole of her foot on the day she was born. Nessa bent down and said quietly, "Remember, Alissia, listen. Don't talk non-stop." In an affectionate gesture, Nessa gathered the little girl's hair in both hands and arranged it down the center of her back. They walked over to Jultje Van Dijk. *Yool-cha.* Nessa had always liked her.

"Jultje, how nice to see you. This is Alissia. She's six years old now." Nessa looked down at her daughter. "Alissia, this is Miss Jultje, Dr. Van Dijk's wife. You know, our dentist."

When Jultje smiled, her eyes smiled, too. She wore a dress the color of lagoon turquoise which set off caramel skin. Black, curly hair tumbled down around her shoulders and she emanated the scent of water, soap and jasmine. As she leaned down to shake Alissia's hand and receive the customary kiss on the cheek, her breasts shifted forward in a neckline split to the waist. It was not the kind of dress that Nessa wore. "You are a pretty girl," she told Alissia. Both island born, at this moment Jultje's and Alissia's skins and lives touched.

A man sauntered up and Nessa turned to greet him. Like raven wings, his dark eyebrows arched over sharp brown eyes. His face was fine-boned and swarthy. He shook Nessa's hand and then boldly slid his eyes up Jultje's contours. He traveled from feet shod in sandals up to the small waist encircled by a sash, lingered on the curves of her chest, and stopped on her face.

Nessa introduced him. "This is André Valenzuela from Venezuela." Nessa laughed. "That's hard to say."

With a nod, André commented, "You said it perfectly."

Nessa smile and commented, "I've been practicing," then continued, "André manages the oil tanker schedules in and out of Sint Nicolaas harbor."

As André and Jultje shook hands, a sudden clatter in the direction of two maids working at a long buffet table punctuated with bright bougainvillea and hibiscus flowers tucked into large conch shells claimed Nessa's attention. "Oh! Excuse me." Nessa hurried toward the commotion and André bent forward in the French quasi-kiss of courtesy, lingering over Jultje's hand. As he rose he brushed his cheek with deliberation along her breast. Jultje flinched and glanced toward her husband. Dr. Van Dijk had his back turned. Jultje quickly regained composure and neither she nor André noticed Alissia's quizzical look. André nodded to Jultje as if there had been no affront and took his leave as the perfect gentleman. Nearby in the garden, a chuchubi bird trilled briefly from a tree branch, hiccupped a few odd notes, and nestled back to sleep.

André joined another cluster of people and poured on charm as he shook the hand of each person. He positioned himself next to Máximo Hirsch who oversaw maintenance for the Mosquito Fleet tankers. A Colombian born in Barranquilla, Máximo's father and a partner had founded the Empresa Alemana de Transporte Fluvial; Señor Hirsch belonged the elitist Club Barranquilla. Máximo parents always spoke German at home and Máximo had learned to also speak it well. Tall, big-boned and blonde, with angular, symmetrical features and icy blue eyes, Máximo had a very masculine appeal. The two bachelors were opposite in looks and personality.

Máximo and André had been friends for a number of years, although "friends" may not be the proper term. At work, they engaged in the practical communication necessary for everyday logistics, but it seemed that what the two men had most in common pertained to narrow aspects of their social life.

With Máximo and André the adage that opposites attract seemed true. Máximo had the deportment of a hatchet and was totally reliable, like it or not. André was perpetually charming, sinuous of movement, and dependably undependable. In fact, there were so many inconsistencies in what he said that one quickly learned not to believe most of it, even though he said things so beautifully. It was bruited about that because of unsavory circumstances he had precipitously fled a few years spent in Puerto Cabello, Venezuela. And because he was a braggart with a penchant for exaggeration, the Arubans who worked with him would comment in low voices among themselves, *hopi scuma, poco chocolate.* Lots of foam, little chocolate. But still, most would agree that André was entertaining.

André leaned toward Máximo and queried softly in Spanish, "Six tomorrow? The Watapana?" In a characteristic gesture, Máximo fingered the antique Colombian coin that glinted from a gold chain around his neck. He always wore the prized 1845 Nueva Granada Diez i Seis Pesos gold coin so that the side with the condor and coat-of-arms was displayed. Máximo thought for an instant and gave a nod of assent. André wandered on.

For the party, Nessa had set up tables and chairs on the sparse St. Augustine grass that, with persistent coaxing, supplemented by choice words on Stass's part, the Saxtons managed to grow in Aruba's dry climate. Torches and strings of lights illuminated hedges of bright flowers; satin-petaled gardenias and clusters of tiny Night Jessamine blossoms wafted streams of fragrance through the air. A well-provisioned table of beverages offered pineapple juice, bottles of Coca Cola, Cuban rum and Curaçao liqueur plus the usual gin, bourbon, scotch and Dutch Heineken beer. The gathering was set up on the sheltered, lee side of the house. The moon was bright, the balmy evening refreshed by the familiar wind that blew through perfumed flowers and the tall stems of the pretty Nerium oleander plant, well-known to be poisonous, particularly so, as local lore cautioned, if some of its leaves are dropped into an alcoholic beverage. Cardiac glycoside is concentrated in the oleander's sap, and even one leaf can deliver enough toxin to cause an erratic-to-fatal heart rate. But this evening's party-goers safely quaffed unadulterated drinks as they stood around the flower-studded yard and patio. Nessa stood with her hands on her hips. She looked around to just enjoy the scene. *I'm so glad I did this,* she thought. *This is what I really wanted.*

The party became more animated as people arrived, singly and in couples, their personal clocks set on informal Caribbean time. Commotion ensued when the jovial Scot, "Red" Burns, and his Cuban wife, Rosa Pérez de Burns, erupted through the gate. Red's flaming thatch of hair and pale skin made a startling contrast to his wife's dark hair and warm-toned complexion. Nessa and her husband Stass hastened to greet them.

"By gosh, it was time fer a party," boomed Red, fondly kissing Nessa on the cheek and pumping Stass's hand with vigor.

Rosa lunged forward and threw her arms around Stass's neck, draping her body against him. "Es-tass!" she cried. "Eet is so good to see you," she cooed. She nodded at Nessa and said, "Hola."

People milled, voices buzzed. Gilbert and Cynthia Williams were there. They lived across the street. Gilbert and Stass had both grown up in Aruba. Their wives, Cynthia and Nessa, had also been brought to Aruba as toddlers. Of the Saxton and Williams children, only Alissia was present. Nessa had allowed Alissia to come to the party for a little while. She found small ways to make up to Alissia for Stass's harsh treatment of the child.

Gilbert Williams helped Stass tend to guests. Nessa was civil to Gil. Early in her marriage to Stass, Gil had made a crass sexual advance to her. His action offended and shocked Nessa. It betrayed the two people to whom Gil owed absolute loyalty--his wife and Stass, his closest, most indulgent friend. In clear words Nessa expressed her repugnance; she chose to tell no one because to do so would wound those deceived. Gil tried to apologize but Nessa cut him off. She was polite to him around others but she would never again trust the man.

Gil was better at socializing than most other things. He loved to announce tidbits of news, usually more entertaining than useful, but people liked entertainment. Although talkative, Gil habitually dismissed Alissia in that pleasant but perfunctory manner that adults so often use with a child. He looked through her as if she were an inanimate and transparent object. Except sometimes, when Gil was not performing and no one was paying attention, he would stand stone still, his mobile face frozen and expressionless. He would lock his eyes on Alissia and if she looked up and caught him staring at her, the intensity of his fixation scared her.

Stass had arranged for a band from Oranjestad. The guitarist plucked strings to tune his guitar, and the others struck some beats on their steel drums. They eased into the music. The smooth cement floor of the patio made a perfect place to dance. After everyone had eaten their fill from the buffet, a few couples stepped out and began to move to the beat of the music. Rosa predictably pulled Stass out to dance a sexy Latin rhythm until it ended and he could escape. Then the band segued into an Aruban version of a fox trot with words crooned in Papiamento. Dr. Van Dijk stood erect next to his wife, Jultje. They made a handsome pair. To Jultje's dismay, André, the smooth Venezuelan, approached them.

"Dr. Van Dijk, good evening. It is always nice to see you, but I must confess that I prefer a social occasion to your dentist's office—in spite of your great skill." André smiled broadly, displaying even teeth, marred only by a small chip on one incisor. He looked at Jultje. "Doctor, would you permit me to ask your wife for this dance?"

"Yes, of course. Jultje loves to dance. She is a better dancer than I." Dr. Van Dijk extended a hand toward the smooth floor of the patio. "Please."

Jultje dared not refuse André. She did not want to be forced to explain her reluctance. They joined the other dancers and she stepped with misgiving into the snare of his arms, but he held her at a respectful distance. Then he pressed his hand into the small of her back and said softly, "You are a fragrant tropical flower. The Doctor is a lucky man." Jultje should have been annoyed by the personal comment but, despite André's earlier transgression, she felt flattered.

Nessa noted that Dr. Van Dijk smiled as he watched his pretty wife walk back across the patio toward him. It's *unfortunate that he rarely expresses his approval to Jultje,* she thought.

A gaggle of people doubled over and erupted with laughter. Dr. Pieter Ritsema, the physician who had delivered Alissia, stood in the group with his wife, Hendrika. The doctor came from the Dutch-speaking island of Sint Maarten; his wife was from the French-speaking half of the same island, where it was called Saint Martin.

"What a name have I got. Hendrika Geneviève Ritsema," Hendrika commented with laughter. "But very fitting for where I was born." She smiled at Alissia, who hovered at the fringe of the group. "So I am lucky, don't you think so, Alissia?"

Alissia nodded. She liked Dr. Ritsema's wife, her mother's good friend. Hendrika taught school in Sint Nicolaas and, after school hours, often came to drink tea with Nessa. Alissia had started calling her *ree-kah,* Rika, when she was small, because she couldn't say Miss Hendrika. Hendrika liked the nickname and encouraged Alissia to use it.

Someone commented to the Ritsemas about how good their English was. Dr. Ritsema said thank you, he was improving, but had to get used to different accents and cadences. "One patient tells me she has a navel problem. This seems a curious condition and I commence to examine her. I soon think otherwise when she tells me no, no, not navel. Nasal. Nasal."

At the center of the clutch of laughing guests, Red Burns exuded good humor as he began to perform from a repertoire of jokes. His red hair crowned a milky-white face sprinkled with thousands of tiny freckles. He paused for breath and extracted an ever-present, oversized kerchief from his pocket. He mopped perspiration beading on his flushed cheeks and neck.

"Red, you should shower at home," interjected Tex.

Red bared his teeth at Tex in mock menace. "Let me tell ye about the fangs of the endemic Aruba rattlesnake, the *Crotalus dorissus unicolor*."

"Oh, no. Please. Not them fancy words again. I'd rather face the durned snake." Tex threw up his arms in a defensive gesture and backed up. Tex was easy-going when off work. Grinning, he quipped, "Forget them varmints. Tell us about the birds'n the bees, why not."

Assuming a disappointed look that was only half feigned, Red retorted, "I'll spare ye this once." In fact, Red knew more scientific names and facts about local fauna than he did jokes. But willing victims for him to indulge his love for zoology were hard to find.

Máximo Hirsch took advantage of the hilarity to press a hip against Red's flamboyant and striking Cuban wife, Rosa Burns. With uncharacteristic discretion, she returned the pressure. André Valenzuela picked up on the fleeting intimacy. English was the lingua franca of the evening and each guest spoke it with a personal flair. Copious accents ranged from rolling Hungarian to staccato Spanish, through the varied English of Scots, Brits and Americans, on to bumpy Dutch and soft Papiamento. After a time, the group that stood gathered around Red fragmented and guests reassembled into different huddles. In one circle, several people stood talking with Dr. Ritsema and his wife. Someone asked Hendrika how many languages she spoke.

"Four," she replied. "And I am fascinated by Aruba's Papiamento. It is the first language of the native population of the ABCs--Aruba, Bonaire and Curaçao," she added for anyone who might not know. "This creole isn't spoken anywhere else and it flourishes." She explained that she was researching Papiamento's seventeenth century origins from a Portuguese-based pidgin in Curaçao.

"My investigations turn out to be a rich language *rijsttafel* for me. A feast of savory dishes," she explained with enthusiasm.

Alissia, whose bedtime was approaching, piped up. "Like a word salad, Rika?"

"Good, Alissia. Yes, like a word salad."

Nessa paid close attention. "Is Papiamento a pidgin?"

"No, a pidgin is not the mother-tongue of any group. People who speak different languages and need to communicate start borrowing words from languages they know. The assortment becomes a common 'pidgin.' Then, when their children speak the pidgin as their 'mother'—and often only--tongue, the pidgin coheres as a creole language."

Dr. Ritsema caught his wife's eye and made a small cutting motion with his index finger.

Geneviève returned a small nod. "Papiamento continued to evolve by borrowing from Spanish, Arawak, French, English and more. Now, enough to talk. Also we must dance." At this point in the party, Alissia's grandparents, who had enjoyed sitting and talking for a while with people they knew, slipped away. It was well past their bedtime.

Máximo Hirsch comported himself with impeccable manners at all times. He first danced with the hostess, then with several of the wives. To dance with Rosa Burns, he chose a slow piece. He drew Rosa close and, from hip to shoulder, she pressed close against him. André Valenzuela endeared himself to several women by demonstrating steps to an unfamiliar beat. He did not dance again with Jultje Van Dijk. Alissia went off to bed and Gil Williams turned his focus to his peers.

Nessa's guests enjoyed the party. Although people mentally or overtly sorted Aruba's diverse population of 49,000 into categories by skin hue, for occasion or for purpose, the evening's mix sparked only lively discussion and sharpened sensory perception. The last revelers reluctantly filed out very late. By the time Nessa and Stass finally fell into bed, a soft pink, the color of the inside of a conch shell, diffused up from the rim of the ocean to fill the pre-dawn sky. Out in the sere *cucunu* the Shoco burrowing owls also returned to their nests from their pre-dawn foraging.

All the adults who would significantly impact Alissia were there that night. Generous, benevolent Hendrika Ritsema, genial Red, duplicitous Máximo--and, of course, Gil Williams.

CHAPTER 25

AN UNACCEPTABLE SPLIT

In 1941, Nessa Gifford turned eighteen. When she ran along the dock at Big Lagoon to dive into the water, her long brown hair swung in waves down to her waist. It glinted highlights bleached by sun and seawater. John Ennis, a young refinery worker imbued with much self-importance, made a one-sided decision. He told the single men in the Colony that he had serious intentions about Nessa and declared her off-limits, bringing disruption into her life. Other men had to challenge his claim with serious intent of their own or back off. Suddenly Nessa found that no one asked her to dance at the Esso Club, no one came and sat next to her to chat—or flirt—at the beach and no one asked her to a Company movie or to go for a ride. She was plunged into a vacuum not of her making, very different from the easy-going social environment to which she was accustomed. She was isolated. John pressed his attentions.

"Come to a movie."

"Come sail with me at Big Lagoon."

Nessa was young and time loomed long; she did not see other options. She accepted John's invitations. He seemed earnest. In just a few months, he dropped to one knee and said "marry me."

Nessa had wanted to go away to school, but that did not work out. The war made travel risky and application by mail to schools difficult if not impossible. Another consideration may have been the high cost for travel, room, board and tuition. On graduating from high school young women were expected to do something. There was nowhere to look for a job, and she could not go away to school. Her only option seemed to be to marry. She could not tell herself she loved John, but he was all right, she supposed. She capitulated. John and Nessa married not long before the attack on the Sint Nicolaas harbor.

For the first ceremony, the civil procedure in Oranjestad, Nessa wore a rose-hued dress of starched cotton and John procured a suit. On his arm, he led her into the small office of the Dutch judge. Their two witnesses followed and squeezed in. With a hand gesture, the judge seated Nessa at one end of his desk and then waved John to the other. He intoned a short litany in Dutch.

"Now sign here." The judge stood and held out his hand to shake Nessa's.

Are we married?" she asked.

"*Ja*," he nodded.

He handed a marriage booklet to John with spaces to register the names of twelve children. "Here. If you have more children, you shall another book get. Also, you can your wife beat. If help is required, request to police."

The second ceremony was held at the new non-denominational Lago Community Church, built in 1939 by Lago, which had to own all structures in its concession area. Nessa had a traditional Protestant wedding with family and friends in attendance. The bride walked down the aisle on her father's arm dressed in white. In one hand, she held a brilliant bouquet that she herself crafted from multi-colored island flowers: red and pink hibiscus, redolent frangipani, bright yellow *kibrahacha*, and Pride of Barbados with rich hues of orange. In vivid contrast to her long white dress, the cluster of color she carried trailed long and supple stems of purple bougainvillea. Thus, the couple received two marriage certificates, one from the Dutch government and one from the local church. Eleven months later, Alissia Aruba was born with the surname Ennis.

Despite the twice-documented marriage, it was an ill-fated union. While John was effective at work, in his personal life he was selfish and overbearing. Within a year of Alissia's birth, Nessa discovered him in bed with a neighbor. Her response was unyielding. She would not tolerate the betrayal and summoned up courage. John and Nessa divorced in Oranjestad.

Such formal splits were uncommon, unacceptable for "nice" women under any circumstances. Nessa left the Oranjestad courthouse in humiliation. With lowered head, she dodged pointed fingers and fled snickering looks. Walking away with burning cheeks, she clutched the divorce decree redacted in Dutch that she could not read.

Even though she was now a divorced woman, it would not be long before Nessa would remarry. She had always been sweet on "Stass"--Eustace Alban Saxton. In the Saxton household, the mention of the surname Ennis provoked stony disapproval or harsh comment. It was not clear whether the taboo was more damaging to Nessa or to little Alissia, who began life with this surname and who bore no personal responsibility whatsoever in the whole matter. By the time Alissia was three years old, Nessa urged Stass to formally adopt Alissia and legally change her surname to Saxton. Stass's responses were typically gruff, so Nessa was surprised when he put his arm around her and said, "OK, if that's what you want." She was even more surprised when, after a moment, he added, "I guess it's probably best for the kid."

"And for me," she said, and her eyes became teary. Nessa safeguarded the adoption papers out of sight together with the related, embarrassing divorce decree. No one ever heard her mention either.

Much to Nessa's dismay, John Ennis began to appear at the Saxton household once a year with a birthday gift for Alissia. Sometimes he brought a book, once a watch. Alissia liked the presents, but a black cloud loomed over the family with the arrival of each gift. She learned not to say she liked a book and most often she read it out of sight. She also did not tell her mother that sometimes John and his second wife—who was really very nice—would invite her in to read coveted comic books on their screened porch. But she stopped going there because that, too, made her feel guilty.

On her eighth birthday, Alissia heard her mother with John Ennis at the door. "Don't bring presents. You're not welcome. Don't come here again. You just cause us problems!" Nessa yelled.

Alissia clasped her arms over her chest and hunched up her shoulders. She tried to shrink. She felt she was somehow the cause of the hostility that John Ennis provoked in her parents. She carried that burden with her mother, just as she seemed to also share other burdens that weighed on Nessa.

It was a relief to the family when Standard Oil transferred John to their office in New Jersey.

CHAPTER 26

NESSA AND STASS

By the time Stass Saxton and Nessa Gifford Ennis married in 1944 and set up their household of three with Alissia, the acute housing shortage of early Colony years had abated. Stass Saxton qualified for a bungalow as a foreign hire. Neither Stass nor Nessa had been born in Aruba, but they had arrived as toddlers with their parents and could not remember ever living anywhere else. Whatever the reason for classing them as "foreign" on this island that had always been their home, they accepted their good fortune with pleasure.

By the time Alissia was born in Aruba, she was the third generation of her family living there: grandparents, parents and grandchildren all lived in the Colony. Everyone had to have a nationality and passport of some sort. Many Colony families maintained a chain of American passports from a forebear, perhaps a naturalized predecessor who had had a foot in the United States long enough to acquire one. Some had worked in Peru, some in Venezuela, and many had been born in some such place. Most Americans in the Colony were, however, what some called *real* Americans. They arrived directly from the United States where they maintained close ties.

When Nessa married Stass, her second marriage was attested to three times. She had a Colombian document from the civil ceremony in Barranquilla where the two had gone to marry, a certificate from the non-denominational Protestant church in the Colony—a small and private ceremony--and by mail they obtained a document registering their marriage with the American Consulate in Cuba. Nessa kept track of a multi-language parcel of family documents which included extensive vaccination records.

Stass's father died when Alissia was an infant. Stass helped his mother move to a small community in Florida said to be friendly. An adult woman, alone, with no work skills, could not remain in a Colony that existed solely to support the processing of petroleum.

With children who represented a well-adapted third generation in an insular sanctuary, like the divi-divi trees, Nessa and Stass had deep roots in Aruba. How would they survive if a transplant ever became necessary? The outside world dizzied with its vast dimension and great dissimilarities. It expanded beyond their comprehension.

CHAPTER 27

WHAT'S COOKING

The kerosene bottle was empty again, signaling the despised chore. How did it get empty so fast? Emily, the maid, was not there, so Alissia was stuck with the job. She voiced a long and quavering "Mom...." To no avail.

"Alissia, just do it."

As a mother, Nessa was loving, fun, zany--but she leaned heavily on Alissia for practical and emotional support that were sometimes beyond the child's years. At least the hated task held no serious menace. Alissia removed the glass container from its seat on the side of the stove, quickly turning it right side up. The bottle was overly large for the hands of a seven-year-old. Drops of kerosene on its sides made it slippery and smelly. Holding it awkwardly out in front of her, she carried it across the kitchen to the screen door. She turned around and pushed it open with her bottom. She went to the oil drum in the yard and filled the bottle from the spigot. No matter how careful she was, this always got more kerosene all over it. Now the bottle was heavy and even more slippery. She always worried that she would drop it. She finally negotiated the bottle back into the kitchen. Alissia always hoped beyond hope that the bottle would get low on a day that the maid came. Emily would always quickly take care of it.

The kitchen stove itself was a simple affair: four burners on top and a small oven fueled by the upside-down bottle on the right-hand side. For Colony residents, the pungent odor of kerosene set saliva flowing. It evoked a variety of tasty foods.

Wonderful aromas came from Nessa Saxton's kitchen. On Saturday mornings, the kids hung around her, underfoot. Stass, if he were at home, usually kept as far away as he could get from anything that could be construed as housework. But on a Saturday, even he hovered around. They all crowded into the kitchen, everyone in the way, as they anticipated the weekly baking process. Nessa mixed and kneaded the dough early. The consistent warm climate was always favorable to the yeast, but to the eager onlookers it seemed that the dough took an eternity to rise. Bread days signified more than just a loaf of bread. Nessa also used the plump, moist dough to make fresh doughnuts, deep-fried in oil, and she also fried the doughnut holes. The aroma of frying doughnuts and baking bread saturated the house

Finally, the baking and frying were done and Nessa opened a cupboard door. From the neat, orderly contents she took a bowl of sugar and set it out in the havoc of the kitchen. Indulgence was not only permitted, it was encouraged. They dipped warm doughnuts and bite-size doughnut holes in sugar and savored them. They also devoured the whole first loaf of baked bread slathered with salty canned butter, to which Stass added copious spoonfuls of saccharine grape jelly--his favorite. Alissia always liked the doughnut holes best.

Nessa was inventive, a free spirit. Her creativity produced delectable concoctions that were a treat for family and friends. Alissia early acquired a taste for savory foods, but the enticing smells that emanated from Nessa's stove acted like a repellent on Stass.

"What *is* this?" he would ask, as he lifted a lid and peered with suspicion into a pot. Stass had unadulterated Anglo-Saxon taste buds that recoiled from anything that was not bland. Duncan emulated his father as closely as he could. In other latitudes, Stass would have been called a meat-and-potatoes man, but most potatoes that made it to Aruba were disgusting. Any potatoes that Alissia remembered seeing were ugly wizened lumps that tasted worse than they looked, and the same went for apples. Rice and noodles and pasta were good, and she loved the tropical fruits from Venezuela.

Aruba had culinary peculiarities that seemed strange to newcomers. Alissia had tasted what passed for fresh milk once. The Company had tried importing for the commissary some "fresh" milk that had been frozen in wax cartons. When thawed, the wax came off the cartons in clumps that sloshed around in the milk, at that point the cow only a dim memory. She remembered when her mom had given her some.

"Here, Alissia, try this."

She had promptly thrown up on the kitchen floor. It was awful. Who would drink that nasty stuff when one could have frothy, sweet-tasting Klim, freshly mixed from powder? No matter that the powder was even farther from the cow.

The first time that Stass saw Nessa prepare to make conch chowder, he was horrified. He heard a pounding racket on the back patio and went to find out what was going on. He found Nessa on her knees with Alissia watching. Nessa had a wooden cutting board placed on the cement floor and with a meat hammer she was beating something white and rubbery. Alissia tensed at Stass's approach.

"What *is* that?" came the stock question.

"It's conch."

"Conch? You mean those slimy things in the big shells that are pink inside?"

"Right."

"What are you going to do with it?"

"Make conch stew." Nessa purposely did not say chowder. Chowder sounded too exotic.

At the hint of family dissension Alissia stiffened. She stood very still, trying not to attract attention. If only she had a Wonderland mushroom, she sometimes thought, she could shrink like Alice and grow too small to notice. She could never predict when anger might escalate to encompass her for the sin of being present.

"Well, don't expect me to eat that crap," Stass said. "Why are you beating it to death? It's already dead."

"It makes it tender."

"Why don't you just make *real* food." Stass marched back to the living room.

"Mom, why do things upset Dad so much?" asked Alissia.

"I don't know, Alissia. He just doesn't like anything different in his life."

Nessa sighed. Her timing was infelicitous. She knew better. It was best if she cooked when Stass was not home. He was always suspicious--with good cause, it must be said. Normally he didn't know if conch was on the table. But even if he did not know that a chowder was made with conch, he was unwittingly safe: he wouldn't eat it because it looked different. And even when he would refuse to eat something, he would sometimes get angry and insist that the offending dish be removed from his table or else he would remove himself. On the occasions that Nessa served something made especially for him that did not meet his idea of real food, he resorted to imported peanut butter with grape jelly.

When she prepared the iguana, at least she had been smart enough to make sure that he was not around. By the time the dish was served, the reptile was no longer recognizable and she could pass it off as chicken. A lot of things got blamed on that domesticated fowl. Stass had been safe from the pseudo-chicken only because the iguana dish had garlic and spices in it and he did recognize garlic, which was not on his short list of Acceptable Foods. On the nights that Nessa fixed fare not approved—at least half of what was available to her locally Stass would not eat--she always made something else for her husband. On the night of the iguana, Stass would have had apoplexy if he had known what the beast on his dinner table really was. But even when he had his own dish to eat, he regularly complained about the smell of garlic. Nessa could tell that "different" food truly stressed Stass. Even living in Aruba, Stass's mother had prepared the bland foods that were to her taste—Nessa called it English-style cooking. One would think that growing up in Aruba would have desensitized Stass.

When Nessa finished pounding the conch she cut it up. Then she sautéed onions and garlic in oil. She added the conch, diced tomatoes and the rest of the ingredients. Last, she added herbs and spices. When the pot began to bubble the chowder smelled heavenly. She and Alissia were in for a treat. Duncan would only eat what his father ate, and not even all of that. Nessa had made enough chowder to share with her more adventurous friends for lunch the next day when Stass was working the day shift. Curbing her culinary forays to keep Stass happy did not occur to Nessa. She was always thinking about what she would try next. It was not surprising that, under the circumstances, Alissia grew up with an adventurous palate that, as an adult, she would have done better to hide in some venues. Those culinary forays with her mother had only increased a desire for other exotic adventure that stayed with her.

On one occasion, the Ritsemas invited Nessa and Stass to try the Dutch colonial version of the Indonesian dinner that became so popular in the Netherlands. For the *rijsttafel,* Hendrika served eleven side dishes to go with the rice—twenty or thirty were too big for what would be a modest gathering. The small group feasted on the spicy dishes served in small bowls that included bits of grilled fish, cubes of pineapple and mango, cooked vegetables, nuts, freshly grated coconut, chopped hard-boiled eggs, and an Aruban version of a fiery sambal sauce made with the spicy Venezuelan peppers, the *ají dulce*, brought by sailing boat to Oranjestad. Stass suffered through the ordeal with a modicum of grace. As soon as they got home, he headed for the peanut butter jar.

With many diverse nationalities and adventurous palates in the Colony, there was a lot of interest in food, at least in whatever could be procured. One year, Cynthia engaged a maid from Martinique. Nicole did not speak English and Cynthia did not speak French. A neighborhood maid who spoke rudimentary French acted as translator.

Cynthia was excited. "I hired a French chef," she exulted. To partake of the formal, upscale cuisine she planned, she invited Nessa and Stass, Rosa and Red, Dr. Ritsema and his wife, Hendrika, and Tex. Tex was older than the rest of them, but with great tales about Lago he was always a comfortable fit. He looked at the group and announced with solemnity. "I'm sorry to have to bring y'all bad news on this grand occasion. The Wagon has passed on. Not even Doc Ritsema could have rescued the patient."

"Oh, no!" exclaimed several people simultaneously.

"I was in love with that car!" Stass declared. "Tex, you made me believe in miracles. Every time the crazy thing ran. You drove me around in it sometimes when I was kid."

Heads were shaking in sympathy when suddenly everyone looked up and stared with disbelief. Cynthia knew she was in trouble when her guests erupted in laughter. The new "chef" from Martinique carefully approached the dining table bearing a whole baked fish on a platter. She held sprigs of parsley in her mouth. Something had been missed in translation. Gil was embarrassed, Cynthia laughed at herself and--since this did not take place in his house--Stass thought the incident uproariously funny. He could pre-empt some of Gil's lame stories with this one. "Wait 'til I tell the guys! If you're going to serve fish, you gotta hold parsley in your mouth." Then he added, "and if I gotta sit at a table that's got fish on it, I hold steak in my mouth." Pleased with his own quip, he laughed even harder.

That evening at Cynthia's dinner, the men were convivial and did not dwell the whole time on cat-cracking or the latest statistics on injury-free work days. Geneviève discussed the best Caribbean fish to eat rather than arcane linguistics. Rosa managed not to appear too bored; she even stifled her flirting. Nessa did not reminisce about her brother Ruddy, which inevitably channeled conversation into wrathful speculation about responsibility for the harbor attack. Red used only two taxonomic Latin names all evening—possibly a record--and Stass happily consumed a serving of leftover beef.

After dinner, the group sat outside under a velvet-and-diamond sky, each person sipping Curaçao, redolent of bitter orange, from a tiny liqueur glass. The trade wind brushed skin and ruffled hair. Stass plucked strings on his guitar to tune it and then sang familiar, sentimental songs. Engaged in the present with each other, hosts and guests enjoyed laughter and good humor. Since he was in the public eye, Gil posed no menace to anyone. Almost a fixture at Colony social gatherings, Máximo Hirsch, a fixture at Colony social gatherings, with his formal, unimpeachable manners, but always reserved, was not included in the evening's gathering. Cynthia appreciated Máximo's social graces and professional competence but she had confided to Nessa reservations about him that she could not pinpoint. Perhaps, she said, her discomfort came from vague rumors that circulated about him, some tangential to that charming scapegrace, André. But, she acknowledged, Máximo shouldn't be condemned based on rumor; everyone knew that gossip was a staple pastime in the small community. And so, on this balmy Aruba evening, the trade wind blew and, at this moment and in this assemblage, no hazards and no tensions surfaced on the right side of paradise.

CHAPTER 28
AUDIO DIVERSION

The coveted new radio arrived in 1949. That day, Alissia had followed her father around to watch. "Make sure you don't get in the way," her mother had whispered softly in her ear. Stass's project needed just a few finishing touches. Bang, bang! Tap-tap-tap. He stood on a ladder outside, up under the eaves of the bungalow. He surveyed his work. "That does it," he declared. His new radio would have been invaluable during the war years. Even though listening to broadcast news would not have protected Aruba, it would have alleviated some anxiety for Colony residents over not getting news from the outside world. Even now, timely outside news was a treat.

Word had seemed to quickly spread around the Colony by *chuchubi* bird that Stass's new radio had arrived and was about to be inaugurated.

"Dad, can Eddie come, too? Please?"

"Sure. Go get him."

Stass's audience had gathered. Red Burns, Gil Williams and a pack of neighbors stood looking up at the antenna, all with necks craned at the same angle.

"I didnae think you could pound that many times without mashing a finger. Congratulations," said Red.

"Will it work?" ask Gil.

"Wise guy. For the price and trouble, it'd better work," retorted Stass.

The wire antenna for his new acquisition stretched the full length of one side of the bungalow. When World War II had erupted in Europe, the well-known Dutch company, Philips, renowned for quality radios, fled from the Germans to the United States to go into production under the name of North American Philips Company. At the same time, the company office moved on paper and with capital to the Netherland Antilles to stay out of North American hands. Canny businesspeople, those Dutch. One of Stass's co-workers had traveled to New York and back as one of the few passengers permitted on an oil tanker and had picked up Stass's treasure for him, a brand-new Philips shortwave radio.

With the antenna installed, the group flowed in the back door of the bungalow, through the kitchen and into the living room. Alissia and Eddie both worked their way through to the front of the spectators. Stass raised both arms, bowed and turned on the radio. It emitted some crackling sounds.

"It's alive," said Tex. "That's a good sign."

With thumb and forefinger, Stass slowly turned the dial to travel through static and a couple of stations broadcasting in Spanish. He heard English and halted. It came in loud and clear. "Git yore gen-yoo-wine sim-a-lated dahmonds," a voice sincerely urged from far-off Texas." Success!

"That's for you, Tex," said Stass.

The radio became a steady companion in the Saxton household. Alissia could always picture everyone fixed in a state of suspense, anxiously awaiting the next installment of a serial. She could replay perfectly in her mind the signature pronouncement, "The Shadow knows," followed by the shady character's distinctive, sinister laugh:

"Ha, ha, ha, haaa..." The laugh portended a story of delicious, imminent and recurring doom.

Audio entertainment was a staple of Colony households. The Saxtons had a high pile of plastic records with bright illustrations of story characters imprinted on them and the children played them over and over on a small manual record player Nessa had set up on her large screened porch. While still very young, Eddie and Alissia could recite whole stories word for word. Stass Saxton liked ballads and popular songs. Nessa--who knows where she acquired the taste in her insular cultural climate--listened to classical music, which she played at stentorian volume whenever Stass was out of the house.

That day it was Bizet's Carmen blaring. Nessa had dreamed up one of her special tasks, one that lay outside of Emily's routine cleaning duties, and she customarily recruited Alissia to assist. Nessa did not seem to see the incongruity of plunging into the intricacies of a complicated and perhaps unnecessary chore in which she took great interest while she ignored the obvious. Rarely were the results of one of Nessa's painstaking jobs even noticeable. Stass's eye was drawn immediately to unwashed clothes in a pile or dishes left in the kitchen sink; the clutter drove him crazy. He must have felt that if he could impose order on everything he saw, this would also put him in complete control of his work and his life.

Nessa seemed to have her own idiosyncratic system of organization and she was consummately skilled in its application. While visible disorder and chaos might bury the kitchen or bungalow, she maintained the insides of things in astonishing order. The contents of her kitchen cabinets, drawers and closet were kept in a perfect, rational arrangement with no extraneous item. One could find anything instantly. *Why doesn't she take care of the stuff Dad can see?* Alissia used to ask herself. What Nessa chose to neglect didn't seem logical. It would have caused her much less trouble if she had reversed what she put in order. Perhaps she was just disinterested in the commonplace. But perhaps whimsy and illogic were what made her so much fun. "There is never a dull moment with Nessa," people used to say. Alissia loved to recall the zany larks that her mother dreamed up. She was glad that Nessa would drop everything to take her swimming in a sudden shower of warm rain. Family and friends and fun took priority over humdrum tasks and when she engaged in routine tasks she tried to turn them into fun. Alissia recalled how her mother orchestrated cleaning the furniture.

Nessa surveyed the living area, contemplating her project. Today they would work on the carved Chinese furniture. First, she and Alissia set aside the pottery, white-and-blue Delft, Gouda in its bold black and yellow. Armed with cleaning cloths, toothbrushes, and furniture polish they began to wipe the elegant Chinese furniture. They used the toothbrushes to clean every minute speck of dust out of the tiny nooks and crevices of the carved figures and scenes. Then, to the thick scent of oleaginous furniture polish, with vigorous arm movements that kept time to the strains of Bizet, they brandished their cloths. Alissia watched her mother's arm pick up the tempo as the needle moved into the Toreador song.

They finished to the sounds of the next record. Caruso filled the air with operatic arias, starting out with La Bohème. Stass and Nessa had stacks of LPs, 78s and little 45s that they played on the big automatic record player that dropped records to play, one by one, onto the turntable. Alissia was permitted to operate it for Nessa. Alissia would hum "*La donna è mobile, Qual piuma al vento...*" She had not the least idea what the words meant. "Woman is fickle, like a feather in the wind" her mother read to her from the record cover. Alissia did not understand the translation much better than the Italian but the pure richness of the music and full voices lifted up and transported them both.

What Alissia especially liked was violin music. One of her very favorites her mother told her was called "Devorjack A-minus."

Strange. It was so beautiful that Alissia thought it should be A-plus. Strains of the violin pierced her brain and she saw the notes in color. Mauve and purple lines undulated from left to right across a black velvet background, forming delicious peaks and sonorous valleys. Rills of sound snaked under the skin of her arms from shoulder to wrist, raising goose bumps, provoking shivers of pleasure.

But the newest source of audio entertainment, the short-wave radio, took everyone to a different place. Daily it siphoned awareness into another realm; it reminded them that a whole world lay beyond the wave-lapped shores of Aruba. In just a few years, that huge, external and unsettling world that had seemed so distant and unrelated to their lives would become an immediate reality for those that the island now protected as fiercely as an ocelot guarding her kit.

In retrospect, Alissia supposed that her mother must have constructed some sort of system based on her own priorities--but perhaps there wasn't any logic to it at all. In fairness, Alissia had to acknowledge that she maintained her own self-deceptions. She constantly tried to herd events and things into an order in which she wanted to believe. She worked at creating the illusion of control in her life. *Like my father,* she thought. *And it didn't work for him, either.* In any case, whatever her mother's sense of order had been, it distressed Alissia greatly when she was a child. She felt like she had to protect her mother. The burden felt too heavy.

CHAPTER 29
BIG LAGOON

Nessa had strewn an assortment of things over the whole dining table in glorious disorder: little jars and boxes, small seashells, glue, tweezers, metal bases, fasteners and large fish scales. She liked to paint small wooden boxes and decorate the covers with seashells to form pretty designs. The fish scales she dyed various colors with great care and they looked like translucent, loose flower petals in diaphanous lavender, aqua, mango orange and sunny yellow. These she used to make earrings, broaches and miniature flower bouquets--delicate and pretty.

Nessa held up the lavender blossom on which she was working. It was almost finished. Two small gaps each begged for just one petal more but she laid the flower down and jumped up. In her bedroom, she pulled on a bathing suit and shorts. Alissia was in school. "Emily, watch Duncan," she called out. "I'll be back." She could get home in time, she thought. Stass's shift ended at four.

After her swim at Big Lagoon, Nessa sat on the diving tower. In general, life was safe and comfortable on her little island. She had friends; she had family; she had all the basics that she needed. But sometimes she mourned faded dreams of going away to school.

She would have learned a profession, maybe nursing; she might have had some independence. There was nowhere that she could get a job in Aruba. In any case, Stass had voiced his opinion on the subject on more than one occasion. "No wife of mine is going to work. A man who can't provide for his family isn't a man."

She wondered what her life would be like if she had gone away. Would she now live somewhere else? She could only conjecture about what she might have missed. She pushed away hazy regret that began to blanket her and let her mind hover lazily.

If she had left Aruba, Nessa thought, she would never have been pressured into her first, bad marriage. At least some good came out of it; it did give her Alissia. But Aruba's small world did not forgive or forget divorce. Nessa fingered her pink gold wedding band. Stass had the heavy ring made for her in Oranjestad. Aruba gold's warm, rosy cast came from its copper content. It was beautiful. Stass was a good man: responsible, hard-working, honest and forthright to a fault. But he was inflexible and he drove others as hard as he drove himself, especially his family who, he said, reflected on him. He was demanding of Nessa--and she recognized with pain that he was unduly demanding of Alissia.

Nessa was very different from Stass. She knew she seemed disorganized. She had so many interests that her attention jumped from one thing to the next to keep up. Her friends and Alissia delighted in her curiosity and creativity, her spontaneity, but Stass required--he *had* to have—a strict order in his house and life that she could not maintain. His intransigence seemed linked to the material stability he considered his responsibility to provide for the family. Stass took for granted Nessa's love and her loyalty. He enjoyed her contagious enthusiasm for living and for people of all kinds. He had, no doubt, married her to bring these elements, which were not part of his own make-up, into his life. But he could only take them in small doses. And it was beyond his comprehension that Nessa could leave a task unfinished to go do something else.

Nessa remembered the disorder that she had left in the dining room. She needed to get home. She looked at the angle of the sun. It was later than she thought. If Stass saw the mess when he got home, he would explode with anger. She most often endured his ire like a rain squall, retreating into the shelter of herself until it passed. But she knew the mess and impending discord would distress Alissia--and Stass's anger would spill over onto the child. Nessa resolved, once more, to try harder. She would try to reign in what Stass called her crazy ideas, to be more organized—more conventional.

When Alissia got home from school that day, Emily said her mother had gone swimming. Walking into the dining area, she panicked at the disorder on the table. Her dad would be furious. She had to fix the havoc, she thought, but there was too much. She didn't know what to put where. She heard the screen door jerk shut in the kitchen. It was too late. She quickly sat in a chair at the table and her father walked in.

"What the hell mess is this!"

"I'm sorry, Dad. I was trying to do stuff like Mom." Head down, Alissia kept her eyes on the table.

"Clean it up. Now. The place looks like a pigsty."

"Yes, sir." She jumped up.

He hesitated, as if trying to decide on a punishment, then turned and stomped off to change clothes.

Alissia made herself picture her Uncle Ruddy whom she had never known. Her mother always said that Ruddy was born happy. She pushed away any thoughts of shadowy Máximo and summoned visions of Red Burns, such a nice man. Red was always so patient, waiting for the little birds to come and enjoy his garden while she hid and watched with delight. Thinking of Red in his garden, the tension in Alissia's body faded away. But that was before thoughts of Red would twist her into knots.

IV

Red and Máximo

CHAPTER 30
HIDDEN TALENTS

It was evening. Rika and Alissia again sat together at the small table in Rika's Sint Nicolaas house. "I think early 1939 it was," Rika explained. "Some news of war from Europe we could get then. But not enough. And not fast enough. We all worried. The only thing the men here could do about the war to help was continue for producing fuel. For this they had to have Maracaibo crude. The Mosquito Fleet ships were essential." Rika paused to sip tea. "Lago brought Máximo Hirsch for maintaining those special tankers. He had much experience in shipping. It was not until the later years, when men went on trips to Baranquilla, that they learned more about Máximo," she said. "They said that Máximo's father lost his Baranquilla business to a dishonest partner. The father did not care if the partner's dealings were bad. He cared if they brought him benefit because he had much debt. He had bought a big estate to live high and could not pay. And when he received an expensive favor, he could no longer return an expensive favor as was local custom."

"What was Máximo like? As a person?" Alissia asked. "He seemed so cold. I always thought he was scary."

"Well, even my Pieter said--God bless him--that very cold Máximo was, and Pieter liked everyone. He always thought only on being a physician. I don't know if the refinery men liked Máximo, but I know he received much respect. Your father said always he handled complicated duties very well. And I'm sure Máximo liked Lago pay, especially with his family's financial problems."

"His family would have been socially disgraced in Baranquilla."

"True. But here people didn't know his story. They liked his Colombian charm for social occasions. He had impeccable manners and he was educated. He could talk about language and history with everyone or about difficult mechanical problems with the men. People said also that he was an excellent photographer. Here he retained status that he had lost in his homeland."

"A big barracuda in a small lagoon." Alissia did not smile.

Rika continued. "Máximo seemed to be good at everything he did. He had many talents. But he left suddenly, you know. No notice to anyone. Things were discovered in his bungalow after he left." She elaborated. "People knew he had a darkroom in the bungalow's big closet. He kept the darkroom locked, maybe because some of his photos were not—not discreet. And he had a Morse Code transmitter in there. No one ever heard he knew Morse Code. He was probably for that expert, too. Like for everything else he did."

Later, Alissia lay in bed trying to understand more about Máximo. She considered what she had observed when poking and prowling around the Colony as a kid, what she remembered from adult talk at the time, as well as new facts just learned from Rika and a probable scenario began to form in some limbo of her consciousness. The scenario played on with a multitude of details that seemed to blow in on the trade wind as she floated away into sleep. The wind saw all.

Máximo was esteemed around the island for expertise, reliability and informed conversation, but certain things he never disclosed.

It was obvious that he spoke excellent Spanish and English, but few were aware that he also spoke fluent German learned from his parents. Six months after his arrival on the island, with World War II well under way, he set up the darkroom to develop his own photos. Although he was accustomed to giving orders, rather than doing manual labor, he crawled underneath the bungalow himself and ran the water pipes he needed to put in a sink. He placed a large filing cabinet inside the closet in which he placed files and a small box that held a pair of gold cufflinks that had belonged to his grandfather. From time to time he looked at the cufflinks for the pleasure it gave him; occasions to wear them for formal dress in Aruba were very rare. To finish set-up of the darkroom, on top of the file cabinet Máximo placed a Morse Code transmitter--a memento of his consuming adolescent hobby. He had trained himself to transmit code in staccato bursts of a good thirty words per minute and he could copy code in his head that fast or faster. Finally, Máximo secured the small room with a new, sturdy door and a good lock, even though he lived in a fenced Colony where people rarely locked the doors to their bungalows.

In the months that followed installation of the darkroom, many admired prints that Máximo made of Caribbean faces and of features of Aruba's dry cucunu landscape. He also composed excellent seascapes in a variety of light and seized on paper the character of vagabond sailing vessels that arrived in Oranjestad from exotic places.

Imposing meticulous order on his files gave Máximo satisfaction. He took pleasure in his collection. To a select few he showed sensuous nude photographs wrested from island women, but no one ever viewed his photographs of the refinery, the tankers in the harbor or his files of detailed notes. Not then.

CHAPTER 31

CAMOUFLAGED

As the steady wind blew across the island, Máximo Hirsch gleaned information of the developments in Europe from every possible source. At certain times, he carefully closed the louvers to his bedroom and stood inside the door of his large walk-in closet where, with the light on, he transmitted and received in Morse code. It was early in 1940 when he received two significant, encrypted messages. These he kept to himself.

Official news channels in Aruba soon confirmed local fears. On May 10, 1940, Germany invaded Holland. On the island, the Dutch government rounded up all German and Italian nationals, as well as any known German or Nazi sympathizers. This included working men as well as families. There was anguish and lament among women and children who had acclimated to their easy-going life. All were transported to the nearby island of Bonaire. Four hundred and sixty-one people from the Dutch Caribbean islands would be detained there, housed in wooden shacks, from 1940 until the end of the war in 1945. There was not much sympathy for their complaints. The Dutch and English on Aruba did not hesitate to point out that conditions in Bonaire were preferable to the internment camps of the Nazis. Máximo was Colombian by birth and spoke flawless Spanish, and so evaded the pre-emptive sweep.

As the island became an ever more important source of fuel to Allied forces, German interest in Aruba grew. Máximo continued to ensure meticulous maintenance of the oil tankers. Under high pressure to produce fuel, all refinery personnel put in long hours. They took their jobs seriously; there were no slackers. In addition to his own long work hours, Máximo invested more and more personal time to stay informed about refinery production and about fuel shipments in particular. He also began to send the occasional sealed courier pouch to his father in Barranquilla via a trusted sailboat captain into whose hands he discreetly pressed a tight roll of bills. The volume of Máximo's communication from Aruba increased.

CHAPTER 32

AFTER THE WAR: RED AND ROSA

1945 was a significant year. It brought so many changes to Aruba that the only constant seemed to be the wind. The war in Europe formally ended on May 8 and Lago produced its billionth barrel of oil. Rika told Alissia that it was that same year, after the war, that Red Burns announced that he needed a break from the years of tension, hard work and long hours at the refinery. He was going to Havana, he said, to celebrate with night life, music and Cuban cigars. There, at a reception held by the British Consulate, he met Rosa. He fell crazy in love with the shapely Cuban beauty and within a month returned to Havana to court her. Rosa was hesitant about this flame-haired, freckled man and moving to a small Dutch island, but earlier in the year she had broken her engagement to a philandering fiancé who had publicly humiliated her more than once.

Red entreated her, promised he would make her happy, that she could have anything it was in his power to give her. He convinced her to marry him. The newlyweds settled into a bungalow in the Colony. For Rosa, life in tiny Aruba and the even smaller Lago Colony was a big change from exotic and bustling Havana. As Alissia would learn, it was not good for Rosa to be so idle.

CHAPTER 33
"DIEZ I SEIS PESOS"

The Lago community was small and in consequence the same people, in varying combinations, frequented social events. Everyone had at least a nodding acquaintance with the other habitués at such gatherings. Máximo Hirsch always attracted attention. He cut a virile and imposing figure, tall with erect posture, a strong jaw and determined, thin lips. He groomed himself meticulously and comported himself formally. Because of his status in the web of transport and refinery operations, his etiquette and social standing in his native Colombia, even though he was reputed to be a distant and very private man, Máximo was sought after for social occasions of any consequence.

Due to his controlled mouth and unfailing discretion, certain personal activities of Aruba's Herr Hirsch during the worst of the war years and outside of his working hours had not been discovered. He continued to be in social demand. It was at one of the island's ubiquitous cocktail parties that his cool, strong looks first caught the eye of Rosa Pérez de Burns.

Flashy Rosa stood beside her husband, Red, sipping a Cuba Libre. Two years into their marriage, Rosa had not gotten pregnant, although she had been vaguely hopeful. She pushed out of her mind any disappointment. She found life in Aruba less than exciting. She was bored. She had no interest in keeping house or in cooking other than to issue arbitrary directives to a maid of dubious ability. The most arduous task she undertook was to communicate in her Cuban English with the Trinidadian English of the maid. Rosa certainly could not pursue shopping as a pastime on this island. One could only spend so many hours lolling on the beach at Big Lagoon and her sporadic visits to B.A. Beach with Red, just the two of them, had become less titillating. Rosa observed Máximo. She was bored and his forceful, brusque manner intrigued her. She liked his blended style of Colombian-European courtesy, but it was more than his style and good looks that attracted her. She realized with a start that she could completely lose her heart to a man like him.

From the fringe of the small group where he stood, Máximo glanced at her. Rosa had found that even aloof men were not indifferent to her tight, low-cut dresses and flirtatious manner. She smiled and slowly shifted her weight from one hip to the other. She tucked her hair behind one ear and held his gaze as she slightly tipped her glass toward him. She took a sip of her drink. He acknowledged the token toast with the hint of a nod. Rosa looked around at her husband. "*Mi amor,*" she said. She laid her hand on Red's arm to get his attention.

"Yes, sweetheart. What is it?"

"We always see the tall one there, no?" She gestured toward Máximo.

"Sure. He's head of ship maintenance. A Colombian, even though he's so blonde."

"*Amor,* let's go talk to him. I have never talked much with him, even though we see him at parties."

"Sure, sweetheart."

Red and Rosa walked over and greeted Máximo. Red asked Máximo for some updates about the lake tankers and nodded at the responses. As always, Máximo was informed and precise in his answers.

"Do ye go to Lake Maracaibo often?" Red asked Máximo.

"Yes."

"Do ye like to fish?"

"No."

Red was not put off by the short replies. He continued with good humor. "I love to fish. Sometimes I go to Maracaibo on a tanker. Fish some on the way over, and then try me hand in the lake. Could ye help me catch a ride with a captain once in a while?"

"Certainly." Máximo paused. "A lot of men like to go to Maracaibo, but many seek a two-legged catch on land."

Red laughed. "I think I'll fish in water, thank ye."

Rosa finished her drink. She held her empty glass out to Red. "Amor, *por favor*, get me another drink. I think just some coca. I'm thirsty."

"All right, love." Red took Rosa's glass and went off to refill it.

Rosa smiled at Máximo and stepped closer. "So, from where do you come from in Colombia?"

"Barranquilla."

Rosa lifted her chin and ran a hand through her long hair. "So, you are *colombiano* from the coast and I am *cubana*. Both from the Caribbean. A good combination, no?"

Máximo looked Rosa over. With flawless skin and thick black hair, she was a sexy woman whose pulchritude always drew eyes. He frankly examined the décolleté that showcased full breasts. "It depends," he said.

Rosa had not expected a parry to her opening. Men were usually flattered by any attention she deigned to give them. Máximo's noncommittal response visibly annoyed her. With a brusque movement of one hand she flipped her hair back from one shoulder. "On what it depends?" Her tone was harder.

"On you."

Ordinarily, Rosa would have just turned and walked off, but she stood and examined his face. Red returned with her Coke and the trio picked up small talk about one thing and another for a few minutes, after which Máximo excused himself.

"Red. Rosa." Snapping heels together, Máximo inclined slightly. "It was good to speak with you both. I look forward to doing so again."

As Máximo walked away, the corners of his mouth curled up and he fingered the gold "Diez i Seis Pesos" coin that he always wore on a chain around his neck. *A married woman can be good,* he thought. *No commitments and, as long as one is careful, no complications. I will leave that fruit to ripen.*

Red, Rosa, Máximo—the triangle that would turn into a trap for a young snoop.

V

Life in the Colony

Strange, strange are the dynamics of oil and the ways of oilmen.

– Thomas Pynchon

CHAPTER 34

THE WATAPANA

The wind knew Sint Nicolaas, as did a number of men in the Colony, although most of them would not want to admit to the reasons for their knowledge. The Village seemed to have forever been recognized as rowdy and, with the advent of the refinery, many men who were living single, if they weren't working or sleeping, couldn't seem to find anything to do but go to there to drink and fight. That and visit what were called--if the speaker endeavored to be polite--houses of ill repute. By whatever name they were called, the establishments were reputed to do a lot of business.

To be fair, even before Lago, it should be said that Sint Nicolaas had always been a hardscrabble town, a place frequented by transient workers, scoundrels, and visiting sailors--as well as raising its own home-grown crop of n'er-do-wells. Then, when pressed hip to hip with the refinery, it grew even more rowdy.

It was the evening after Nessa Saxton's 1948 garden party when, as agreed, André Valenzuela waited for Máximo in the ramshackle Watapana Bar in Sint Nicolaas. The refinery was sandwiched between Sint Nicolaas and the Lago Colony.

André took a swig from his bottle of cold Heineken and set it back on the scarred wooden table. Over the years, hands and forearms and sagging heads of imbibers had polished the table's wooden surface smooth to the touch, except for carved rivulets and initials that, without thought, André traced with his fingertips. He had frequented similar bars in many other places. He glanced at his watch. At precisely 6:00 Máximo Hirsch strode through the open door into the Watapana. André noted that Máximo carried slung from his shoulder a bag of camera equipment. A curious accessory to bring for the evening's activities. André and Máximo often met at the Watapana, the Arawak word for the tree known as the divi-divi throughout the region. It was a good name. Customers, looking off-balance like the lopsided little trees, exited the bar canted to one side as they lurched in a zigzag down the street.

Máximo pulled out a chair from the table. "*Saludos*, André." He sat. He beckoned for service. An elderly and crooked Aruban waiter shuffled over, hands and elbows as gnarly as divi-divi trunks. He stopped and waited, bent in silent resignation, like the trees, to forces beyond his control. "The same as my friend," snapped Máximo.

The old man soon returned and carefully set a second beer down on the table. "Anything else, *señor*?"

"No." Máximo quaffed a large mouthful of the frothy liquid, held it in his mouth a moment to savor it, and swallowed. The two men gazed around the Watapana's dim interior at nothing in particular. "No use to discuss weather," declared Máximo. He turned his beer bottle around on the table a few times with the fingertips of both hands. "Sun, wind, infrequent rain. The usual."

"Not all is usual. I did not miss your connection with Rosa last night," said André. "What do you have going? She is such a hot one, why are you here? Red is working tonight."

Máximo looked at him without changing expression. "She is always around."

The two men sat in silence, one slim and bronzed with sultry good looks, the other fair, imposing and solid of body. The

Watapana's patrons interacted as usual. Voices of men mixed and tumbled about the bar, occasionally punctuated by an angry obscenity or a raucous laugh. Here and there the voice of a woman shrilled, a piccolo above the lower-pitched rumble of male sounds. It was not late, but tones already slurred drunkenly in an off-key cascade. Beer flowed copiously and accompanying tumblers of cheap rum stupefied a few of the patrons more quickly. André and Máximo, as was their wont, drank their beer at a deliberate and slow pace. André kept his mind clear so he could manipulate with charm, Máximo his in order to impose control.

"So, which shall it be, Máximo? Hija del Dia or Hija de la Noche?"

Máximo turned his gaze toward André. "Hija del Dia. Filomena told me she has a new girl from Cartagena. A little younger and prettier than the usual."

"Well, then I want the *venezolana* Efigenia."

"What? Not sampling new flesh?"

"I need another helping of the same. Efigenia can do things for a man with a bowl trick of hers. It's shallow and made of wood. She rubs it with coconut oil. When she lays those hips in it she can writhe slowly like a snake or gyrate like a wild thing. With music, she danced me all the way to heaven. My dusky Santa Efigenia." André rolled his eyes back theatrically. "She warmed me up with a *joropo* and finished me with a *salsa*."

Máximo laughed and took another swallow of beer.

"But you, amigo. The camera," queried André. "What's the matter? Maybe you can only take pictures now, eh?"

Máximo cocked his head. "Pictures first," he said. He paused and thought. "The woman can detach her soul from a man, but she doesn't know how to hide it from the camera. The camera penetrates to what she hides inside. It exposes the wick of the candle. That excites me." He tapped his fingers on the table. "And it excites her, too, even though she tries never to show her core. I am terrible. I strip from her everything when she tries to protect so little."

"Máximo, you can actually speak in more than monosyllables. Those pictures I would like to see. Photos of souls clad only in flesh. That sounds even more arousing than the bared Aruban beauties you've already shown me."

Máximo's expression answered nothing.

After so many years, André reflected, he still did not know Máximo and it was not just about his women. Preceding and during the war, Máximo seemed to have had daily need of information and specific details about the shipping and loading schedules of all the tankers, more than was warranted to coordinate work and maintenance. Máximo would quiz André at length. As soon as the war ended, his interest plummeted. There had always been something about the focus of Máximo's questions and their sudden cessation that did not seem right to André. He could never quite coax the hovering, amorphous idea into an intelligible thought.

André returned to his banter. "I don't understand, Máximo. I woo women. I warm them and charm them and they come to love me madly—at least until I abandon them, and then they hate me. Now, you, you are a cold one. You treat women badly. You insult them with indifference. And they come to love you madly—even after you throw them away. It doesn't make sense. But I guess *así son*. They are just like that. Lucky for us."

Máximo looked André over for a moment, then said, "At the party I watched you dance with Jultje Van Dijk," he said. "You should try your charm on that beauty. Dr. Van Dijk is so stiff and proper, it would make good sport." He took another drink of his beer and studied André. "In fact, André, I challenge you."

The two men sat a moment while André seemed to consider Máximo's dare. Then he pushed back his chair. "Well, Máximo, I'm ready. I say let's go see Madame Filomena and put our talents to work."

CHAPTER 35
JEOPARDY

The morning after the Watapana and the evening's activity, André relaxed with a swim at Big Lagoon. Eventually, he waded out of the water and dried off. He put on his watch and checked the time. Máximo had asked him to come by to see some recent photos he had taken and André was late. He headed on foot for Máximo's bungalow. Máximo was punctilious. He would be waiting, probably annoyed and impatient. André quickened the pace of his walk.

Máximo's greeting was curt. Without comment, he motioned for André to come in. He laid three photographs out on the dining room table, then went to his darkroom. "I'll get a couple of others to show you." André only glanced at an excellent photo of a Shoco owl. It was an unusual subject for Máximo. He must have laid in wait at dawn at the entrance to a burrow to get it. André considered the other two photos with more interest. In them, a pretty young woman reclined nude on the trunk of a divi-divi at the beach. Then, unbidden, André followed Máximo to the darkroom. He stepped into the open doorway of the converted closet. The bright overhead light was on, illuminating the closet set up as a dark-room complete with water, sink, a work table and a file cabinet.

"*Caramba.* I thought you just worked on photos in here. It's an office."

As André stepped over to examine some photos of the refinery tacked to the wall, something on top of the file cabinet caught his attention. "What's this?" He reached up to finger the Morse code transmitter.

Máximo bucked. "Get out. Out!" He advanced with physical menace. He thrust his face to within inches of André's and shouted, "How dare you walk in here uninvited."

André backed up a step. He held his hands up, palms forward. "*Lo siento.* Sorry." He wheeled away and returned in haste to the living room. He had never before seen Máximo lose control; the man's cold, calculating style was more than sufficient rebuke at work.

Máximo followed André. "You are *not* to discuss my private affairs with anyone." Again he advanced on André. Máximo was furious. "Never. With no one." With the heel of his hand, he shoved André in the chest causing him to stumble backward a step. "*¿Compriendes?*"

The uncharacteristic display of anger unnerved André. "No problem. No problem. I understand." André again raised his hands in defense. "Máximo, no one is interested in your technical things." He tried to jest. "Just your photos of Aruba beauties, *amigo.*"

Máximo harnessed his wrath. With characteristic and deliberate coldness, he made a direct verbal threat. "Make very sure you watch your mouth, André. If I hear that you have been talking, I assure you that certain men will learn what you have been doing with their women." Máximo had a dangerous look in his eye. "And that is not the only problem I will give you. You can count on it."

Outside the trade wind blew. André's visit was truncated. Having passed on refinery information during the war without detection, over time Máximo had relaxed his vigilance. He had grown privately arrogant over his impunity. Although it was illogical, at times he wished for recognition of his clandestine skills and success during the war. At least his father knew—and his family in Colombia had well benefited financially. Máximo did not like the unease that he now felt about what André had seen. He thought that he had put any vulnerability on this count long behind him. Everyone knew that André had a loose tongue. Always anxious to please, the man prated without thinking; he would blurt out anything to sound interesting. Others might make the ruinous connection that André seemed to have missed. Discovery would put Máximo in sure and immediate danger. Hotheaded refinery men were well known to administer their own harsh punishment and they had been specific about how they would retaliate. The competent Dutch would show no mercy in meting out peremptory justice to a wartime spy.

Máximo considered his options. André engaged in a number of questionable pursuits and the man knew that Máximo was privy to this information. Máximo could put André in serious jeopardy if he were to reveal André's unsavory activities. He would reiterate his threats to ensure that André did not forget them. André was no match for him. In addition, the man abhorred and avoided confrontation. Intimidation should shut André's mouth so that Máximo would not have to take more drastic measures.

CHAPTER 36
PERKS AND SNOOPS

At various points in her quest for the answers she had to have, Alissia needed to break the tension of her tight focus. She would turn to her good memories and bathe in the happiness of being back in Aruba. She loved the island itself--and she had loved all the different people. Even as a child she realized that the Lago refinery had thrown together an unusual potpourri of nationalities and ethnicities and the seemingly endless variety of languages they spoke had always fascinated her.

Now Alissia walked on the beach at Big Lagoon, stopping to examine a shell here and there. She picked up a piece of driftwood. Running her fingertips over its grey, smooth surface, she thought back. Adults had often discussed the subject. Apparently, refinery hires classified as "foreign" were housed in the Colony, where complexions ranged from the predominating pallor of northern Europe to Mediterranean bronze. Alissia had always wanted to believe there was no racial tension in the Lago environment but her mother's attitudes must have shielded her. With the distance of years, she discerned a divide. There was a de facto sorting. Lago employees classed as "local" lived in Sint Nicolaas where she recalled faces that averaged a richer, deeper brown than those in the

Colony. White and black visages dotted the edges of the Village color spectrum. The color line, however, was imprecise. Pale white Dutch, who by circumstance were hired in Curaçao, were classed as local. As a consequence, they lived in Sint Nicolaas. However, the Company considered the Dutch who arrived in Aruba directly from Holland to be foreign hires and these pale complexions, no different from the Dutch in Sint Nicolaas, lived in the Colony. Whatever the rationale--with the exception of ubiquitous André Valenzuela who seemed to interact with everyone and to troll for women everywhere--only Colony residents attended Esso Club gala dances. Even so, the mix of people at Club dances, though more homogeneous and lighter in average color than refinery employees as a whole, was lively. These gatherings generated ample spark and intrigue. Alissia remembered how her mother and Miss Cynthia used to look forward to an Esso Club dance. They would talk about the event with anticipation for a week.

Alissia had walked out to the end of the T-dock at Big Lagoon where she sat, picturing preparations for an Esso Club dance. A few days before the event, her mother Nessa and Miss Cynthia had laid out long taffeta dresses on their beds. They checked them carefully to make sure there were no stray spots, no stitches needed here or there. Miss Cynthia's dress was a deep rose; her mother's was inky black. Alissia had run her hand the length of the smooth, shiny fabric of her mother's gown.

On the morning of the event, he two women began in the morning to get themselves ready by washing their hair. Cynthia's hair reached just to her shoulders; Nessa's was very long. It hung down her back past her waist and had soaked her green blouse until the fabric, almost transparent, clung to her like a second skin. With backs to the sun, they sat in chairs in the Saxton backyard and murmured in conversation as they let their hair dry. The bungalow sheltered them from the full force of the wind, but there was enough of a breeze to aid in the process. When their hair was dry enough, they went inside together for a cup of coffee.

They seemed to enjoy the anticipation and preparation for formal dances and all the commentary afterwards as much as they enjoyed dances themselves, thought Alissia. She could well imagine what the gala was like.

Expectant excitement and talk always rippled through the Colony at the prospect of an Esso Club dance. "They seem so civilized—and the men look their very best," the women would say. They enjoyed dressing up, a change from bathing suits, shorts, and simple cotton dresses. Everyone knew that some would flirt. They also knew that the occasion presented, if one paid close attention, the opportunity for some to exchange malicious information or cultivate furtive connections.

That evening the general mood was lighthearted. Stass danced a showy waltz with Nessa. Turning in wide circles with expansive flourishes, he put on a show that drew laughter and applause. Interspersed with dancing, with drinks in hand, people clustered and chatted. Tex speculated on what new movies the Company might bring in. Stass reported with enthusiasm that the Commissary had just received some new hardware.

Red reflected out loud, one hand supporting an elbow, the other cupping his chin, "Ye know that Lago treats us well," he said. "We enjoy a colonial lifestyle."

Faces turned toward him. The term colonial sounded novel.

Cynthia considered this for a moment and laughed. "Well, we do live in what is called the Colony."

People began to list advantages and disadvantages to living in Aruba. Stass and Nessa listened. They had lived here first with their parents, now with their children, too. They could not recall having lived anywhere else and the concept of colonial seemed foreign.

Stass thought a moment, then affirmed, "From what I hear, it's true that the Colony gives us a standard of living that's better than most in the Caribbean."

Some commented on the constraints of the island's size, the heavy demands of work, scarce commodities and the limitations of a fenced enclave that housed only Lago employees and their families.

"And we all know that many turn to heavy drink," added Red. This was too close to the truth for some. A few listeners sidled away to other conversations at moments they thought inconspicuous.

While confinement to a small area and the solace of alcohol may have dumbed down the interests of some Lago residents, it struck Nessa that circumstances in Aruba seemed only to wildly stimulate the imagination of others.

"It seems to me that a lot of people in the Colony are pretty inventive," she said. "Think of all the interests and skills people have."

"We've got some purdy interesting cars, for sure," said Tex. "Guys stick together the darndest hunks and pieces. Most surprising thing is, some of us can actually drive them around. The Wagon lasted me a mighty long time."

"And we sure have guid fishing," proclaimed Red with enthusiasm. "Just about any day of the year. And there are the golf and flying clubs. They're quite a challenge with this wind."

Rosa stood beside Red and listened. She shifted her feet to back up just a few inches. She made brief eye contact with Máximo, who stood at the edge of the conversation group. Máximo, with obvious respect, pointed out that one man ground his own telescope lenses to gaze at the stars that pierced the velvet expanse of night sky. Playing bridge and the construction of kites of astonishing complexity and shapes to fly in the ever-reliable wind were added to the list. But even with the wide range of conversation at the Esso Club that evening, no one thought to conjecture about what it might mean to all of them if they were ever expelled from their sheltered small world.

André, bored, feigned interest in various conversations but did not comment. Throughout the evening, he cultivated general goodwill as a gallant and accomplished dance partner but, assessing tonight's particular assemblage, he deemed it too hazardous to engage in the usual seductive interaction that he masked in graciousness.

Inventive pastimes and gossip had always provided an ample number of topics for discussion in the Colony, a place with little stimulus from the outside world. However, it seemed that not even the busiest snoops--whose main talent and focus it was to ferret out the most guarded and secret of information--uncovered the questionable interests and covert activities in which a circumspect few engaged.

Alissia still sat on the dock and her mind returned to the present. Bits and pieces of certain incidents came to her unbidden. Somehow, they related to each other and to what she needed to know. One insistent scene took over the foreground of her ruminations, clamoring for attention. She held a hand over her eyes to better focus. It was something she had witnessed on one of her daybreak prowls as a little girl. *Máximo's behavior was abnormal. And was too early in the morning,* she thought. She remembered that he had first looked around in every direction, but he didn't see her crouched in the hedge. In retrospect, she recognized his behavior. *He looked just like me and Eddie when we were about to do something we knew we shouldn't.* The incident inflated with significance. What did it mean? Another piece to fit into the picture and she had very little time. Her heartbeat accelerated. She abruptly stood up and hurried back along the dock toward the beach and then up the cliff.

All of what Alissia heard and saw and lived in Aruba, everything that she smelled and touched, felt and thought, had begun to cohere into some kind of rough order for her, an amalgam of the details that formed the tableau of what she knew about this place. At least what she thought she knew.

CHAPTER 37
WHEELIES

It was another beautiful day and after conversation and a late breakfast with Rika, Alissia continued her search. She parked on the side of a street in the Colony and got out of the car to proceed on foot. She did not walk in a straight line, but wended her way in shallow curves and detours around small pools of black asphalt that bubbled like molten lava here and there in the glaring, perpendicular rays of the sun. The asphalt radiated the heat it had soaked up. She stepped off the paved surface and, at the touch of her sandal, talcum-fine kaliche dirt spurted up in rosy puffs that faded away on the wind. Yellow dots of small wildflowers bobbled in the wind at the end of spindly stems, punctuations on the side of the road. Alissia walked over to the pipelines. For nostalgia's sake, she took off her shoes and, with caution and bare feet, arms akimbo, she stepped carefully along a stout pipe that ran like an alley between the rows of bungalows. She had lost her skill. She feared tumbling (again, sharp memory told her) onto the jagged coral. Being on foot brought to mind the wheelies. What fun. Alissia laughed out loud. She and Eddie had spent endless hours playing with their contraptions, suspended outside of time in a place free of care for them both. It was the wheelie that had led her what was intended to be well hidden, a peculiar occurrence that, at odd times, returned to her, asking for explanation.

Colony households produced a steady supply of Klim cans and Alissia and Eddie found endless uses for them. Broomsticks, however, were another matter. These were a treasure hard to come by and Alissia and Eddie needed two of them. On the prowl, they eyed imported brooms and mops, entreating their surrender, so far without success. They were rummaging in the garage at Eddie's one day when Eddie had to go into the house.

"Have to go in," he mouthed, clutching at the front of his shorts. He ran off.

Unexpectedly, Alissia found herself face-to-face, alone, with Gil Williams. With a tight expression, he started around the car toward her. Alissia bolted out of the dim garage into the bright sunshine of the yard. Not a word was spoken.

Eddie came back from the bungalow and the two children moved on. A little later, without permission, they appropriated a broom from the Saxton household which the two of them declared to be worn-out. When the sawed-off, discarded end of the broom was discovered, this caused enough of a fracas with Nessa that they did not try that tactic a second time. Instead they were forced to beg one more long, smooth broom handle from a neighbor. They gloated in success.

Stass Saxton was not thinking of play when he had come up with a good use of his own for a broomstick. He sawed the used-up brushy end off and threw it away. Securing the handle in a vise on his workbench, he hammered part-way into the blunt end a heavy, long nail that extended in line with the stick. He gave it to Alissia to pick up leaves in the yard, one of her regular, assigned chores. Their bungalow faced toward the sea and inside the low cement wall that surrounded the front yard was a ring of Seagrape trees which continually dropped plate-like, tough leaves. With her father's fabricated implement, Alissia no longer had to bend down to pick them up. Standing in the yard she could see the lagoon. She pretended that she had a harpoon and was stalking fish. She posed with one arm up and the opposite leg extended out behind as she leaned forward to spear and skewer leaves with the nail. When the nail was full, she pulled off the sheaf of leaves and deposited them in a bag. Her elaborate theatrics transformed the chore into her own, solitary game.

Eddie and Alissia were ready to construct their new invention. To make a wheel, they tried to attach a Klim can lid to the side of a broomstick's end by driving a heavy nail through the center of the lid. Stass found them frustrated in his workshop with smacked fingers and unsatisfactory results, especially when the nail fell out and the can lid went flying. With rare patience, he helped them get the nail centered in the lid and driven straight into the hard wood. They each had a new toy, a wheelie Alissia called it, and it held together. The can lids actually rolled instead of lurching along unevenly. Each grasping the end of a broomstick, the two children spent countless hours wheeling the home-made contrivances around the streets with appropriate and varied sound effects. The wheelies speeded up. *Vroom, vrrooom.* They screeched to a halt. *Irrrk!* They raced and they set up obstacle courses. Eddie liked best to stage as many accidents and crashes as possible which annoyed Alissia and she most often succeeded in evading. The wheelies did not work well in sand, they found, and they were unsuccessful in walking the top of the low cement walls of their yards with them. Nor could they figure out a way to use the wheelies in the Seagrape trees, but they could not be faulted for lack of imagination. They escalated the skill level needed for their play. After tentative forays, they could soon run along the pipelines while rolling the wheelies one-handed out in front of them along the pipe. It took no little coordination to accomplish this without teetering off into the sharp beds of coral.

The makeshift toys provided the two children with hours of great pleasure and it was on one of Alissia's solitary early-morning forays that her wheelie had led her to see Máximo Hirsch slip silently into Red Burns's house, an incident that provoked ongoing questions still had to be answered.

VI

Gravitas

Never attempt to win by force what can be won by deception.

–Machiavelli

CHAPTER 38
WORRIES OF WAR

Dawn approached and, at Rika's, Alissia slept. Chittering *chuchubi* birds cavorted in a dream as she watched gregarious Red Burns in his garden. The peaceful scene she had always loved somehow turned suddenly ominous and she jolted awake drenched in sadness.

It was too early, not yet light. She lay in bed and redirected her thoughts to the day ahead. This place was so much a part of her. She knew the answers she had to have were here and she was determined to find them. She turned on the bedside lamp and reached for the notebook.

> August 3, 1938. Yesterday Gus introduced me to Red Burns, the latest newcomer. He has a thatch of bright red hair and is a bachelor. His Scottish accent is so heavy I can hardly understand him. I don't understand many of the expressions he uses, either. He loves to tell jokes. He carries on and laughs so hard himself when he tells them that everyone laughs with him, even if we have no idea what he said. I wonder how he'll get along at work. A lot of the men only speak basic refinery English.

Alissia's parents had always said that over time Red tamed his accent and dropped many of the expressions that confused listeners. *That may be true,* she conceded, *but he was still quite clearly a Scot.* She had always loved the lilt of his speech. She laid down the notebook. She could almost hear Red speak.

The Saturday-afternoon group stood gathered on the Saxton back patio. In addition to talk of what was currently happening, they all loved to listen to the telling of Aruba stories. The newcomers paid rapt attention and the long-time regulars seemed to enjoy the stories more every time they heard them. That day Red recounted life on the island when he first arrived.

"The climate here was totally different from what I was used to—not much like Scotland. It was not just dry with warm temperatures--Aruba was different in every way. At the time, we didnae realize we were living in paradise. Well, deep doon, I think we did. Food at the mess seemed good, but I think we would have eaten almost anything, we were always so hungry after work. In those days, a Scotch and soda cost us 13¢ in American money. A bottle of Tanqueray gin only $2.50. They put me in the Bachelor's Quarters--what we still call the Sheep Sheds. It was a long line of rooms built of wood up on stilts. We each got a room, a bed, a chest of drawers and a wee table. The Company built loos and brackish showers in a separate row. After a night shift, most days we sure didnae sleep late, I can tell you. The goats discovered our garbage cans and they came to knock them over at the break of day. What a racket. Can you believe I even had a Chinese houseboy? I could leave dirty clothes in a pile on the floor. Even me own mother wouldnae let me do that. Lam Ming cleaned and washed me clothes. He even folded and put them away for me. And the island looked like a picture postcard. At Palm Beach, I usually didnae see another living soul. Life was good." He paused a moment. "We didn't know then what would hit us. This place seemed so safe, so far from the rest of the world." He stood silent.

No one spoke. The men looked somber and waited for Tex to continue. Finally, he picked the conversation back up. "Those days, the late '30s, we was shipping to all of Western Europe—even clear to China. Not Japan, though. Word was we would go to war with the Japs. 150,000 barrels a day was going out of here. But to ship more, we needed a bigger harbor and more docks. The Company spent a million dollars on that, then another a million and a half to build the large still we needed. Over in Venezuela they just kept on drilling wells." He ran his hand over his forehead and hair. "At work, they was pushing us real hard. We sure worked, but I have to agree, we still had life pretty darn good."

"In '39 things sure changed," Stass commented.

By the late 1930s, Alissia knew, multiple declarations of war had been made and life in Europe was not so good. The chaos of the time spilled across the world. She picked up the Notebook and read further.

> October 28, 1939. Last month Germany, France and the UK all declared war. This affects us, too, even though we are so far away. Here all people can talk about is the fuel needed to fight the Germans. Buyers are lined up and pressure to produce keeps increasing. Gus says Lago can't get enough tankers of oil from Maracaibo to keep operating at full production. The biggest problem, though, is getting the fuel shipped out. The Dutch here are talking about putting in anti-aircraft guns and big guns to defend the coast. They act like Aruba is as close to Germany as Holland.

Alissia's thoughts turned to Tom. She wondered if he missed her. She hadn't thought much about Tom. She reassured herself. *Maybe it's because I'm focused on what I need to do here. And right now, I need to get up.* She sat and placed both feet on the floor. *I need answers to my three big issues. I need to get control of them all.* She stood up. *Why does a war so distant in time weigh on me so much? Then there is what I brought on myself.* She hesitated before adding the third to her list, but continued. *His death. I was responsible for his death. And there is a fourth. I hardly dare think about it. I have too much invested in my present life. But maybe I could. Maybe I could just jump ship.*

CHAPTER 39

CAT CRACKING AND SAILING

Alissia stood in the shower for a long time, letting the refreshing water run over her back as her mind moved through war and refining. After a while she turned around and lifted her chin to let water pour over her face. For as long as she could remember, Alissia had heard stories about the pressure during the war for the Lago refinery to produce fuel. She recalled her father explaining once when she was young that, in 1942, the year she was born, the Company had implemented a new process called "cat cracking" which would further increase the productivity and importance of Lago's Aruba operation. She had felt confused--and the term cracking alarmed her. She asked why cats had been in the refinery. Her parents laughed. Their simple explanation put her at ease.

Stass Saxton was a process man. He had always been a diligent and conscientious worker, but then, with a war going on, Lago converted to the new method for refining oil. This forced an accelerated learning curve which required his constant, intense focus. Under great pressure, his temper flared faster and higher. His impatience exploded on the job. "Damn it, man. Move. Use your brains!" Stass watched Máximo Hirsch make complex calculations and diagrams to come up with even more efficiency. The situation made Stass feel even more keenly his lack of formal education beyond high school. It increased his hidden feelings of inadequacy.

Traditionally the refinery had relied on thermal cracking to break—crack—the heavy molecules of crude oil into desired lighter materials. Oil was heated to nearly 1,000°F at pressures of up to 1,000 pounds per square inch, creating a serious risk of fire. The new technique of fluid catalytic cracking used a catalyst that flowed through a "cat" cracker with the feed stock oil. The process could be carried out at lower pressures with better results, higher yields and less danger. While Axis forces suffered severe shortages of fuel, with its additional increase in production, the refinery was able to supply to the Allies even larger quantities of the essential gasoline that was in high demand for the war. The fuel the refinery supplied to the Allies was directly affecting its outcome. The efficiency of the new process would also impact the lives of those who had lived so long in the Colony.

Time felt taut. Maintaining and operating the refinery was more than just a job to the men. They felt they were fighting a battle, too. People sizzled with tension. After long, hard hours of work, men dragged home bone-weary from their shifts to drop into merciful, dreamless sleep on their beds.

Over the years, people in the Colony enjoyed almost any event that was unfamiliar and broke routine, incidents that were ritualized as stories to recount and entertain. Now, with the high stakes of the war at pressing them at work, the refinery men sought out frivolous diversion even more. If nothing materialized, they dreamed up ridiculous pranks. Gil Williams came up with some that were used more than once, such as wiring the light switch in the bedroom of newlyweds so that it could not be turned off. For good measure, someone would attach bells to the bedsprings. And they could always rely on something eventually washing up, so to speak, from warm Caribbean waters.

The newest buzz was the arrival of a sailboat. Gil hastened to report to a group on their lunch break: "They're Norwegian and they have a pretty good boat. It's a forty-footer."

"They must not know there's a war going on," said Stass.

"Maybe they're happy to be so far from Europe," conjectured Red.

Gil continued. "They took off to go around the world. No schedule. They spent a year in the Canary Islands and had a baby while they were there."

"Purdy busy people," drawled Tex.

"Guy's name is Aksel. The boat sprang a leak and they had to put into Sint Nicolaas harbor to see if they could make repairs."

"Just the three of them?" asked Stass.

"Yup. And a dog. I talked to André and Máximo and they figure we can help them out. They'll hoist the boat with the big floating derrick so's the guy can work on it," replied Gil.

When word got around, people trooped down to the overlook on the harbor to see the boat. Refinery men speculated and opined on the repair. Some used their small fishing boats to get close and offer more free advice than anyone could possibly use.

Gil arranged with Cynthia to invite the family to their house. "I'll bet they'd like some time on shore. We'll have the guys over for beer and something to eat.

"I wonder what our visitors will think of Spam." Cynthia laughed.

At the gathering at the Williams's house, they learned that the name of the transient visitors. The woman was Hella, the baby Goran. They just called their dog Hund, or "Dog." According to Aksel, the dog had developed good sea legs and loved to ride standing in the bow as the boat cut through the water, always on its way to some new port. Before they went back to the boat, Gil invited them to take showers while they were at the house. Hella was effusive in her thanks.

"What a great kindness! You cannot imagine. And Goran, he loved it."

The couple said the opportunity to bathe at length in a real shower was their greatest luxury in a year. Gil smiled ear-to-ear.

"Well, you know the water's brackish."

"Brackish is heaven!" exclaimed Hella.

Aksel, Hella, Goran and Hund enjoyed the hospitality on shore and the help with their boat. They traded what they had: stories of their sailing adventures. After a few days, the small family sailed away with their dog, still unconcerned about the war. The visitors had provided a brief distraction from grueling work, but great distress was imminent.

Alissia loved that story. It still had the power to tempt her to embark on an exciting escape, but that's not why she had returned. She had come back to Aruba to salvage the life she had built for herself—a stable conservative life. She wrested her thoughts from a vision of sailing off to adventure and refocused her attention. The war was an issue. It had always been an issue.

CHAPTER 40
THE WAR

Alissia's understanding of the war came from varied sources. Old books, pamphlets, and written records were ostensibly objective sources of information, but all the emotional oral accounts she had lived with weighed heavily. And there was the notebook, so close to her in many ways. It was clear that 1940 was a portentous year. In the Colony, Japan no longer seemed so far away, with Japanese ships traveling from port to port in the West Indies to scavenge all the scrap iron they could find. German forces overran The Kingdom of the Netherlands in Europe. Through 1945, first Britain and then the U.S. made Aruba a protectorate in an effort to guard Lago fuel production. However, the formal preemptive measures by Allies and the island's distance from Europe were insufficient to protect the island from catastrophe. From people living in the Colony during the years leading up to what happened, Alissia had heard many accounts of the tension with which they lived.

Dutch families in Aruba were horrified by the invasion of their homeland and worry about relatives in Holland consumed them. Communication with Europe had always been slow, but now they suffered even more from no news at all. To support each other, they gathered in each other's homes to eat with legendary Dutch appetites. They drank copiously to allay strain.

In Grandma G's notebook, Alissia read:

> We are observing black-outs at night. This might be more dangerous than a possible attack. Gus asks how the men can work safely at night in a refinery without lights. It is good there are not too many cars because we drive without headlights and hope the moon is bright. The favorite entertainment in the Colony now is at night in dark bedrooms. We'll surely have an explosion of babies born in nine months. Merchant ships in these waters are being attacked. We worry about having enough food if our supplies are disrupted. People are stocking extra tins of Klim, Spam and vegetables. But there is more to worry about in Europe. We just received shocking news. The passenger ship S/S Simon Bolivar was sunk off the coast of England on November 18. There were a number of local people on board. Of one Dutch family of seven, I hear that only two children survived. What a terrible tragedy for this small place.

In 1940, the Vichy regime took over in France. On July 4 of that year, while the trade wind blew, Red was at work in the refinery when the captain of a French warship stationed in Aruba, the Jeanne d'Arc, burst into the office of the Company manager on duty. Stomping through the door he spouted loud and rapid pronouncements, all the while waving his arms to punctuate them with wild gesticulations in every direction. Ire inflated the captain's accent and made his expletives as incomprehensible as they were impressive.

"*Nom de dieu*! We 'ave a grand problème wit' zee salauds à Vichy!"

The big *problème* was that he had received an order from the Vichy "bastards" to scuttle every British ship on sight. The captain abhorred the Vichy government and had just cabled his son to join General De Gaulle's Free French Forces. Nonetheless, he was a captain in the French Navy, which was now controlled by Vichy. To disobey orders was treason. His quandary was serious. The French had been sent to Aruba to help defend the island—the refinery, to be more accurate—from the Germans and now the puppet Vichy government was issuing orders. Most of the French assigned to Aruba favored De Gaulle. The Company manager said he had no authority in such a matter.

"Go talk to Lieutenant Governor Wagemaker."

The captain and the Dutch Governor met privately. They must have come to some understanding. The French took no action for two days until, early on July 6th, 1940, a Dutch cruiser, two destroyers and a submarine that had deployed from Curaçao were able to reach Aruba and give an ultimatum to the French. The troops and the warship Jeanne d'Arc had until noon on the 6th of July to surrender—or the convenient alternative to immediately evacuate. Not surprisingly, the French captain chose to leave—*tout de suite.*

"The last we heard of the Jeanne d'Arc," Red recounted, whenever he told the story, "was that it was anchored in Martinique "for maintenance" where, conveniently, there were no British ships around that they would have to scuttle.

With the departure of the French, the Queen's Own Cameron Highlanders were deployed to Aruba. Alissia often heard her grandparents and parents speak of them. The Highlanders were the backbone of the island's war defense. A high-spirited and jovial lot, they were well remembered after their departure.

Nessa's brother, Ruddy, who was working on an oil tanker of the Mosquito Fleet, became close to two of the Scottish Highlanders. He spent time with them when he had leave on shore. The three young men shared stories and recited hopes. Ruddy took Aengus and Farlane sailing; he guided them around the island. They, in turn, invited Ruddy to join the high-spirited and boisterous group of Scots for evening gatherings of song and drink.

The Scots dressed in kilts, interesting garb to wear in the brisk Aruba trade winds. Men speculated with laughter and Alissia had heard her mother and Miss Cynthia whisper with giggles about what was or was not worn under the kilts of these virile men. Rika confirmed to her that one tenacious account was true: the Highlanders took to sewing fishing weights in the hems of their kilts to keep them from constantly flying up about their necks as they walked, marched and maneuvered. Ruddy would tease Aengus and Farlane about real men wearing skirts and they would swell up with mock bluster.

Reaching for the hem of their kilts they cried, "Crivens! We'll show ye a real man!"

Ruddy would clap his hands over his eyes and laugh.

The Highland regiment used its stint in Aruba to train for desert combat. When not drilling for war, they paraded playing bagpipes, the now-tamed kilts swinging but not flying, as islanders enjoyed the stirring sound.

The Japanese attacked Pearl Harbor on December 7, 1941. By December 11 the United States was at war with Japan, Germany, and Italy, fully engaged in World War II. When the United States sent men to protect the refinery, the Scots were transferred to North Africa to engage.

The news soon came. It was a somber day in Aruba. Stass was the one to tell Nessa's brother. He and Ruddy had been classmates. "Ruddy, sit down," he said. Ruddy's smile faded and he seated himself with foreboding.

The trade wind seemed to moan as Stass began. "I'm so sorry, Ruddy. We're all in shock." He thought of the amiable Scots, full of high spirit and laughter. He cleared his throat, then continued in a thin, constricted voice. "Most of the Cameron Highlanders have been killed in action by Rommel's troops." He paused. "Ruddy,

Aengus and Farlane didn't make it." No one there realized that more tragedy was to come.

> *The war so far away in Europe charged this place with emotion,* thought Alissia. *It still fills me with emotion today. And somehow it tangled together the identities of Uncle Ruddy and Red for me. It confused and mixed my feelings.*

CHAPTER 41

SUSPICION

Germany mounted a concerted objective to disrupt oil operations and lines of supply in the Atlantic. U-boats now prowled the American coast and in the first three months of 1942 they successfully sank many times the number of new oil tankers that were put into service.

Further to the south, an Axis wolfpack consisting of five German and two Italian submarines, the Neuland Gruppe under the command of Werner Hartenstein, prowled the southern Caribbean and the Gulf of Venezuela. Hartenstein's mission was to attack refineries producing aircraft fuel, as well as to attack oil tankers and merchant ships wherever he could find them. The attack on the Aruba refinery was part of the Axis focus to disrupt oil operations in the region.

Stass commented to co-workers, "Just think, if that U-152 had hit the refinery, Lago would have been out of production here. What a catastrophe for the Allies that would have been." He stopped and looked down. Then in a low, choked voice he squeezed out, "But hitting the tankers was horrible for us. For as long as we live, that night will live with us."

The refinery went on to successfully supply millions of gallons of gasoline to Allied forces for the duration of the war, in particular the critically important high-octane aviation fuel. Despite the tragedy of the Aruba attack, the loss of life could have been far greater. Later the men learned that after successfully torpedoing the oil tankers in Sint Nicolaas harbor, the German submarine surfaced to better target the refinery and storage tanks on land. A Lieutenant von dem Borne was in charge of the deck gun crew. When he ordered his men to fire, the 105-mm cannon exploded, blowing off one of his feet. In his haste, he had failed to order the crew to remove the cannon's watertight muzzle plug. The submarine cleared its decks and went down.

On the same day as the attack on the refinery, two more lake tankers were torpedoed between the sand bars of Maracaibo Lake and Aruba, with heavy loss of life. Destroying oil tankers was a priority because, even if the refineries continued to operate, the fuel they produced could not then be transported. Submarine warfare had entered the Caribbean where it continued for the duration of the war.

That moonlit Caribbean night during World War II remained forever burned into the consciousness of all associated with the Lago refinery. It deeply affected those who personally witnessed the grisly sights and sounds of the disaster. Aruba had been the target of the first torpedo fired in the Western Hemisphere during the war. The specific threat of fiery retribution that was made at the scene of the torpedoed tankers against anyone connected to the attack became common knowledge in the Colony.

Reliving the 1942 tragedy became an island ritual. Sometimes, on a Sunday afternoon, Alissia and Eddie's families would go on what had become a traditional Colony outing. They would all stand on the cliff overlooking the harbor. With eyes wide, the children would listen to their parents bring to life the sights, the sounds and the smells of that terrible night. The children experienced their parents' emotions with them. They went to examine the damage from torpedoes that could still be found on structures.

"Here, Alissia, put your hand in this hole in the cement. A torpedo hit here. Lucky it didn't take down the building."

Alissia would finger the rough edges and chipped areas of the cavity. Once her father took them all to feel a dent in one of the huge oil storage tanks which, by luck, was not punctured. Alissia ogled and exclaimed as she examined still visible scars. She palpated rough areas with her hands. The children begged to have the scary details of the shelling recounted over and over.

"Tell us again what happened."

"You must have been really scared," they would exclaim with horror.

Alissia sat on the cliff and looked out over Sint Nicolaas harbor. The sounds of those explosions seemed to follow her all her life. They still felt so real her heart began to pound. She could smell the smoke, see the ships in flame. She still carried in her fingertips sensations of raspy concrete and jagged stone. *We children lived the attack through the telling and retelling of the gruesome story in our families and at later gatherings so many times that the tragedy passed into the consciousness of our generation*, she thought. *As if we ourselves had lived it.* She knew that the rancor and suspicion of those who actually did witness the catastrophe did not much diminish with time.

"How did the sub know there were loaded tankers sitting in the harbor?" was always the recurring, angry question.

"Yeah, and it's no coincidence that the Germans got the two loaded tankers between Maracaibo and Aruba the same night," was the typical retort.

"What son of a bitch passed information? How?" was spit out with wrath.

Alissia knew she was not privy to all of the speculation about how a few submarines could have so exactly located and hit in one night four loaded tankers in the small area from Aruba to Maracaibo when they had the whole of the Caribbean to patrol. In the Colony, the question about who could have been the traitor always came back. And in Alissia's family, thoughts of the war always played sad, bass notes, a lament for the death of Ruddy. For Alissia, Ruddy, the uncle she never knew, became embodied in the person of the jovial and generous Red Burns. He was a benevolent, approving figure that, as a child, she had needed.

CHAPTER 42
UNTHINKABLE

The rising sun was still low in the sky but, even so, Alissia wore the straw-hat Rika insisted she use. She sat cross-legged on the beach at Baby Lagoon and watched the day come in--diaphanous, clear and pure. The morning air bathed her with the scent of the sea. She picked up a handful of sand and held it out, palm up, spreading her fingers to feel it softly sift between them. Time was also sifting away and she assessed her situation. The whole, secure, ordered life she had built with such focused effort was at stake, the key to her security and happiness. She summarized for herself the issues she had come to resolve—the place and time, the context for what happened, the whole hangover from the war. The war was scrambled up with what happened to Uncle Ruddy and it all connected somehow to what happened later. She could see that now. Then there was the ugly incident. Her part in it, her willfulness. She stopped for a moment. Her eyes moistened as she thought of the worst. She made herself to put words to it. Red's death. A heavy, tainted shadow of guilt passed over her. Its opacity blocked the pure rays of the sun. *Is it even possible to forgive myself?*

Alissia sat quietly for a while then returned to the car. She read in the notebook, not only its words, but looking for anything that might be contained between the lines. She had revisited places in the Colony to stimulate memory of things she had forgotten—forgotten or intentionally suppressed. She had talked for hours with Rika and filled her head with fresh recollection and new information. She saw clearly that it was her wonderworld that had shaped her unconventional identity, that filled her with the disparate desires that threatened to tear apart her safe life. With new, adult understanding she could picture how many of the past events in question might have unfolded and she plunged in.

VII

Alissia in Her Wonderworld

Paradise, one day at a time.

CHAPTER 43
THE BIG RULE

Although in the 1940s, everyday life in Aruba was for the most part idyllic, turbulent and rough realities nonetheless disrupted the Colony's daily hedonistic world. Periodically the legacy of the submarine attack surfaced to feed unsettling conjecture about sabotage and betrayal from within the community. It tugged down like a strong undertow, drowning carefree mood. After the day shift, men often joined Stass Saxton on the back patio of his bungalow to drink a beer and switch into low gear. They just wanted to hang out, to banter and engage in entertaining talk. But sometimes, when someone injected a hot topic into a conversation, they burst into anger. Barred from these gatherings, Alissia would listen from her secret spot in the nearby bushes, close enough to hear the adult, male conversation peppered with colorful speech. Some discussions she could only try to decipher. She always recognized Tex by voice as well as by sight. He was tall and lean and his speech had a lazy sound that belied quick-thinking competence—he was a lots-of-chocolate, little-foam kind of guy. Red Burns almost always came. His voice and Scottish cadence were distinctive, a signature to his boisterous enthusiasm. Alissia had always loved the lilt of his speech. The tall, blonde man came rarely. He was punctilious in manner, stern and stiff. He never seemed to quite fit with the others even though her father said he was really smart and valuable to the refinery. She knew his name was Máximo. One of her father's friends said that he was not only a cold bastard but that he was "a mean sonuvabitch"--eavesdropping expanded her vocabulary. Máximo's name was always disquieting to her. He still evoked a menace she could not define. Gil Williams was present as always, always dissembling.

Now, trying to salvage her job and her relationship with Tom, Alissia poked around the streets in the Colony. When she parked the car on the Three Hundred Row in front of the bungalow where she had lived, she felt tangled in a surge of jumbled feelings. She tried to unsnarl them. She looked across the street at Eddie's house and thought of him with a mixture of affection and compassion. She played back an incident, seeking to decipher its reality. She and Eddie had been very young then.

What Eddie did still seemed bizarre and incomprehensible. Although she vividly remembered that day, the mishap now seemed removed in a way that made her feel as though she were watching images not of herself, but of someone else who was there, someone whom she knew quite well. Many who lived in the Colony could always recall the tension caused by the accident, if it could be called an accident. She knew that her mother was rough and angry with her that morning. She had been confused because she had not been doing anything wrong. It was a shock when Alissia found Eddie.

The day had seemed innocuous at its outset. Alissia chafed to cross the quiet street to look for Eddie, to ramble in play, to explore outside for as long as possible—at least until she got hungry. She was always a compulsive wanderer. As soon as she could walk she had begun to watch and pull at the back gate. She had learned that she could escape if anyone left it unlatched. She would lurch in unsteady steps down the street, pumping wobbly, pudgy legs as fast as she could in an effort to keep up with the forward cant of her body. When Nessa ran after her baby girl and snatched her up, Alissia would writhe and protest, intoxicated with the excitement of her freedom.

"Mom." Alissia patted her mother's hip. Nessa had not answered her. Her mother was frowning and seemed distracted.

"Can I go now, Mom?" Alissia asked again, tugging at her mother's arm to get her attention.

Nessa responded with a swift admonishment. Her tone was unduly severe for the simple question.

"Alissia, don't you *ever* go to Eddie's unless Miss Cynthia is at home." Again, Nessa insisted. "Not if just Eddie's dad is home. Do you understand?"

"Yes, Mom," Alissia responded in automatic agreement, her head still turned toward the street.

Nessa grabbed her daughter roughly by the shoulders and shook her. "Do you hear me?"

Startled, Alissia stopped still and, eyes wide, turned her head to her mother. "Yes, ma'am," she replied.

Nessa was angry. "Look at me and tell me 'Only if Miss Cynthia is home.'"

Alissia tried to respond to Nessa's sudden wrath. She focused on her mother's tense face and she repeated haltingly "I can only go... ummm—I can go, only go, if Miss Cynthia is home."

At an early age Alissia's inquisitive nature had to be reined in with some rules. Nessa was not a martinet but transgression would bring a reprimand. Then there were the Big Rules. These were few, but Nessa tolerated no infraction of a Big Rule, such as wandering off to the lagoon alone before Alissia could swim. It was quite clear to Alissia that the Miss Cynthia Rule was a Big Rule.

Alissia remembered the Big Rule admonishment with perfect clarity. Her mother had been emotional, her harshness out of character. Even at the memory, Alissia still felt surprise. What had caused such disproportionate reaction to an ordinary request? With hindsight, she wondered what Nessa might have known about Gil Williams. Alissia understood now that her mother felt tainted by divorce and went out of her way to avoid pointed fingers. In addition, Miss Cynthia was also her mother's good friend. Did those things hold Nessa back from confrontation of any kind over Gil Williams? She pictured her mother abruptly backpedaling from her anger that day.

"It's all right, Alissia. This is something girls should learn. It's important. You shouldn't go to anyone's house if the mom or wife isn't there. OK?" Nessa put her arms around her daughter in a protective circle and hugged her. "Go ahead. Go play."

CHAPTER 44

THE KEROSENE DRUM

Cynthia and Nessa had both grown up in Aruba. Because the two women were close friends and also neighbors, Eddie and Alissia had played together from the time they could crawl. The two children seemed to understand each other without words. Since both were seen frequently with one mother or the other, people who didn't know them easily mistook them for fraternal twins.

Edward Thomas Williams had hair that, much to his chagrin, bounded in rebellious curls. It attracted unwelcome comments and provoked an irresistible urge in adults. They would advance on him and rumple his hair with their fingertips. Eddie hated the attention; he hated the comments; he ducked and dodged the intrusive hands, which he hated even more.

The two children were similar in coloring, although Alissia's hair was a shade lighter than Eddie's, a honey-blonde. Its curl was looser--less unruly than Eddie's. In personality, however, the two children were opposites, perhaps complementary. Alissia was gregarious, whereas Eddie was taciturn. Eddie may just have been a loner by nature, but his problems made him even more withdrawn and eccentric. Eddie dodged responsibility. Alissia bent to adult directives when she had to, but she would then search for any small way to make the obliged compliance serve her own ends. And, for better or for worse, the expectations of Alissia's parents compelled her to always endeavor to perform at the highest possible level. Either by consequence or by innate inclination, she developed early a precocious impertinence that often made adults bristle.

Alissia was four years old--"almost five," she would insist. Nessa supervised as Alissia ran across the street into Eddie's yard. She looked around and called out, "Eddie." No answer. "Eddie, where are you?" She heard some odd sounds and walked around the bungalow. Eddie lay on the ground by the kerosene drum, writhing on his back. He gasped, making raspy noises, and clutched at his throat. Alissia let out a loud wail. "Eddie's hurt, Eddie's hurt." Cynthia rushed out the back door of the bungalow.

"Oh, dear God, please help us." She grabbed her son up in her arms. "Alissia, tell your mother we're going to the hospital. Run!" Cynthia ran with Eddie for the garage. The keys were always in the car.

When Nessa heard what had happened, she called to the maid. "Emily, take care of the children until I get back." She ran out to follow Cynthia and Eddie to the hospital.

Nessa sat with Cynthia and the two of them waited while the physician attended Eddie. Silent, Cynthia stared out the window. Then she began to weep quietly.

"I worry so much about that boy. He was born with difficulties. He can be so withdrawn. He seems healthy and active, but he disconnects from people."

Nessa nodded. "I know."

"Ordinary things get complicated with him. Now the kerosene. Why?" She put her head in her hands. "Oh, Nessa. I hope he'll be all right."

Nessa put her arm around Cynthia's shoulders. "He's in good hands, Cynthia. Dr. Ritsema will do everything that can be done."

Later, when Nessa returned home, Alissia ran to her. "Mama, where's Eddie? Is he all right? Is he home? What's wrong?"

Emily stood beside Nessa and Alissia in the kitchen. Nessa crouched down to reassure Alissia. "Eddie's sick. He has to spend the night in the hospital. But Dr. Ritsema says he'll be all right."

"But he looked awful. He couldn't talk. He made horrible noises. Why can't he come home now? I'm scared," she cried.

"Well, honey. He swallowed kerosene from the drum spigot. The doctor took it all out. He can get better now."

"Why did he do that? It smells awful. It's greasy."

"Kids just do strange things. He'll be all right. He should come home tomorrow."

Over the years, the Aruba hospital had pumped the stomachs of numerous small children for the ingestion of kerosene. It was an exceedingly unpleasant procedure. It was also dangerous because of the risk of aspiration--one child had died from resulting pneumonia. People often stored the fuel in corked Coke bottles, not a smart place to keep it, but convenient. The kerosene was used as a fire-starter to grill meat and fish outside at home or at a beach picnic. Children found the bottles too tempting, access too convenient. The hospital staff stood ready to rebuke Cynthia for leaving such a hazard within her son's reach, but just shook their heads when they found out that he had laid down on the ground and let the kerosene dribble into his mouth from the spigot on the barrel.

That evening, when Nessa went back for a second time to the hospital to check on Eddie and comfort Cynthia, Alissia climbed into Emily's lap. Emily came on weekdays to clean and help cook. Emily was as relaxed as Stass was tense. She would throw her head back and lose herself in her own hearty laugh. Now Emily bathed

Alissia in her low and throaty Trinidadian voice. "It's all right, Alissia. Eddie will be all right. Come sit on my lap." She stroked the little girl's hair. Alissia inhaled deeply. Every person had their own scent, she thought. The good, familiar smell of Emily's skin comforted her. She ran her hand over Emily's black arm, beautiful, as smooth as the satin of her mother's evening dress. Only Emily's face had been cratered and ravaged by the smallpox that scourged the islands. Alissia pillowed her head against the expanse of Emily's soft chest.

"Why did he do it, Emily?"

"The Lord knows, Alissia. Kids do crazy things."

"Is it my fault? Today I didn't go early. He always waits for me to come play."

"No, it's not your fault. Things just happen. You probably saved Eddie's life."

Alissia's eyes widened and she looked up at her. "Really?"

"Yes. Don't worry. Hush, now." Emily rocked back and forth with Alissia in her arms and began to softly sing the mockingbird song she always sang.

"Eddie gets sad. Then he won't talk. Not even to me," Alissia said, and tears spilled down her cheeks. "I try and try, but I can't fix it."

Emily comforted Alissia in mellow tones. "You don't have to fix nothing." She continued to rock her and croon the mockingbird song. Exhausted, Alissia nestled down into her arms. Being responsible for everything wore her out.

CHAPTER 45
HAIRCUT

A few days after Eddie's bout with kerosene, Cynthia sat reading in the living room. Gil was working the evening shift. Cynthia looked up from her book as Eddie came out from his bedroom. Cynthia looked up from her book. The boy was moving and walking in a very strange manner. He took one short, halting step at a time, his body as stiff as a plank. His arms pressed like rigid sticks against his sides, not moving, except for the flapping of the fingers of his left hand.

"Eddie."

He did not respond or turn his head. He just stared straight ahead as he progressed awkwardly across the room. The fingers of his left hand snapped open and closed. Cold sweat beaded on Cynthia's face. Her stomach clenched. Maybe the kerosene had damaged Eddie's nervous system. Something was very wrong.

"Eddie." No answer. No reaction at all.

"Eddie."

Eddie stopped his ungainly advance. He stood immobile, eyes fixed ahead. He still did not move his head or his arms, nothing but the fingers.

Cynthia stood up and walked over to him. She put her hand on his shoulder. She opened her mouth to say something and then snapped it closed. She stared with disbelief. A dense curl tumbled off Eddie's head and she watched it float to the floor. It lay there inert in a small, accusing clump. Then another curl rolled off his head and fell. And another.

"Eddie!"

She looked closely at his hair. It looked odd. She took hold of a tuft of curls with the tips of her fingertips and the small bunch lifted off.

"What's this?" she exclaimed.

Eddie turned his head to look at his mother. The movement spilled more loose curls to the floor in little rolls. He had cut off all the hair on the top of his head and then, with great care, piled it back on.

"What did you do? Did you think I wouldn't notice?" A pause. "Are you crazy?" she blurted. She winced at her choice of words.

"I hate my hair. People make fun of me."

Cynthia hid her face with her hands. Her shoulders shook. It was so ridiculous. She tried to suppress spasms of laughter as she hid her smile. Relief poured over her. She dropped her hands and tried to assume a stern expression. She would have to use clippers to even up the shorn, irregular stubble on top of the boy's head. She needed to get that done before Gil came home. She would just say that she had cut his hair shorter because he wasn't a baby anymore and that she got it a little too short. Gil would not think the curl incident was funny. If he got angry, he might take it out on both of them.

People didn't know Gil. He acted pleasant and helpful around others, but he could be brooding and unpredictable at home. He would flare like a spark to a gas leak for no apparent reason. Once when she was coming out of the bedroom they met unexpectedly as he was coming in. He shoved her aside so hard that she gashed her head on the door jamb.

Well, the haircut wasn't life-threatening and eventually it would grow out. She would keep Eddie's hair clipped short from now on.

Cynthia sat back. Her face grew grave. Eddie seemed so fragile. She repeatedly agonized over his disfigurement, feeling guilty, as if she could have had control of how the child was formed in her body. She had wanted more children but maybe it was better that it had never happened for her. She knew Eddie was odd and he did not seem to relate to people. He only suffered Alissia as a playmate and sometimes he withdrew from her. There was also the involuntary finger-flapping of his left hand and his manic focus on things. If Gil yelled, Eddie would bend over, holding his hands over his ears as if in physical pain. He looked like a hermit crab retracting into its shell. He had started to draw but even that was different--no misshapen bananas or awkward stick figures like other kids. He only took interest in drawing endless, tightly convoluted lines, all squeezed together, which did not look like anything.

With Eddie, there was always something strange in store.

CHAPTER 46
NIPPING PROBLEMS

It was now afternoon and Alissia drove to Big Lagoon and walked out to the end of the T-Dock. She sat for a few moments and then lay down to bask in solitude in the sun and wind. Her mind skipped back to Eddie and the kerosene incident which led her to thoughts about the hospital. In the notebook, Grandma G had written about the Lago Hospital.

> April 17, 1940. Gus gashed his head and went to the hospital for stitches. The Company built it for the people they brought in. They lance boils, deliver babies and treat job injuries. Two men we know had emergency operations for appendicitis. Gus says we're lucky there has never been a major refinery disaster, but Lago is pretty strict about safety. Locals who work in the refinery can go to the hospital, too. Dr. Ritsema says that most Arubans who show up get real medical treatment for the first time in their lives. He says they are grateful, stoic patients.

Alissia remembered the hospital, mostly because of her own mishaps resulting from escapades, both solo and with Eddie. The incident that sprang up most vividly in her mind was falling forward when running, her hand landing on a board with a long nail protruding from it. The nail had gone clear through the palm of her hand and stuck up from the back. Dr. Ritsema attended her. He just shook his head and commented, "It is good that you get your tetanus shots."

Alissia had heard one patio forum discussion of the merits of the medical treatment provided by Lago. The group had declared it competent.

"And don't forget. It's also inexpensive," her father had said. "For guys at the lowest wages, the Company provides care at no charge."

"Well, they sure treat all sorts of stuff," responded Tex. "At one point in 1930 some forty guys got dysentery so bad it almost stopped work. The hospital finally figured out that it was being spread by a Chinese cook in the mess hall. They nipped that problem in the bud." He went on to consider a more common affliction: the venereal disease contracted in active Sint Nicolaas brothels. He enjoyed the reaction he provoked when he added, "guess the docs couldn't nip what caused that." Unobtrusive, listening in, at the time Alissia did not understand why all the men laughed.

Apparently, other ills also came from Sint Nicolaas. In addition to women of both day and night, the Village offered the consumption of alcohol as a regular off-work pastime to an unruly community of refinery workers. In consequence, the battered regularly trooped through the hospital to be patched up for injuries sustained in drunken brawls. "In the Village," said Red, "ye never ken whether provocation is real or imagined." Unfortunately, the Lago hospital could not cure all ills. Deaths occurred from sundry causes, including peritonitis and tetanus, neither of which was uncommon.

As on most days, the sun had been shining the day of the hospital discussion and from the Saxton yard one could look out to sea to see the crests of small waves sparkle with specks of its reflected light. Alissia looked out to the horizon of this similarly sunny afternoon and turned her thoughts from medicine and mishaps back to her own dilemma.

CHAPTER 47
PLANTAIN CHRISTMAS

Alissia was on a mission to find peace for herself. She had a deadline to meet--Tom's ultimatum. She tried to figure out what questions she should be asking, where she should look but, instead of answers, visions of Christmas filled her mind. Her mother had dreamed up even more inventive decorating projects and preparation than usual one year and Alissia's excitement had built up over many weeks. Above all else she wanted a specific present which had to be ordered from a catalog and shipped to the island. She just *had* to have it. She had been about five years old and she remembered having such high hopes that she thought she would never go to sleep on Christmas Eve. She had pestered Nessa for months with persistence. Tenacity--obstinacy might be more accurate, she admitted--was still one of her characteristics.

"But Mom, I really, really want a swimming mask. Do you think Santa will bring it?"

"Maybe when you're older."

"But I can swim some now, Mom. And I'm almost six. I can learn to use it."

"Santa's pretty busy. Maybe not this year."

"But I really, really need one."

"You'll probably have to wait."

"But--"

"Alissia, enough!"

Alissia's mouth hung open to continue her plea. She closed it.

That afternoon Alissia had helped her mother make cookies and in the evening, just before bedtime, they set them out for Santa Claus with a glass of the Klim milk that Nessa mixed from powder. In bed, Alissia restlessly turned over so many times that she got wound up in her sheet and had to unsnarl herself. Finally, she succumbed to sleep. At dawn her eyes popped open and she was instantly awake. She put on shorts and a T-shirt. She walked slowly as she passed through the living room. Her excitement mounted as she eyed all the presents under the tree. She entered her parents' bedroom and pressed on her mother's shoulder several times.

"Mom, Mom," she said quietly.

Nessa didn't know eyelids could be so heavy. With a groan, she forced them up.

"Can we open presents now, Mom?"

Nessa stretched, then yawned. The clock read 6:35 AM. She could see the pre-dawn light outside and the sun would soon rise up over the horizon. Not too bad for Christmas morning in a house with children. "OK, honey. Let's wake up Dad and I'll get Duncan up."

Alissia went and sat cross-legged on the polished wood floor in the living room. She gazed with admiration at the tree. She thought it was beautiful. It was really tall, higher than her dad's head. The fake tree sported sparse, disheveled needles and stood misshapen from storage in a box in a hot attic for most of the year. Alissia had lovingly helped to bespangle it with sundry ornaments. At the top, a small home-made angel perched precariously at an angle as it tried to bless its balmy environment. The tree dripped silver tinsel which emulated the icicles of an unknown distant winter where people said it got as cold as the freezer compartment of the refrigerator. The overabundance of ersatz silver icicles helped camouflage the tree's structural shortcomings. Just for Christmas Eve the prized string of multi-colored electric lights had not been turned off when the family went to bed. All night they had cast their auspicious glow.

The living room boasted showy homemade decorations. Nessa had collected branches of Seagrape trees. She filled an empty Flit can with aluminum-colored paint that Stass had brought her from the refinery and thoroughly sprayed the branches and leaves using the hand pump. Outside, the trade wind quickly dried her handiwork. She added red crepe paper bows. Now, festooning the living room walls, the decorations announced Caribbean Christmas cheer.

Nessa appeared with Duncan. Stass joined them. While the children slept, presents had mysteriously appeared and now they seemed to beckon. Alissia noted that some of the cookies were gone. Santa must like oatmeal cookies, like her Dad.

Duncan was young enough that tearing the paper off his wrapped gifts was as interesting to him as the contents. Alissia got a new dress, which didn't excite her much—especially since she most often wore shorts, sometimes with a T-shirt. From some relative, there was a doll which she would place with care on a shelf and never again touch--when Alissia wasn't reading, she ran and swam and played outside with Eddie climbing trees and doing other interesting things. Dolls were sissy. An auntie she had never seen had shipped to her the usual, hoped-for and eagerly-awaited gift of books of which she never had enough. She finally opened her last gift with both dread and hope. She was elated. It was what she most wanted, what she had asked Santa for in her carefully written note. She danced around waving her gift in the air and then ran to hug her mom and dad. She knew that they were really responsible for Santa, but she was not yet quite through with maintaining the fun of the myth.

"Santa brought me a swimming mask!"

As they did every year, early in the afternoon the family trooped off to Grandma and Grandpa Gifford's for Christmas dinner. Food was plentiful, but Alissia eagerly awaited the special dessert. On the quay in Oranjestad, Grandma G and Nessa had purchased plantains from one of the sailboats from Venezuela. They let the fruit ripen until it looked rotten: squishy, black and ugly. The flesh inside turned deliciously sweet. They fried long, limp slices and Grandma arranged the gold and brown strips, now firm, on a large oval platter. She sprinkled them with sugar. She carried out the platter of still-warm plantain to the dining-room table and Grandpa Gus brought over the bottle of rum.

"Get me the matches, princess," he told Alissia.

He poured a measure of the fragrant Cuban spirits into a large serving spoon. Holding it carefully, he had Alissia steady the box with both hands so that he could strike a match. He lit the rum and poured the flaming liquid over the amber fruit, then added another lighted spoonful. Blue flames ran and danced the length of the platter, melting the sugar and then, slowly, they died out and Grandpa served everyone. To Stass, Grandma G served a slice of lemon meringue pie which he considered quite exotic enough.

"Here you go, princess," Grandpa Gifford said, as he handed Alissia her plate.

With her fork, Alissia placed a morsel of plantain into her mouth and held it there for a moment, unctuous against her tongue. She could smell the scent of rum and sweetness of plantain as she breathed out through her nose, adding to its rich taste. She held the heady blend of flavors in her mouth, tasting it, before she chewed and swallowed. She would forever associate plantain flambé with holidays and special occasions. The dish was predictably delectable. Audible sighs and murmurs that evidenced pleased palates and replete stomachs rippled around the table. There was no better dessert to culminate this meal of celebration.

Only one traditional activity remained. Christmas day was always warm and they always ceremonially finished it at Big Lagoon. Even Stass made a rare appearance at the beach. Since it was late afternoon, he shed the broad-brimmed hat and long-sleeved shirt he always wore so the sun would not fry his fair skin. Normally he saved any exposure for fishing, for which no sacrifice was too great. Since Aruba lay so close to the equator, there was no great difference in the length of days and nights at different times of the year. The sun, which would soon set, cast long, persimmon-colored streams of light over the water. Ending this Christmas day, the members of the contented group talked softly and lazed in the warm shallows of the blue Caribbean lagoon on the right side of paradise.

In retrospect, Alissia recognized that she had had a keen sense for how far she dared venture out of bounds without attracting attention. With stealth, she deliberately broke rules when she thought it worth the risk of being noticed. It had been a mistake to break the Big Rule. Thoughts of Uncle Ruddy, tales of war, the incident and the death all gnarled in an obscure, guilty murk that made her body stiffen. She made herself replace the shadowy snarl with an image of Grandpa Gifford and the tautness began to melt. *The thought of Grandpa Gifford makes me feel safe. If I will see myself like his much-loved princess, I can overpower the turmoil in my life.*

CHAPTER 48
BARRACUDA

With her swimming mask at Big Lagoon, Alissia swam from dock to dock and could see the bottom clearly. In one area, undulating arms of seaweed reached up for her as small shapes darted in and out of its dense bed. At first it was frightening and she would put up her mask so she couldn't see so well--just as she chose not to see disturbing incidents in her life. It was more comforting to have everything look blurry and familiar. She knew it was silly not to look with the clear vision of the mask because everything was still there. Eventually, she was able to force herself to brave the new perspective of her underwater world.

Even so, swimming alone around the docks was intimidating. Alissia thought of all the stories she had heard about barracudas, recounted with the best embellishment and gory details the storyteller could muster to impress his audience.

There was good reason for her to give the stories thought. Silver barracudas, long and slim, are voracious, opportunistic predators. Relying on short bursts of speed up to twenty-seven miles per hour, these solitary hunters tear off chunks of flesh to kill and consume large prey. They sometimes mistake things that glint and shine for quarry.

"Don't wear anything shiny when you swim," Alissia had heard. "The barracudas think the glint of a ring or bracelet in the sunlight is a small fish. They go for it. They're so fast, they can rip the arm off a grown man."

The great barracuda species that is common to the Caribbean normally strikes once, a lightning quick, fierce hit. Two parallel rows of sharp, cutting teeth in their upper and lower jaws cause deep, slashing wounds that damage nerves and tendons and sometimes sever large blood vessels.

"Boy, do they have a mouthful of teeth. If you catch one fishing, it'll bite you even after you land it in the boat," avowed Stass. "The Arubans say that sometimes one will jump out of the water to attack a fisherman." But despite the prevalent fear of these predatory fish, the reports of attacks on humans were infrequent.

The first time that Alissia went swimming by herself at Big Lagoon she thought she caught a streak of silver from the corner of her eye. With a spurt of panic, she swam to the wooden ladder and shot up onto the T-dock. She peered down into the clear lagoon. She could see tight schools of small fish make synchronized swirls through the water but she couldn't see under the dock. She sat for a while. On the far end of the dock, two men sat talking in hushed tones. It was a good place for André Valenzuela and Máximo Hirsch to talk with no danger of being overheard. Alissia could not presage the harm that, like barracudas, the two men would inflict on others. She did not know the damage Máximo would cause her or how André would affect the fate of pretty Miss Jultje. The men soon left.

On subsequent trips to swim at Big Lagoon, as Alissia gained in confidence and strength, she ventured farther. Within a few months she could swim clear to the raft anchored between the docks and the reef. Her boldness grew. Making herself acquire new skills--and especially making herself face fears--taught her to push boundaries in her life. It instilled in her a boldness

Although she did catch occasional glimpses of a barracuda, the predator's attention never turned to her. It was not the sea that held the threat to Alissia. The closed environment of the Colony itself fomented graver dangers.

CHAPTER 49

ARUBA DAY

Alissia led a life well shielded from most menace. The daily events she experienced on the island might range from innocuous to perilous, but since most were benign, the majority of her misadventures were usually inconsequential—but not all.

A light scratching sensation wriggled into dim consciousness. Alissia sighed and turned from her side onto her back. The intrusion faded away. Floating in blissful and dreamless oblivion, she had no perception of time when the small wriggly movement on her stomach again pierced the gauzy veil of sleep. Reflexively she laid her hand on the spot that seemed to move. Nothing. Then it moved again. Awareness streamed into her head, filling dark corners. She knew she felt something. It was a crawling sensation. She felt it with her fingers. A small, hard shape was trapped in a fold of the bed sheet at her waist. The shape was alive. From groggy slumber, she exploded with a yowl into sitting position. She leaped out of bed, teetered, then caught her balance. She yanked back the sheet. It was a moonlit night and dawn was approaching. From the folds of the sheet she saw a scorpion tumble out.

Nessa, awakened from a dead sleep, ran into the room. "What's the matter, Alissia?"

"A scorpion!"

"Where?"

"In my bed."

"Did it sting you?"

"No. Get it, Mom."

"Get me a shoe. Quick."

Alissia ran to the closet and came back with a sandal. The scorpion had crawled back into a fold of the sheet. Nessa uncovered the creature. She pushed at it with the sandal and brushed it off the bed onto the wooden floor. She smacked it sharply, twice—but not so hard that she would have to scrape it up. Alissia ran to get toilet paper. Nessa picked up the feebly moving remains of the intruder with care. She carried the wad of paper into the bathroom and flushed it down the toilet. She turned up her right hand and cradled the back of it in her other hand.

Red Burns had told Nessa that local scorpions were a subspecies peculiar to Aruba, the *Buthidae centruroides testaceus arubensis*, he was pleased to specify. Nessa walked back into the bedroom looking at the white scar in her right palm. She rubbed the small, hard knurl with her left thumb. The knot was a battle scar inflicted on her the year before while hanging up clothes to dry in sun and wind. She had a shallow clothespin bag that tied around her waist. When she reached in for a wooden clothespin, the scorpion got her. It felt like fire being injected into her arm. The hand throbbed, her arm became red and swollen. Pain traveled up into her armpit. The sting made her sick. She didn't feel like doing much of anything until the next day. It took a few days for the effect of the venom to dissipate.

Nessa put her arms around Alissia and hugged her. "It's a good thing it didn't sting you, Alissia. That's a scary way to wake up." She took a deep breath. The venom would surely have had a stronger effect on the body weight of a six-year-old.

"Well, you might as well get up," Nessa said. "It will soon be time to get ready for school."

Dressed to go, which included binding, hated shoes, Alissia headed across the street to get Eddie. They usually left in time to walk, even though there was a school bus. Their cache was not far from the house. They quickly removed and stashed the stiff instruments of torture they wore on their feet and continued on, happy and barefoot. On the way home, they would retrieve the shoes and put them back on.

That day, in class, after being repeatedly hushed when she wriggled, waved her hand, and volunteered an answer to every question the teacher posed, Alissia put her head down and tackled the next assignment. The children had to do multiplication and division problems and hand in their papers. Alissia worked fast. When she had almost finished she pressed down hard and broke the point off her pencil. She went to the sharpener on the wall and cranked the handle to re-sharpen it. On her way back to her desk she walked by Eddie. He had been admonished not to fiddle with his marbles in class but, as she had guessed, she could see that he was not absorbed by arithmetic: he was penciling another drawing of tight, curvy lines that clung together for safety. She steadied herself with one hand on his desk as she passed by, leaving behind a small, folded piece of paper which he palmed. She gave him answers to just enough questions to keep him out of trouble. She felt a twinge of sadness. It seemed like she always had to watch out for him. She worried about her mom, too. The load felt heavy. It was hard enough to keep herself out of trouble. And she worked hard for perfect grades to try to buy approval at home. If she just worked harder, if she performed and excelled, surely then she would be loved or liked or accepted by others.

In the evening, after dinner, Stass gave Alissia an empty Cuban cigar box with which he had just finished. "Here's one of those boxes you like."

The boxes were a wonder. The wood was so thin and light that when she picked one up it felt as if it had been planed from air. When Stass was a boy, he used to tell them, he would cut off the lid and stretch different sizes of rubber bands lengthwise across one of the cigar boxes in an effort to fabricate a guitar. He'd pluck at the bands to see if he could pick out a tune. He soon progressed to the real instrument. Now, at small Sunday afternoon gatherings in the Colony, he often played and sang for family and friends.

Alissia opened the lid of the cigar box and put her nose down into it. She drew the heady residual fragrance of the tobacco in through her nostrils. It was intoxicating. Sometimes her dad would hand her the paper ring off one of his Havana cigars when he picked it up to clip the end and she would sport the adornment on a finger for the short time that it lasted. She would choose good treasures to store in this box. She stored the handkerchiefs she sometimes received as gifts, so pretty and so useless, in one. They were now permeated with the heavy redolence of tobacco.

Stass was in an expansive mood. He began to sing "I could have danced all night..." and grabbed Nessa in his arms. With grandiose movements, he twirled her in circles around the gleaming wood floor of the living-room in her bare feet and shorts. Nessa laughed. Alissia felt light and happy. Dad could be so much fun sometimes. She felt like she was a part of this family merriment, for once not standing outside the circle of light looking in.

Before she went to bed that night, Alissia went outside. There was just enough light for her to clamber up to her perch in the fork of the Seagrape tree. She sat suspended in the perfect temperature of the evening. The trade wind sang to her as it wafted the light fragrance of flowers across the garden. The night sky dropped falling stars that left sparkling trails to mark their trajectory. It was good that there were plenty of falling stars. Alissia had plenty of wishes. She wished she would grow wings. She envisioned herself rising up into the sky and it seemed as if she could feel the freedom of flight.

CHAPTER 50

THE BANANAQUIT

The next morning, the soft, pale dawn diffused through Alissia's consciousness. She moved her small body slightly to feel the texture of the light cotton sheet graze across her skin. She slept in just panties and the sheet felt good against the breeze that whirled in, blowing through the window screens, sliced into streams as it passed between the wooden louvers. Alissia lay still a few moments to enjoy the safe, comfortable feeling of her bed while she listened to the morning crescendo of twittering birds. She rose quietly and slipped on a pair of shorts. She padded in bare feet across the wooden floors of the bungalow and then across the kitchen floor, feeling the cooler linoleum on the soles of her feet. She reached the back door of the house. Unlatching the hook of the screen door, she slipped silently outside, taking care not to let the spring on the door slam it shut. The sky had lightened now to shell pink and the sun would soon appear. She wanted to get there in time to watch. She would hide where she could not be seen. She only had to go two blocks. In the muted light of early morning she traveled quickly along the familiar, fat pipeline that lay inches above sharp grey coral. Her practiced bare feet turned out slightly to hug the curve of the pipe. Holding her arms out for balance, she speeded up to a run. She travelled everywhere through the Colony on the network of water pipes that, instead of an alley, ran inches above ground between the bungalows constructed in tidy rows. She and Eddie always took care not to fall on the savage, jagged points of the coral that had ripped their flesh more than once. At the end of the first block, she took to the asphalt street.

When she reached the house, Alissia crept silently around to the back. There she burrowed into the hedge and sat down out of sight, cross-legged on the sandy ground. Good. He wasn't out yet. She settled in to wait. Shortly she heard a screen door creak open. Red Burns emerged into the sun's first rays. The Scot stretched his arms up to greet the sky, then walked to the middle of the yard and sat down in a low wooden garden chair. He shifted his weight around to get comfortable sitting on the slats. Then he took a small jar out of one pocket and poured a little mound of white granular sugar into his hand. He rested his forearm on the arm of the chair positioning it with his palm up. Red's eyes roamed around the garden as he sat quiet and motionless with his offering.

Usually Alissia did not see anyone on her solitary forays out to greet the arrival of the day. When she had chanced by Mr. Burns's house on one of her early wanderings the week before, she had crouched hidden in the hedge to see what Red was doing out in his yard so early. That is when she first saw it. Now she stayed iguana-still, controlling even her breathing as she peered through the leaves. She hoped it would come again. She waited expectantly. A flash of black and white flitted in a bush near Red and she heard the whispery, silvery trill. The call was followed by swift movement. The bird darted in, alighted on the back of Red's chair, then flitted to his hand. She watched with sheer delight as it began to eat sugar from Red's hand in small, short pecks. She held her breath. The showy little bird bobbed, displaying bright yellow patches in its plumage.

Alissia wondered if she could do that, have a bird come and eat from her palm. How long would it take for a bird to get used to her if she sat quietly every morning? As she watched, her nose began to tickle. She tilted her head down and rubbed her nose against her upper arm. The urge to sneeze built up and then slowly subsided. The pressure built up again more insistently. *Oh, no!* She pressed her lips together and held her nose to stifle it. She couldn't stop. Air exploded out loudly through tightly-pinched nostrils and pressed lips. The bird darted away and Red started. He got up and walked over to the sound. Bending down, he saw crossed legs on the ground and a small shape filtered by leaves.

He chuckled. "I think I caught me a little spy. Who's this?"

Alissia stuck her head out.

"Why, it's Miss Alissia Saxton."

"I'm sorry I scared the bird." She dipped her head in embarrassment. She felt she had intruded on something private. She knew who Red was, of course, but she had never talked to this adult except to greet him politely when she was with her mother.

"What are you doing here so early? I didnae think anyone else was up, much less out and about. Did you see my wee friend?"

Yes, sir." She debated whether to say more. "I watched you before."

He laughed. "So, you like the quiet of early morning, like me. My Rosa sleeps late. If I'm here and not working, I like to sit in my garden for a while to see the sun come up. Later I take coffee to Rosa in bed. I saw these little birds fly into the Kibrahacha Restaurant and eat sugar out of a dish. They set it out for them on the back of the piano. So first I lured this little fella to a dish. Then I wondered if I could get him to come to my hand. It took him a while, but he decided sugar is too sweet to pass up, even if I am scary." He laughed.

"What kind of bird is it?"

Red smiled. "It's a bananaquit, a *Coereba flaveola*." He rolled the Latin name off his tongue for himself. "Some people call it a sugar bird. That's an easy name. The Arubans call it *chibichibi*. It eats insects and fruit and it sips nectar from flowers. It loves sugar. Smart bird. I'd like sweets better than bugs, fer sure. There are interesting birds and bats in Aruba, and lots of other critters, too."

"I'd like to know about bats." Alissia fidgeted. "I need to go. My mom worries when she wakes up and I'm gone."

"Be off with ye, then. We'll talk more about critters another day."

Alissia crawled out of the hedge. She nodded good-bye as she rose to her feet and scurried away. She liked Mr. Burns. He was comfortable. Not rough—and not scary like Eddie's dad. Maybe Mr. Burns would tell her more about birds and things.

CHAPTER 51
JUMPING CACTUS

"Pull it off! Pull it off," Alissia screamed. It burned like fire. Eddie stood next to her but didn't move.

"Eddie, pull it off!"

He stuck out a hand and pulled it back.

Alissia started crying. She held her left leg out at an angle, touching the ground with just her toes. The large cactus leaf covered almost the full length of her thigh. She had not run into it, just barely grazed it.

They were threading their way through a cactus patch in the coral between Baby Lagoon and the church on their way home. People sometimes talked about jumping cactus. At the lightest possible contact, it seemed like the cactus really did jump. When Alissia's thigh grazed the leaf, it instantly detached and sank a profusion of needles into the flesh of her leg. Each sharp tip burned into her and she was too terrified to move. Alissia cautiously pulled at the top of the leaf, away from her thigh. The angle drove the lower needles in deeper and she yowled. It would take two hands, one at the top and one at the bottom, to quickly yank the large oval straight out and off her leg. Eddie backed away, both hands behind his back.

"Eddie. Help me!"

A car approached. The children saw few cars in the Colony when they were out and about. It slowed down and stopped. With relief Alissia saw Red Burns get out.

"Begorra, lassie. Looks like you're in a bit o' trouble." He went to Alissia, and with two hands in one quick jerk he ripped the cactus from her leg.

Small drops of blood welled up in a grid on her thigh and she could feel the sting of each puncture. Red walked a few feet away and took out a pocket knife. He sliced off two chunky leaves of an *Aloe vera* and took them over to her. He squatted and held the wide ends toward her. They oozed a thick, clear sap.

"Rub this on your leg. It'll help ye."

Alissia spread the Aloe's gel thickly over the affected area.

"There you go, lassie. That cactus has a bite." He patted her on the top of the head. "Do ye want a ride home or do ye prefer to walk?"

"No, we'll walk. Thank you, Mr. Burns."

Aloe sap was used in generous measure on the island for scrapes, sunburn, wasp stings, nettles—not to mention cactus—and more. It was good the plants were so easy to find. Alissia was relieved and grateful for the rescue. The Aloe gel did help some. But, from experience, she thought it helped more for sunburn and nettles than for cactus.

After dinner that night Alissia sat up in the fork of the Seagrape tree. She looked out over the lagoon that reflected the crimson of the sunset and beyond to the blue expanse of sea. For a while she imagined herself flying, wondering how far could she could go. She brought herself back down to her perch. She felt sad that Eddie wouldn't help her. She did lots of things for him. He acted like he didn't care about her.

She leaned back against the trunk of the tree. She liked being outside. *Maybe he just couldn't,* she thought. *That's how he is.* She turned her thoughts to Red Burns and anticipation replaced her sadness. She hoped he would tell her more about birds--and other stuff, too.

CHAPTER 52
INTO THE CAVE

Alissia was still on her mission in Aruba to salvage the perfect, staid life she had built, but she set aside thoughts of work and of Tom to contemplate the tall wire fence she faced. It surrounded a deep, open cavern. Standing here she realized that it was when they went to the Cave that she really connected to Red Burns. The man's expansive, caring nature had filled an aching, emotional void for her.

In the children's minds, the Cave loomed large in the middle of the Colony, surrounded by bungalows. *Stay Out,* the sign admonished. Stories about the Cave both repelled and attracted them.

"There are gases that can kill you."

"Beware of the poisonous snakes."

"There are scary, dark tunnels. You'll get lost and never get out."

"I heard there was a fierce ocelot."

"Bats live in there."

Thus had the cavern taken on a disquieting personality of its own. The roof of the Cave had collapsed at some distant time, leaving it open to the sky. The large hole thus created at the surface was some twenty by forty feet across with a twenty-foot drop to the bottom. To preclude falls by accident and discourage climbs down by design, the Company had surrounded the cavity's large opening with a tall chain-link fence. A large tree grew up from the bottom, its canopy reaching up just above ground level. Lacing their fingers into the metal mesh of the fence, Alissia and Eddie pressed their foreheads against it. They gazed down intently for a while. When they straightened up, they both wore a diamond pattern indented on their foreheads. They moved around to examine the big hole from various angles, trying to see as much as they could wherever foliage did not obscure their view. At the bottom, they could see sand and clumps of pointed grey coral. The regular method of access was to climb down the limbs of the Seagrape tree—an enticing activity in itself. Once one reached the floor of the cave, the openings into passages and tunnels that were reported held a lure of their own. Temptation trampled fear.

They knew, of course, where the hole in the fence had been cut at ground level by some Colony interloper. On hands and knees, they crawled through it, then shimmied down the Seagrape tree. They dropped onto the sandy floor at the bottom of the cave. Standing close together, pressed back to back, they peered around. Tree branches cast moving shadows. Dark crevices, nooks and crannies surrounded them, harboring chimeras of their imagination. Some of the openings led off into Stygian passages. Abruptly something flapped about their heads and they threw up their arms and ducked. A form flew up and out of the cavern. They were jumpy and nervous and their hearts drummed in their chests.

"A bird?" whispered Alissia.

They didn't know what might be down here. Neither said a word as they bolted as a unit for the tree and scrambled back up to safer grounds. After fearing the Colony Cave for so long, just venturing into to it was adventure enough. They had made a start.

Alissia wanted to know more about the Cave but she didn't want to ask her parents. Better not to show too much interest and provoke an interdiction. Red Burns would probably know. She hung around his yard until she could ask him.

Alissia told her mother that Red had offered to tell them about the Cave in the Colony and what lived in it. He had even said that he would take Eddie and Alissia down there sometime if their parents gave permission. Since the Colony did not have telephones, people went to each other's bungalows to communicate. Nessa walked over with Alissia to the Burns's place.

"Can we go, Mom? Can we? Please!" she said, skipping along and lifting up onto her toes with each step. She did not mention her brief foray down the big Seagrape tree with Eddie.

Nessa would herself like to see the Cave. And she didn't think the two children should pester Red Burns.

She knocked on the door of the bungalow and Rosa answered. Nessa explained why she had come. That Red was going to talk to the children about bats and things, and that they might slip down into the Cave to explore. Would Rosa like to go if she and the kids went? Rosa said no, she didn't think so, but that she would get Red. He loved to do things like that.

"Especially weeth company," said Rosa.

The hole in the fence was a tighter squeeze for the two adults than for the children. With Red in the lead and Nessa last, each in turn scrambled down the Seagrape tree.

Standing in dim light on the sandy floor of the cave, Red told them softly that they might encounter snakes.

"Watch where ye step. Check dark areas before ye step in."

They stood close together and looked around.

"All this used to be under the sea," said Red. "A geologist from Maracaibo told me that this island comes from volcanic activity over ninety million years ago. The molten rock that flowed up is called the Aruba Lava Formation. Have ye seen the round black lava on the north end of the island? What we call pillow lava?"

Nessa and the two children nodded assent.

"We see the round stuff sometimes when Dad takes us for a drive," said Alissia.

"Those round shapes were formed under water. Then movements of the earth's crust pushed up the sediment of underwater coral reefs. That's the surface limestone we see everywhere. We all just call it coral. There's plenty of jagged coral all around the Colony."

Eddie and Alissia were intimately familiar with the jagged black lava and sharp grey coral that covered the surface of the island, a ripping menace to bare feet and flesh.

Red continued. "Limestone is very porous and water has made caves and tunnels everywhere in Aruba." Red pointed to the tunnels that branched off in different directions from where they stood.

He continued. "We probably won't see an ocelot," he said, "even though there are a few on the island. People brought wee kittens from Venezuela for pets. Now they're grown and roam wild. The body of a grown cat—not including the tail—is only about two-and-a-half to three feet long." He held his hands apart to show the length. It looked plenty long to the children. "They prefer the *cucunu* and areas on the windy side, where we dinnae have many people. If one hears us, it will disappear through some tunnel. But ye dinnae want to corner one. They're scrappy fighters. They mark their territory with urine. Phew. It's strong. It'll knock ye over."

"I'd like to see the little kittens," said Alissia.

Red mopped his neck and face with his kerchief, even though they were out of the sun. "Well. Here's the thing," he continued. "Each female usually has only one kitten and only every two years or so. We need to protect the species if we don't want ocelots to disappear. They're bonnie animals."

I like this stuff better than Pilgrims and Indians, Alissia thought.

Eddie fidgeted. When no beam of attention focused on him, some subjects could entice him to engage. Like a hermit crab, he tentatively ventured out of his shell. "Are there bats down here? Something flew past us the other day." He caught Nessa's quick glance. He looked at his feet. "We were just walking by," he lied. "Up top."

Nessa raised an eyebrow, but didn't say anything.

Red continued. "I'll get to that. We have special critters in Aruba. Some only live here, nowhere else. Like our rattlesnake. It's a rare kind. The Arubans call it *cascabel.* It's usually on our end of the island. It's pale in color, like the ground. It almost looks pink. The babies don't hatch from eggs. They're born live."

Eddie and Alissia listened intently.

"The baby rattlers are venomous from the minute they are born. Ye know venomous means poisonous?" he interjected.

The children nodded.

"Their venom is one of the most toxic of all rattlesnakes." All three listeners were duly impressed.

"And our little owl, the one we call Shoco, only lives in Aruba. It burrows in the ground. The *Athene cunicularia arubensis,*" he specified. He could indulge his love of taxonomic names when he held people's interest with his narrative. "We have special kinds of bats, too."

"Do they suck blood?"

Red spread out his arms and swooped down toward the kids. "Time for dinner!" They shrieked. "Just kidding. There're a bunch of bats in the world, almost a thousand kinds. Only a few feed on blood. Bats are important. They fly at night and they go to the cactus flowers and such that only open at night here because it is so hot and dry. They carry pollen. The cactus and other deserty plants here couldnae survive without the bats. And our birds eat fruits that ripen from flowers that the bats pollinate. A couple of kinds of bats live in this cave. Maybe that's what ye saw, Eddie. Something must have disturbed it, if it flew out in daylight. Wonder what that coulda been." His eyes twinkled and he looked at Nessa.

I feel like Alice, falling, falling, falling down the hole, thought Alissia. *Into another world.* She liked this. It was more interesting than a lot of things that she and Eddie did by themselves.

"We have quite a few species of bats in Aruba. I'll give ye some easy names." There's the long-tongued bat." He clowned, sticking out his tongue long enough to provoke chuckles. "The long-nosed bat." He grabbed the end of his nose. "And leaf-chinned bats," he said, stroking his chin. The last two only live in Aruba, Bonaire and Curaçao. Nowhere else in the world." He concluded, "Bats here eat different things. Nectar from night-blooming flowers, insects...even fish."

"Let's explore." Red removed the flashlight he had hanging from the belt that anchored his khaki shorts around his robust middle. "Stay behind me. Stay close and step where I step." Lighting the way, he led them into one of three caverns that opened into the area where they were standing. He illumined the dark space to show them stalactites and stalagmites. Then he moved the beam to show some deep holes. His tone changed. "These wells were dug by phosphate miners." In the dim lights, he looked at Eddie and Alissia in turn. "If one of us fell in," he said gravely, "it would be a really big problem." They all nodded. They gazed around in awe. They had not realized that the system of caves and tunnels was so big. They were standing under the bungalows of the Colony.

"Well, I think it's time to go. I'm working the four-to-twelve shift. When they stood at the base of the Seagrape tree, Red had a serious look. "Dinnae come down here by yourselves," he admonished Eddie and Alissia. "If one of ye goes down a well, it's big trouble. Ye understand, right?"

Alissia and Eddie nodded again, impressed. "Yes, sir."

"Now you've looked around. Come with your mom or dad. I could come back sometime, too. Better not to talk too much about our little visit. The fence is up there because the Company doesn't want us down here. But some of us come down anyway. It's too tempting. Right?" He winked and smiled.

I wish I had an uncle just like Red, Alissia thought with longing. *Mom talks about my Uncle Ruddy who died in the attack, just before I was born. I bet Red is what he would be like.*

In her head Alissia carried an abstraction of Nessa's brother, Ruddy, someone she had pieced together from photographs, family reminiscences and occasional tossed comments. She began to overlay her perception of substantive, present Red on the distant and illusory person she knew only in her mind. She shaped for herself a surrogate Uncle Ruddy. Her new Uncle Ruddy was present and real, embodied in the ebullient Red who never criticized her and was never harsh. She felt an immediate bond with this tender-hearted, living uncle, her new uncle, an uncle whom she could lose.

CHAPTER 53
WHAT THE DEVIL?

Alissia's trek back to the island distilled moments of pure pleasure as well as sparks of euphoria that scattered her attention. The odyssey also plunged her into moments of heartache that clouded her concentration, but she made herself keep focus.

Alissia and Rika talked over lunch. "Time then seemed unhurried," said Alissia. "One week resembled another. They just floated by in leisure."

Rika nodded. "Yes, always sun and sea—and the faithful breeze."

"It was any unusual event that seemed to mark the passing of time for us. People looked forward to any incident out of the ordinary. Anything that brought a change of pace."

"Ja," Rika replied. She seemed to look off in the distance for a moment, then said, "But some things were too much out-of-ordinary."

Alissia was quick to respond. "Well, no one wished for job injuries, that's for sure. Like the water contamination or the war catastrophe. Just little things to break routine. People inflated trifles to gigantic proportions. Then they laughed at themselves. We all did."

"I liked your mother's phrase for that. 'A sense of the ridiculous.'"

"Rika, do you remember the big scare about criminals?"

"Of course. We all worried."

"Anyone who was here still talks about it," said Alissia. "One more story of legend. I overheard it discussed many times on our back patio."

"Ah, yes. You heard many interesting things from that group. But I think overheard is not the right word. No?"

Alissia tried to contain her grin. "Ach," she said, imitating Rika's Dutch. "You know me too well. In any case, we both know what happened."

Although it provoked legitimate consternation at the time, after the fact the story held value as entertainment. It was told and retold with enthusiastic relish and exaggerated embellishment. Alissia had listened to more than one recounting of the incident.

Eager to talk about the event that certainly deviated from daily routine, the usual clutch of refinery men congregated on the Saxton patio at Bungalow 362. Stass passed out chilled Cokes and beers. The men stood or sat in the shade, laughing and talking. They had arrived by car and by scooter. When they removed their hard hats, the bands inside emanated the rich, earthy smell of warm leather, damp with male sweat. Most of the men sported the common insignia: a tidy row of pens and pencils lined up in their front shirt pockets. The ubiquitous slide rules were too long or they would carry them there, too.

Gil looked pleased. "Well, you heard what showed up in Sint Nicolaas harbor yesterday. Pretty unlikely." He paused for effect. "Ten convicts. Would you believe it? They escaped from the penal colony on Devil's Island."

Tex did not like the sound of that. "I heared a bunch of guys showed up. Didn't know they was jailbirds." He scowled. He had long assumed the role of watchdog for the refinery and the Colony. "Devil's Island is bad news."

"Well, these fellows arrived in a wreck of a sailboat. It's only fourteen feet long." Gil shook his head. "I don't think I've ever seen such an unseaworthy pile of sticks afloat."

"Why did they head for Aruba?" queried Stass.

"They didn't," Gil answered. "They didn't know where the heck they were. They thought Colombia sounded like a good place to go."

The men chuckled.

Tex pursued his point. "Are these convicts running around here loose?" he asked.

Máximo Hirsch was in the group. He nodded to acknowledge Tex's concern. "I checked. The Dutch stepped in and put them in jail overnight. They will not be causing trouble."

Stass had seen them. "Those guys couldn't cause trouble if they wanted to. They're just skin and bones. They were probably happy to see the inside of that jail because they got fed." He laughed. "Heck, even I might be willing to be locked up for a square Dutch meal. You know how they heap food on a plate." He eyed Tex's lank form. "You know, Tex, you could use some of that Dutch cooking."

"Well, wherever these scoundrels be, I think ye'll agree that any Aruba conditions are a wee bit better than Devil's Island," said Red.

Reporting on the boat, Gil said, "A couple of the guys are repairing it. Plugging holes, mostly. Should be ready tomorrow," said Gil. "I'll talk to everyone. We'll get them some water and food to take off with."

"Well, I suppose the French'll hear about this little visit," said Stass. "There'll be the devil to pay with the French over any help they get here. Pun intended." He laughed and shook his head. "I'll tell you, those guys are one sorry looking lot."

Alissia well remembered the details of what had happened. After a night in jail, the Dutch released the convicts. Even imperturbable Máximo displayed sympathy for their plight. He had the refinery's pilot boat tow the patched-up vessel out well beyond the reef to send the escaped convicts back on their way. Just minutes later when the two men on the pilot boat looked back, the small sail had disappeared. They turned around and went out again, only to find the craft capsized with the recidivist unfortunates clinging to its bottom. They fished the bedraggled derelicts out of the water and brought them back again to dry land. All they had left were the rags on their backs. The Dutch clapped them back in jail.

This time Gil took up a collection among the refinery workers and the men even convinced the Company to pitch in. The miserable sailboat had sunk. The convicts were shortly provided with another small craft and again sent off to sea with a few provisions. They were last seen heading in the general direction of Panama and were never heard from again.

When the French heard of this they protested vigorously to the Dutch.

"You have aided and abetted desperate criminals!"

Dutch authorities in turn blamed the sentimentality of some local Americans. But, of course, as Stass pointed out, the Dutch did release the men from jail—more than once—allowing them to twice embark on their voyage of escape. And refinery men from a dozen countries had contributed to the cause for which Gil solicited.

The general consensus around the refinery and the Colony was that it was well worth whatever was donated for the entertainment that the whole episode provided.

Alissia had heard Red Burns laugh about it.

"Seeing those blokes was a lot more fun than the last movie that the Company brought in, if I could even remember what the devil it was," he had said. He then guffawed his contagious laughter and, for the time being at least, Colony life had apparently resumed an uneventful course while the refinery cranked out fuel.

Alissia sat very still. She looked off as if trying to discern something, somewhere beyond Rika's kitchen.

Rika waited. After a minute or two, she asked "What is it, Alissia? Where did you go?"

"It was the escape, Rika. The adventure. The story just makes me picture flying away on a great adventure of my own."

CHAPTER 54
HERMIT CRABS

After lunch, Rika had to run an errand.

"I'll be here for a while," Alissia told her. "Then I'll go back out around three or so."

"Later I will see you then," responded Rika as she left.

Alissia lay stretched out on Rika's comfortable couch. Years ago, she had started out with little adventures here in Aruba, but her fixation on taking off for a major adventure had taken over her life. It threatened everything she worked so hard for. *Have I become too driven? Too serious?* she asked herself. A further thought came to her. *My desire to escape is because I feel trapped. That's why I want out!* She took a deep breath. Maybe she just needed to put some carefree, plain silliness back in her life. She pictured herself in the past, going off with Eddie on one more of the busy, trifling little forays with which the two had loved to fill their days.

Eddie and Alissia must have been five or six years old and they stood together in the kitchen at Alissia's. "Mom. Mom. Can I go to Baby Lagoon?" Alissia entreated. Each gripped a large, empty can with both hands. "Can I, Mom? Eddie can go. We want to look for hermies."

"You sure love those hermit crabs. Go ahead--but be back in time for lunch, OK?"

"We will, Mom." Alissia turned to Eddie. "Let's go!" They ran out the back door, and the wooden screen door whacked shut, snapped back by its stiff wire spring. "Oops. Sorry Mom," she called over her shoulder.

It was two blocks to the Lower Road. There they ran down a sandy dune of tangled morning glory vines flaunting violet blossoms. Through the soles of her feet Alissia felt the soft sand and sharp twigs that lay under a jumble of vines as thick and tangled as the intrigues in the Colony. One of the vines snagged her big toe and tumbled her forward, knocking the breath out of her. She jumped back up and continued down the dune.

The two children crossed the narrow unpaved road to the beach. As usual, there was no one to be seen at Baby Lagoon. The sand was white and clean and fine, and shallow light blue water beckoned one to loll in its warm and safe embrace. At the east end, the sand had been formed from lustrous, petal-pink interiors of shells. Pink Beach really was pink, its pale and delicate roseate hue beautiful against the turquoise of the lagoon. She and Eddie sat down to watch a cluster of small hermit crabs scrabble around.

The crabs had left trails where they had toiled across the sand. Alissia got on her hands and knees to more closely examine the traces that crisscrossed willy-nilly in every direction. She liked to see the symmetrical, spidery pattern formed by scratchy little legs. In no time, both children had a swarm of captive crabs scratching around in the bottom of their tin Klim cans. They set the cans down. Each found a short stick for poking, and they walked to where the short beach narrowed and stretched into a thin arm of coral that curved around to protectively embrace the lagoon. The water on the shallow reef was only inches deep, and on this protected lee side of the island small, friendly wavelets plashed around their ankles. The myriad creatures that populated the reef fascinated them without end. Using her stick, Alissia prodded a small octopus that squirted ink. She watched the dark liquid swirl out into multiple tendrils in the water. The children examined starfish and picked up snails. Alissia inhaled the scent of the Caribbean. She then exhaled her whole being outward into the air. Ankle deep in the salty water, she stood in just that moment, suspended in one place and time, with no thought or worry outside of that one long, fixed instant. The sun insistently warmed her arms and back. She and Eddie often just co-existed beside each other with no need to talk, each child barefoot and free in an individual and isolated bubble of time.

Reliving that scene made Alissia feel an ache of longing to just be, to feel herself light, expanding into space and time. *How do I recapture moments of just existing, of being who I really am? I know I'm an adult, not a kid, but I need to recapture at least some of that feeling of burden-free existence, to feel as free as if I were flying.*

There was more to the story of the "hermies." Eddie and Alissia made their way back to the beach, retrieved their cans with the crabs, and headed home. Alissia stopped by her house, and pressed her face against the screen of the kitchen door. It smelled faintly of dust. "I'm going to Eddie's, Mom" she called out. Can I eat with Miss Cynthia? We'll play over there."

"That's fine, Alissia."

After sandwiches and fresh lemonade, Alissia and Eddie tried hermit crab races, set up little ramps, and experimented with various small obstacles to see if the crabs would go around or over them. The hermit crabs were good for another hour that Saturday, and would merit their attention again on Sunday afternoon.

Sunday morning brought Sunday-school, only bearable because it was held in the shade of a high stone wall beside the church. At least it was outside where there were birds and a few bugs to look at. When she was obligated to attend the endless, monotonous service inside the church, Alissia would push in ahead of her family. One might have thought she was eager. She would head for a pew toward the back, on the right-hand side, and then sit at the far end, next to the windows.

On entering the church, on first impression the interior appeared distorted. Although it seemed disproportionately long from front to back and much too narrow from side to side, whoever had designed the building should have won awards on several counts. The two sides of the structure had a tall, uninterrupted line of contiguous, clear glass windows—a rarity in Aruba--so that on the lee side one gazed out at a panoramic expanse of sea. All of the windows opened wide like doors and the trade wind blew through the church from the windward to the leeward side. Nessa had been married in that church and Alissia was christened there.

Alissia survived the drone of the preacher by watching the white sails of small boats as they tacked back and forth just outside the lagoon edged by reef, trying to make headway upwind, always seeming to call to her. Cottony clouds changed shape as they floated without effort, herded quickly southwest by the wind. If she narrowed her eyes and concentrated she could just discern the faint shape of the Santa Ana mountain peak in Venezuela. Alissia endured the monotonous, weekly, Protestant indoctrination with escapes to imaginings in bright colors. Then, as now, she survived by dreaming of ways to break free.

That Sunday, after church and lunch, Stass, Gil, the families and a friend visiting the Aruba refinery from Vera Cruz, Mexico, gathered on Gil's large screened porch. Stass had his guitar. A few Heinekens and some Cokes sat on a low table. Cynthia and Nessa chatted and the children played. The men strummed and sang an eclectic selection of American Western songs, wailing Mexican ballads, Venezuelan love songs and happy island tunes in Papiamento. "Git Along Little Dogie" was followed by "Cielito Lindo." In his fine tenor Stass hammed and delivered a maudlin rendition of "Blue moon, you saw me standing alone…" Then everyone sang "La Cucaracha" and the children laughed and staggered to the stanza when the cockroach could no longer walk… "*Ya no puede caminar*," they hooted. Gil seemed unaware of Alissia; his guests consumed his attention. She was conscious and relieved that she did not feel the focus that she could always sense shroud her even before she saw Gil's eyes.

The comfortable Sunday afternoon drew to an end. The next day it was back to school for Eddie and Alissia. They looked at each other.

"I don't think we should leave them in the Klim cans," Alissia said. "They don't have enough room. And you know they always crawl out of their shells in the cans. Ugh. I hate to see them naked. They look so ugly."

"Come on," said Eddie. "I know where we can put them." Alissia followed Eddie to his room. He pulled out the bottom drawer of his dresser and crammed his shirts in with the neatly folded shorts in the drawer above it. He indicated the empty drawer. "Put them in here. They'll have plenty of room." The crabs were accommodated in the drawer, which they then closed. Alissia crouched down with one ear against the drawer and listened closely. She could hear the faint scraping sounds the crabs made as they dragged their shells around.

Monday came and the hermit crabs were forgotten. Life went on with breezes and the island's consistent warm temperatures. By Wednesday, Cynthia thought she could smell an odor in the house. She checked the kitchen, but it was immaculately clean and any perishable food was in the refrigerator. She thought she must be imagining things. By Thursday the smell was stronger. She went outside and peered under the house from different vantage points, sniffing as she did so. She couldn't see anything. The smell came from inside the house. By Friday the rotten stench permeated the house and nauseated her. Before Gil left to work the four-to-twelve shift, she asked him if he could smell it, and even Gil, who was oblivious to anything domestic, and whose olfaction had been diminished by exposure to chemicals and gases in the refinery, could detect it.

"You're right. Something really stinks!" he said.

Cynthia prowled the house. The odor was definitely strongest in Eddie's room. She sighed a sigh of exasperation. *I should have known*, she thought, placing hands on hips.

"What have they dragged in now!" she exclaimed. Cynthia checked the closet and under the beds. Nothing. She pulled back the sheets on Eddie's bed and looked under his pillow. She still did not find anything. The room had wood floors and was neat, clean and sparely furnished. As she was about to leave the room, she turned back. There was the dresser. She started through the drawers from the top and worked her way down. When she pulled out the bottom drawer, an effluvium of rotten crab rose into her face and almost bowled her over. The creatures had predictably crawled out of their shells, died and decomposed into a foul, gooey mess.

Cynthia quarantined the offending drawer outside on the scraggly St. Augustine grass. She had finally finished scraping the remains of crab out of the wooden drawer using a putty knife that she found among Gil's tools in the garage. She dragged over the hose and, using her thumb to form a hard spray, she washed the drawer out at length. Then she scrubbed the bottom hard with powdered soap and a stiff brush. She rinsed the drawer thoroughly and left it to dry in the hot Aruba sun. *A few days in this sun might do the trick*, she thought. She looked at the brush with disgust, then threw it in the trash.

Cynthia repeated the cycle of soap and water and drying in the sun for three weeks before she returned the drawer to the bedroom dresser. Despite Cynthia's efforts, even after the drawer had dried, when Alissia and Eddie opened the drawer, they could smell the putrid odor of dead crab and it would cause them to retch. And Eddie, who was not in the least fastidious, would not wear any article of clothing if anyone put it into that drawer.

Alissia woke up and after a moment understood where she was. She got up from the couch, went to Rika's kitchen where she drank a full glass of water, then left the Sint Nicolaas house. She drove to Baby Lagoon. There, sitting on the beach, she thought of the hermit crab escapade. She had been surprised and grateful that it had not provoked the usual degree of her father's anger. He had been generous with affection to Duncan--no matter what he got into, Stass thought it was funny--but to her he poured out wrath. She understood now that she was part of the package her father acquired when he married Nessa and that his attitude then still affected her now. She chose to consider him responsible for his own behavior and found she was able to let it go. Even so, it was more difficult to understand how to manage her present concept of self, her situation at work--and Tom. She had to take back control of her life. She needed to claim all that she had accomplished on her own.

An errant cumulus cloud passing over splattered a few fat raindrops on her head and shoulders, drawing her into a different scene.

That day the clouds that had gathered overhead brought with them thunder and lightning, an infrequent occurrence in Aruba. They loosed large, warm drops of water that plish-plashed as they plopped here and there. Alissia ran outside. She loved the excitement of a sudden squall. The rain began to pour down heavily in an abrupt afternoon shower and the smell of wet kaliche dust wafted up from the ground. Nessa called out the door. "Come put on your bathing suit."

"What for?"

"Let's go swimming."

"In the rain?"

"Sure," said Nessa. She cocked her head. "Do you know why people don't go swimming in the rain?"

Alissia looked puzzled. "Why not?"

"Because they're afraid they'll get wet."

They laughed, raced each other to get into their bathing suits, and, barefoot, headed off at a trot for the lagoon.

Alissia had reveled in that rain squall with no intrusion of any other concern. She had loved Aruba's short storms. She could always feel the barometric pressure fall and it exhilarated her, as if she were expanding, bubbly and weightless, rising up into the sky. Just recalling the past swim in the rain and water and wind isolated her for a brief moment from her present search for answers. The cloud moved on. There would be no squall today as she sat at Baby Lagoon. The only dim cloud that lingered was her need to find the right key to the future.

CHAPTER 55
THE FISH FIASCO

The trade wind streamed in through the windows of the classroom. Alissia was in second grade and it was another glorious, wonderful, unexceptional school day. The sun shone brightly, eclipsing all shadows of concern and life felt perfect. The children settled into their seats. No one could have imagined how Alissia and Eddie would apply what they learned from that morning's simple lesson. Perhaps it was in jest but, in later years, some even speculated about whether it was the venture resulting from that class that led Alissia to the career path she chose.

"Today we are going to learn about Thanksgiving," the teacher had announced. "The Dutch have special appreciation for it." She explained that the Dutch felt a connection to the American holiday because, on their way to the New World, the Pilgrims sojourned in Holland for some years. Even so, Thanksgiving was never a Dutch holiday and the Lago refinery did not interrupt its seven-days-a-week operation. Men all worked their scheduled shifts and, in the Colony, American families planned a special, traditional meal, adapting the foods available to them and scheduling the repast on a day that was convenient.

The lesson about Pilgrims and Indians had proceeded. The Pilgrims landed on Plymouth Rock. They seemed pretty boring. The Indians planted corn. More interesting, they buried a fish in each mound for fertilizer. In the illustrations Alissia viewed, neither people seemed to bear much relationship to her experience. The Pilgrims were completely covered in mountains of bizarre clothing and some of the Indians depicted wore even less than Aruban fishermen. The class was not much impressed. When Eddie and Alissia were finally released from the classroom, they retained at least one piece of information that made sense to them: fertilizing corn.

During the school year, Saturdays signified free time for Alissia and Eddie. This Saturday the twosome came up with yet another plan. They would go fish at Baby Lagoon. Stass had a narrow, very long net, only some two feet high, that he dragged through shallow water to catch bait fish.

"Can we use the bait net, Dad? Please. We want to fish at Baby Lagoon." Alissia bounced on her heels.

Stass kept his belongings in strict order and perfect condition and fishing was a serious activity. His first reaction was negative. He stiffened. Alissia stood very still. She looked away from her father, trying to hide her disappointment. She knew better than to ask again. Stass frowned at the two children. He looked fierce. Alissia braced herself for the outburst she knew would come. Then, with a half-smile, Stass said, "OK." Alissia looked at her father, eyes wide. His face turned stern again. "Don't you drag it on the way there and back. And don't snag it. I don't want to see any holes. Do you understand?"

Alissia nodded, serious. She fully understood. "Yes, sir. We'll be really careful."

Alissia wanted to take her father's unexpected acquiescence as an approval of her, but maybe, she thought, it was just that anything to do with fishing put him in a good mood. Whatever the reason for his consent, her animation returned. She and Eddie scampered off to Baby Lagoon taking turns at carrying the folded net, each carrying a Klim can tucked under one arm. They started at the end of the lagoon on the side toward the refinery. They stretched the net across, from one side almost to the other, and slowly they dragged it through the lagoon toward Pink Beach on the Light House side where the water became progressively shallower. As they neared the edge of the lagoon they could see small fish darting around in front of the net as it herded them toward the beach. They both bent low. The net was long and only two feet wide. Each of them held one hand down to drag the bottom side that had lead weights so that it brushed along the sandy bottom of the lagoon. With the upper hand, they steadied the top side with the floats to help keep the net vertical. Little fish trapped in front of the advancing net milled frantically. Small streaks of silver boiled up from the surface of the water in erratic, crazy jumps. Reaching the beach, with the net Eddie and Alissia scooped the fish up onto the sand where they danced in glints of panic.

"Wow, Alissia. We got a bunch!"

"Let's drag them farther. So they can't flop back."

Eddie ran and brought the Klim cans over to the net. The cans were large, about three-fourths of a gallon in volume. The two children scurried around picking up the slippery thin fish, at most a scant inch long. They filled their cans to overflowing.

"We've got to rinse the net and fold it. Otherwise we'll get in trouble," said Alissia. They took the net into the water and swooshed it back and forth. They folded it into a small bundle and Alissia set it on the packed wet sand at water's edge. The two lay down and lolled in the warm water, rolling over a few times to rinse off. Then Alissia picked up the net and they headed toward home, each proudly carrying a Klim can full of catch.

"What will we do with them?" Alissia asked as she and Eddie walked. "I don't think Mom will cook them. And Dad won't eat fish."

"My mom won't want them, either." They walked on in silence. "Can we sell them?"

Alissia brightened. "I know. Let's sell them in the Village. We can get some money." This was an exciting idea. "We can buy something in Oranjestad."

"Or we can order from the Sears catalog," said Eddie with an unusual display of enthusiasm.

They walked for a few minutes in silence.

"How do we sell them in the Village?" asked Eddie.

Alissia thought about that. "They're really little. Like those sardines that come in a can. Maybe we can sell them to the sardine factory."

They both brightened. A factory would probably pay a lot. They could get more money than they had ever had. They tried to think of the best, most expensive thing they could buy. Eddie said a bicycle. Or maybe a boat. They could use all the money and get a sailboat. "Our own boat!" How far they could sail?

After a while, Alissia began to frown. "You know, Eddie, I don't think there are any factories in Aruba. People always say the only jobs are at the refinery. And the Company has to bring stuff on a boat to the Commissary for people to buy. They sell those sardines in cans there."

Eddie shook his head at "factories" and nodded agreement at "Commissary." He shrugged. "Yeah. I don't think we can sell 'em. What'll we do? They'll get smelly fast." They trudged on.

They reached the 300 Row and were coming up to their houses. "I know," chirped Alissia. "We'll put them in the garden. You know, like those Indians in the States we learned about. They'll make the plants nice."

Eddie's beaten expression took on life. "Yeah! Let's."

They replaced Stass's net in the garage with care and then went to the garage at Eddie's to get two garden trowels. They proceeded to very carefully hide a fish or two at a time under a sprinkle of soil in the flower beds all around both houses.

As they worked, Alissia speculated on the results of their endeavor. "The plants will probably get really tall. They'll have more flowers. Bigger ones, too. Do you think the colors will be brighter?"

"Maybe."

They finished up at Alissia's, the gardens at both homes well fertilized.

"Done!"

Alissia turned on the garden hose. They rinsed the dirt and slime off their hands, then rinsed the trowels and trusty Klim cans. Lunch time. Eddie went home and Alissia went inside.

At the first smell of fish, Alissia began to feel queasy, not from the odor, but in anticipation of her father's ire. What would he do? It smelled really bad. Within the week the block around Bungalows 362 and 363 reeked of rotten fish. It would be impossible to find and remove the hundreds of tiny fish camouflaged under thin sprinklings of dirt. The trade wind carried the thick, foul odor through the Colony. It did not take long for the explanation to spread through the neighborhood. Blocks away, Red Burns laughed with gusto and Máximo Hirsch scowled his displeasure at the stench carried on the wind. Eddie and Alissia slunk around, trying to stay out of sight for the weeks it took the disgusting smell to subside.

The obvious culprits had confessed during immediate and ritual interrogation. It had not been a big leap to link the pair's fishing expedition to the ubiquitous bouquet of fish. Stass's initial, eruptive choler, uncharacteristically and to Alissia's great relief, subsided right away. In fact, that evening, in discussing the escapade, it amused the Saxton and Williams adults more than it upset them. Gil seemed to think that the fish made the goat manure that Cynthia and Nessa were always hauling home for the garden seem aromatic by comparison. Stass loved the children's explanation of their commercial aspirations--which may be why the antic so amused rather than angered him—that and the number of fish they said they had caught. He shook his head. "The sardine factory!" The four adults were careful to smile and laugh and discuss the incident after all the children were asleep.

"Wait until they are teenagers!" admonished Cynthia, with a display of horror not totally feigned.

Stass snorted. "Well, at least we know they listened in class. Pilgrims and Indians. That's a long way off."

"What next?" said Nessa.

The sardine escapade entered the Saxton family repertoire of favorite stories and in later years, they never failed to refer to it as it Alissia's first business venture. Once someone asked her if she had written a paper on it when working on her degree in business. Alissia always remembered the incident with a layer of amusement herself. But under her amusement lay recalled apprehension and the subsequent relief at her father's reaction. She realized that neither had been under her control. *He was so domineering*, she thought. *But Tom is strong-willed, too. He has to be or he wouldn't want to be around me.* Her smiles over the fishing fiasco faded. *What about Tom?* she asked herself. The small question inflated until it filled her with a sensation of pressure. What were Tom's expectations? He was more demonstrative—in a good way—than her father. He was affectionate, not so harsh. But what would he be like if they married?

CHAPTER 56
THE MAZE

It was Sunday afternoon again. Alissia and Eddie had homework to do most weekends and they were running out of time. They went to the screened-in porch at Eddie's. They had ten arithmetic problems.

They sat on the floor. "Eddie, I'll do the first five and you do the other five. Then we'll trade answers." Alissia began.

Eddie fiddled. He got out his box of marbles. He rolled several around in each hand, palpating the cool, round shapes. He put them all down and began to examine the marbles one at a time. He sorted them into three groups, then selected two which he set aside from the others, a privileged duo. A brilliant orange cat's-eye winked from the black one; the other was larger than all the rest, his best shooter. He called that one the Green Cannonball.

Alissia finished half of the problems. "Are you done?" she asked Eddie. He didn't answer. When Eddie played with his marbles the colored spheres seemed to hypnotize him. Alissia checked his paper. It was blank.

Alissia lost her usual quiet patience. "You didn't do yours." She spoke loudly, in an accusing tone.

Eddie laid down on the floor. He curled up on his side like a hermit crab, clutching his ears. When he finally dropped his hands from his ears, his left fingers began to flap. After a while the flapping spasm settled and Eddie lay still. It seemed like a lot of time passed before he finally sat up again. Not even glancing at the homework, he turned his attention back to his marbles. Eyes fixed on the small round spheres, he sorted and re-sorted them into different groups. Alissia couldn't tell why he chose which marble. She worried. Sometimes, if his father found out that Eddie didn't hand in his homework, she had seen him cuff Eddie. It seemed like she worried more about Eddie than he worried about himself. It wore her out. When she pressed Eddie, he just retracted back into his shell, as if he could not bear to even hear her words. Then he wouldn't talk at all. As usual, Alissia worked through the rest of the problems and gave Eddie the answers to copy. She wished that someone would take care of her like that.

Homework done, Alissia asked Eddie if she could read one of his Hardy Boys books.

"Yeah."

She read a while, then checked on Eddie. He still had not copied the answers.

"Eddie, you'll get in trouble." She pressed him in an accusing tone. "Just copy the answers." With a wave of his right arm Eddie shooed her comment. "I hate arithmetic!" he blurted. "I hate it. The numbers won't hold still. They switch places."

Alissia stared at him for a moment, uncomprehending. Then she went back to reading. Eddie began to draw on his paper. When the adults came out to the porch to sit and talk, both children were engrossed. Stass looked down at Eddie. Complex lines almost filled the whole sheet of paper over which he was laboring. They all hugged together in a tight, defensive pattern.

"Can I see that?"

Eddie handed it to him. Eddie would doodle for hours sometimes, totally absorbed, but Stass had never paid more than passing attention to what he did. On close examination, he saw that what he expected to be a jumble of random squiggles was actually a tight and intricate maze of tiny blind alleys and complex narrow passages. In the center, there was a little blob that might be a bug and to one side, outside the lines, there was a circle with what looked like legs poking out.

"Is this where you go in?" Stass pointed to a tiny gap by the spidery figure at the edge of the labyrinth.

Eddie nodded.

"Well, I'll be damned. Gil, look at this. We always thought he was just scribbling and wasting paper."

Gil came over.

"This is complicated. Unbelievable. It's more complicated than refinery blueprints." He handed the paper to Gil. The two men tried in turn to follow the maze to the center with a forefinger without success.

"Beats me," said Stass. "Do you know how to get to the middle?" he asked Eddie.

Again, Eddie nodded.

"Show me."

With the tip of a skinny finger, Eddie traced the route for him.

"OK. Does the maze keep the spider from getting the bug?"

A quiet "Yes."

Stass laughed. "Nice touch."

Gil examined the drawing again. "Can I keep this?"

Eddie nodded.

"Well, if the boy can come up with something this complicated, there's hope," Stass said to Gil. "You've got to show that to the guys." He looked at Eddie. "Maybe you can get a job as a draftsman someday, kiddo."

Eddie did not look up. He had gone back to rolling his marbles around in both cupped hands.

Gil shook his head. "I don't know how his mind works."

Cynthia brought out a platter of sandwiches for everyone and set it on a low table. Alissia went to help herself. Miss Cynthia had made egg-salad sandwiches on home-baked bread that Nessa brought. *Yum,* Alissia thought. She glanced up. Gil stood to one side. Arms folded, eyes narrowed, he watched her. Alissia shuddered and dropped her eyes.

CHAPTER 57
TWO SIDES

Fairy tales tell us dragons can be slayed.

–G. K. Chesterton

Alissia again sat on Pink Beach at Baby Lagoon. She picked up a handful of fine sand to enjoy the soft tickle as she let it sift through her fingers and listened to small waves break on the nearby reef. She lifted her face to the sky. The wind blew her hair out to one side in a stream as she inhaled the scent of the sea. Re-immersed in familiar sensations and the Aruba Colony, the murky suspicion that blurred the edge of her thoughts spread into more clarity. There were two sides to life on this island, both paradise and perdition, she thought. Now a similar and parallel polarity existed for her between what, at a deep level, she really wanted and what she believed to be her obligation. But between these antitheses a realization took form in her thoughts. *Life is not confined to extremes; we live the extraordinary along a continuum of the ordinary.* Pitting these opposing forces against each other was causing the tumult that fed her demons of guilt. When she thought of confronting these extremes, of trying to negotiate a truce, a rush of fight-or-flight stole her breath. What if she reconciled sides only to irrevocably reconfirm her culpability?

Buoyed by the warm water of the tropical lagoon, caressed by the soothing breeze, it occurred to Alissia she could have learned her multiplication tables in any colorless place. Two-times-two-equals-four had no taste in her mouth; universal numbers did not titillate with island flavor. She swam toward the warm current of her comforting memories of this unique paradise and understood how the right side had nurtured and molded her. She comprehended that both the ugly and the sublime of this place were integral to who she was. They could not and should not be excised. *Identity is the bundle of each person's experiences, trivial and weighty alike,* she thought. *We are made up of our memories, each person's discrete package differentiating us one from another.* She understood that only here, in this place, could she have become who she was.

From a young age, she had ventured and wandered on the island. The confines of her small world had then seemed limitless as she satisfied her compelling desire for freedom. She wondered if it was the leisurely and sunny, breeze-cooled habitat that ignited her need to live unfettered, or did this part of her just thrive in the physical and cultural climate of her insular, tropical enclave?

A cloud passed over the sun and for a moment dimmed the light. She never felt that she really belonged to any group around her and so she had sought her own path. *I became willful and selfish,* she thought. But surely frolics in pleasure and joy were good. She knew that, in fairness, most of her pastimes were innocuous, mischievous at worst. She still could not believe that she had dared to circumvent so many rules. She smiled as she thought of crazy pranks—trying to run with the wheelies on pipelines, storing hermit crabs in Eddie's dresser drawer... She lived carefree and unafraid then. When did that change?

Two dark shapes crossed the sunscape vision she contemplated. They embodied the reprehensible acts, her loss of innocence. She had strayed too far out of bounds. It was Gil's predation and her part in Red's death that had brought fear and guilt into her carefree world. She didn't believe that assuming such burdens had to be the universal cost of growing up but there was a side to her paradise that exacted tribute. She knew that she caused what happened through deliberate choice and now she had to pay the price.

Alissia was torn by her dilemma. She felt confusion, fear about again choosing. If she could reconcile what she wanted with what she *should* do, if she would play by the rules and marry Tom, maybe she could fit in. Why couldn't she be accepted, loved unconditionally, just as she was? Why was the cost so high? And no matter how far down she pushed it, the temptation to follow desire, that past habitual indulgence, clamored against perceived duty. She was tired of the fight. She wanted to again feel as if she were riding the trade winds, flying off to unlimited possibilities. She wanted to save who she was, to claim the essence of her identity. Tom and a job couldn't do that for her.

Facing the issue, Alissia's real fear loomed larger. Maybe she wanted to delude herself, she thought. The illusion that her Eden was perfect and one-sided was a shield. To impose order on her life she had to give up that protection. To reconcile the two sides of paradise she would have to face the guilt she fought to suppress. She gasped as she sank into an emotional quagmire that threatened to swallow her and she summoned visceral courage, the fortitude not just to revisit her island but to find and face the truth. She had to *understand* what she wanted. A thought struck her and she panicked. What if the essential fragments of who she was had been misassembled? Maybe the shock of the harm she had caused skewed her ability to perceive and understand, trapping her in a false counterpart. It was too confusing. All the pieces of what happened exploded into erratic flight in every direction, a flock of panicked, darting birds. The maelstrom made her dizzy.

CHAPTER 58
BALMY WEATHER

Alissia cruised and probed around the Colony, its sights and sounds and scents triggering further recollection of things forgotten. She reveled in the weather--another perfect day--and remembered her father's project to monitor Aruba's reliable temperatures. She chuckled out loud and smiled. Her father had delivered his report to a back-patio gathering of men who were enjoying it.

As if work did not keep him busy enough, Stass puttered at sundry activities, some with better results than others. He had decided to monitor, on the first and fifteenth day of every month, the ambient Aruba temperature that varies little. He set up a thermometer inside the bungalow and another outside in the shade. Again unobserved at a back-patio gathering of men, Alissia listened to her father report on his two-year findings.

"The coldest I got was 76°F."

He took a sip of his Coke and continued. "We usually get our warmest weather August through October. You know how the temperature goes up when a hurricane hijacks our winds.

The men nodded.

"The hottest reading I ever got was 91°F. That was on September 21st during this year's hurricane season. We had hardly any wind at all that day."

"Sure don't see many days without wind," said Tex. "Gives me the creeps. It gets so quiet it seems like the world has stopped. I can't sleep if that breeze don't croon me a lullaby."

"What's the average?" asked Gil.

"About 81°F," Stass replied. "It's God's most perfect weather when the trade winds blow. Love that wind!"

Tex shoved his hands into his pants pockets. "Well, those sure are some sorry results, Stass." He hung his head and shook it. "I'm disappointed in you."

Stass bridled.

Tex went on. "For so much work you shoulda at least come up with readings hotter than hell and cold as ice."

Stass gave Tex a mock punch in the arm. "You ornery son-of-a-gun."

Gil snickered. "Well, Stass has a better project now."

"What's that," asked Red.

"He got a BB gun at the Commissary."

Tex snorted with a dismissive gesture. "What's he gunnin for on this island? Big game?"

Gil turned to Stass. "Go on. You tell him." He paused, then continued. "He's shooting at tarantulas. They're always some in the palm trees, but a couple got into the bungalow. So he was trying to shoot tarantulas in the house."

"I didn't know you were so brave," said Tex.

Gil continued. "Well, that's over." He chuckled. "Nessa found BB holes in the walls and that's the end of that."

"Yeah, when I said brave I was thinkin about Nessa, not the tarantulas," retorted Tex.

"Well, Stass. Here's the thing. Dinnae shoot any of me birds," admonished Red.

Stass asked, "Which ones are those?"
"All of them!" Red exclaimed.
"Better watch out," said Tex. "I think he really means it!"

As a detail of that day came back to her, Alissia's smile faded. Her mother had been busy. She had called for Alissia and asked her to carry out more cold drinks. With perfect clarity Alissia recalls her revulsion when she had to hand a Coca Cola to Gil Williams. She had made sure to avoid eye contact. Alissia loathed that man. He was evil. He tainted her island memories, but what happened must have been her own fault. She had provoked it when she chose to break her mother's Big Rule about going to anyone's house. Now she had to find a way out of the polluted cloud of guilt formed by her deliberate choice. It was choking her.

CHAPTER 59

ORANJESTAD TREK

It was a quiet Tuesday morning and the sky stretched and yawned awake overhead. Alissia had always liked going to Oranjestad. The air was soft and Alissia felt as if she were skimming, light as a *chuchubi* feather, on breeze and sunshine. She followed her mother across the street to Miss Cynthia's. Today Nessa wanted to leave early enough. This time, she wanted to be sure not to miss out when the fishing boats came in.

Nessa called through the screen door. "Cynthia, ready?"

In the kitchen, Cynthia jangled car keys. She came out carrying two baskets. "I'll drive this time." Eddie and Alissia were already disappearing around the corner of the bungalow. "Eddie, Alissia, come on, let's go," she called, and they came back.

As they walked toward the car, Alissia tugged at her mother's skirt. She began in whining tone. "Mom, why can't I go to school..."

"Alissia, stop it!"

"But…"

"You are *not* going to school in Sint Nicolaas."

Alissia recognized the tone and cut off her wheedling. She often thought of the school in Sint Nicolaas. She knew they taught different languages there, and the kids were different, too, and the possibility excited her. Usually her mom seemed to like anything different, but she thought that Sint Nicolaas was too rough. *But wouldn't I be OK in school?* Alissia wondered. She knew better than to bring it up again because more than once she had been made to understand that the subject was non-negotiable. She turned her attention back to the Oranjestad trip.

"We're in luck," Nessa commented to Cynthia. "I hear a Chinese junk is in port again. We'll stop there, too. Emily is taking care of Duncan, so we can take our time. Eddie and Alissia will hang out together and follow us around, like they usually do."

Cynthia beckoned. "Come on, kids, pile in."

Nessa and Cynthia loaded Alissia and Eddie into the back seat of the Williams's car. The 1941 teal-blue Plymouth had been Gil's pride and joy in its early years but, despite meticulous care, salt air and Aruba roads had taken their toll. It was well past its prime. Once outside the Colony fence and gate, the old Plymouth bumped and rattled along in a northwest direction. The sun, low-lying behind the car, angled higher, brightening the pale morning light that muted the landscape. They drove by the refinery. Through the open car windows the pungency of petroleum whiffled through the air. They bypassed Sint Nicolaas, that rowdy little den of sin. The road surface was sometimes thin soil, sometimes sand—or a mixture of the two, with areas of exposed lava here, patches of rough coral there. It wended its way along the coastline. Further on, they drove past the fishing village of Savaneta, the first capital of Aruba, then by the water desalination plant and Spanish Lagoon.

"Mom, can we get mangos today? And bananas?" asked Alissia.

"Sure," said Nessa.

"Why do the sailboats come clear from Venezuela?"

"To sell fruit and vegetables. Not much grows here. It's too dry. Venezuela gets more rain."

"We're lucky they come. I love fruit," said Alissia.

"We *are* lucky."

The car descended into the depression of Frenchman's Pass. The vehicle bounced and complained over the deeper ruts and potholes and then gradually rumbled up and they continued to travel northward.

After a short distance, Cynthia veered to the right. They drove past scrubby trees, cacti, and an occasional foraging goat. In some places, they looked across bare and arid vistas where it seemed miraculous that even tough divi-divi and scrappy cacti could survive. They came to aloe fields where the spiky plants marched in orderly lines across the *cucunu*, pointing needle-sharp tips of fleshy crenate leaves at the sky. In rectangular fields scattered workers labored in stooped position. With machetes, they hacked off one fleshy aloe arm at a time, standing them all in sheaves to drip their juice into drums. Some men tended fires of cactus leaves. The smoke spirals thinned as they trailed away downwind. The workers cooked down the viscid sap of the aloe to form dry cakes used for export. Arubans claimed that the island's fierce sun and aridity intensified the healing qualities of the sap to make it the most potent in the world. But aloe was never a significant cash crop.

Cynthia slowed down for a donkey and a little further, she stopped for an Aruban crossing the road on foot. She pointed.

"It looks like he has dinner."

The man carried a large *yuana crioyo* slung over one shoulder. The creature swung back and forth as he trudged.

Nessa looked at Cynthia. "You know why they like the Aruban iguana species so much, don't you?"

"No, why?"

"Of course, it's food, and they fix it in soup. But they believe it has special properties."

The car lurched through a dip in the road, then resumed its bumping pace.

Nessa continued. "It's supposed to have healing powers. But the main reason they like it is because the male has a peculiar-looking member. Red Burns told to me that the penis has a split and the locals believe it's actually two. So they think that when men eat iguana it doubles their virility."

Cynthia laughed. "I'm surprised there are any iguanas left on the island."

"Well, I'm sure there are a lot of male fantasies about the iguana's powers." Nessa chuckled.

From the back seat, a voice asked, "Do all Aruban men have two penises, Mom?"

Nessa took a breath. "None have two, Alissia."

"But you said they did."

"I did not. I'll explain it to you at home."

"But--"

"Enough, Alissia. I... said... later."

Nessa and Cynthia looked at each other. Nessa raised her eyebrows.

They watched the thin man with his iguana set off across the arid *cucunu* to some lost shack. Solitary Arubans could be seen trudging without end from one unknown place to some other lost place, along dry river beds and rock paths that wound through a dry landscape that seemed forever unchanged and disconnected from time.

After what seemed a long drive to Eddie and Alissia, the little group arrived in Oranjestad. Cynthia parked on a side street by the harbor at Paardenbaai, named for the horses that used to be shipped from Venezuela. When a vessel arrived, islanders would bring a horse and hold it by the reins at water's edge. Crew members would push one horse at a time off the boat into the bay. The floundering animal would swim toward the horse on shore and clamber onto land--a practical offloading solution.

"Today we're early enough," said Cynthia. The fresh fish that the boats brought in were always in short supply relative to pushy demand.

A short walk took them to a throng of people who pressed forward, body against body, preparing to grab for fish the moment the morning's catch was hauled off the boats. Nessa positioned Alissia and Eddie near the edge of the group of pushing buyers and handed the two baskets to the children.

"Wait right here." Raising a finger, Nessa admonished the pair. "And don't you move."

Nessa looked at the expectant faces surrounding her. They well reflected Aruba's racial blend. She thought of the seafarers and visitors from far-off places who, over centuries, had mingled their genes with those of island people. She commented softly to Cynthia.

"You can really see the Arawak in Aruban faces."

"Yes, it's a handsome look," Cynthia responded quietly.

"I love Aruban names," Nessa said. "Like soft, Spanish Mario that slides off the tongue. Then for the last name you get a mouthful of Dutch consonants. Like Mario Kleinheksel at the shoe store."

Cynthia nodded.

"Oh, speaking of names, there's Fernanda Hoogaboom," said Nessa. She lifted a hand and waved. "*Con ta bai*," how are you, she called out in Papiamento.

"*A mi ta bon.*" Fine, came the answer with a smile.

Alissia paid close attention to the short phrases. She had already learned most of them, always drawn to anything different, anything that departed from routine. The Aruba environment imbued her with a fascination for the exotic. It stimulated her imagination which already ran at high speed.

Around Nessa and Cynthia, Arubans chatted. The two women commented on scattered English words and slang expressions common to the Lago refinery that they could hear interjected into Arubans' Papiamento, evidence of the constant evolution of language.

"Stass told me the other day that Standard Oil has a policy worldwide of using local language for refinery operations," Nessa commented to Cynthia. "But Papiamento doesn't have many words for technical terms. That's how English ended up as the common language for the mix of nationalities at Lago."

Cynthia grabbed Nessa's wrist. "Here they come."

Although not typically aggressive, the two women had come away empty-handed from the harbor too many times. This was no place to be timid. Determined to be in the race, they shoved their way between pressing bodies to the forefront of the crowd.

Baskets of fresh fish were plopped down. Plunging both hands into the baskets, each managed to grab two medium-sized fish by the gills. Nessa jockeyed her two into one hand and with slippery fingers extracted some guilders and coins from her dress pocket to pay. The two women extricated themselves from the throng of people. A few unlucky buyers tried to strike a bargain with those who had been successful. They were unlikely to find a seller at a price they were willing to pay.

Victors beamed as proudly as if they had caught their fish themselves. With fingers hooked in the gills of their "redsnap," women began to lumber away, some with fish so large that the tail dragged behind them. The first houses in Oranjestad had been built at random and the streets that came later meandered their way between them. Slimy, winding trails followed the women as they disappeared with their booty into the labyrinth of side streets.

As Fernanda broke away from the crowd to head home, she called over her shoulder to Nessa and Cynthia, "*Te aworo.*" See you later. They waved good-bye.

Nessa and Cynthia unloaded the four fish into one of the baskets the children had been holding. When they got home, that basket would be thoroughly hosed out with brackish water and left in the yard to dry in hot sun. Their maids would be happy: they would beg the heads of the fish to cook in a Klim can on the kerosene stove, a delicacy for lunch.

"Has Stass started eating fish?" asked Cynthia.

"Not a chance. He loves to fish, but he won't eat them," Nessa replied.

Nessa, Cynthia and the two children walked along the quay to the boats that waited with appealing fresh produce from Venezuela. It was nothing like the wrinkly stuff in the Colony Commissary that came who knows when or from where, and it was a very welcome change from the canned goods that ranged from nasty spinach to the Spam that reigned at the top of a tinny hierarchy. Nessa and Cynthia loaded up the second basket with bananas, mangos, papaya and passion fruit. They purchased summer squash, carrots and tomatoes. They were pleased. They regularly bought produce from the boats but less frequently were they able to buy the coveted fresh fish, having to fall back on catch from their husbands' sporadic fishing expeditions. Any reference to fresh fish at the Commissary was a contradiction in terms.

Their last stop was at the Chinese junk. The traveling vessels peddled carved wooden furniture, ivory statues and other wares from port to port in Caribbean waters. In many living rooms in the Colony sat chests, bookshelves and screens, carved with intricate, low-relief Chinese scenes. The beautiful pieces supplemented the plain, sparse furniture with which the Company furnished the bungalows. Atop Asian buffets and coffee tables stood distinctive Delft and Gouda pottery from Holland in proud display. The juxtaposition of Chinese and Dutch culture typified Colony homes and if residents left the island, the unusual combination migrated with them. Friends visiting friends who had lived in Aruba could walk into a living room in Norway, Mexico or the United States and for an instant live the illusion that they were entering a familiar island bungalow.

Nessa selected, a small, delicate vase inlaid with carved ivory as a birthday gift for her mother from the rich assortment of ware displayed on the quay. The vendor spoke an astounding Spanish-English pidgin slathered over with a Chinese accent, sufficient nonetheless to conclude his sale. Nessa and Cynthia, kids following behind, moved on to their other errands. The small man gesticulated in disappointment, brandishing various items in an effort to tempt them back.

They lugged their purchases to the car. Nessa wrapped the basket of fish in burlap bags while Cynthia bought a chunk of ice at a nearby store. She placed the ice on top of the burlap bundle in the metal wash tub she had stowed in the trunk. This would give them a little time to enjoy a visit to Oranjestad shops.

On her infrequent trips to Oranjestad, Alissia looked forward to the traditional stop at the De Vries bookstore where, surely, she would get a new, imported Burgess animal story book. She started her begging the day she heard they were going.

"Can I, Mom? One Burgess book?"

When Nessa acquiesced, she tried again.

"Mom, can I get two this time? Please."

"Just one at a time, Alissia."

"But, Mom--"

"Alissia!"

"But--"

"If you ask again, you won't get any."

Alissia could tell she had reached her mother's limit of patience. The imported books were a luxury.

At the De Vries bookstore both Mrs. De Vries and Jultje Van Dijk assisted customers. During the war years no books could come in. After the war ended came an exciting day: De Vries received their first shipment in years. Among the new books was a translation of *The Little Prince* by Antoine de St. Exupéry, which Nessa had purchased.

Alissia liked to have Miss Jultje help her. Jultje knew what Alissia liked and brought her the next book in the Burgess series.

"I knew you would want this," Jultje whispered. "When it came in, I put it on the side for you."

Alissia nodded and said quietly, "Thank you." Then, in an even softer voice she repeated in Papiamento, "*Danki.*"

Jultje patted Alissia's shoulder.

The next stop was for salty Dutch licorice and traditional *speculaas* with almonds, those cinnamony, gingery cookies that crunch between the teeth. Nessa gave Eddie and Alissia each a square nickel, which they hastened to spend for ice cream. For their last stop, they went to a store to replenish the Saxton's and Williams's two households' supplies of Curaçao.

"We are down to nothing. People really like it." Nessa said.

Cynthia agreed. "We need some, too."

Curaçao liqueur was a staple in any ABC home that could afford it. The bitter-orange flavor was much prized. "It really is a specialty of our region," Nessa commented. "Geneviève Ritsema was in Curaçao for language research. She said she met the family that makes the liqueur. They are descendants of Spanish Jews. The Valencia orange tree was brought from Spain but wouldn't grow in the dry climate and horrible soil. A stunted tree evolved. It's called Laraha Citrus. The fruit is acid and inedible—nasty little knobs. The peels are tougher than leather. But the family noticed that the oil in dried peels smelled orangey and pungent."

Cynthia nodded.

"They figured out a way to use them. They soak the peels in alcohol and water and then filter the brew. Geneviève said they end up with a crystal-clear liquid. They add some spices and that's how they make the liqueur. They named it simply 'Curaçao'."

"Well, people love it," said Cynthia. "It has such a distinct, semi-bitter flavor. A lot of people use it for mixed drinks."

"Well, many people have acquired a taste for it and this at least gives Curaçao something to export." Nessa leaned toward Cynthia and said in a lower voice. "For Curaçao, it's a big step up from selling slaves."

On the bouncy trip home, Alissia examined her new book. First, she opened the front cover to smooth it flat, then the back cover. She riffled through the pages and smelled them. Then, before she began to read, as Grandma Gifford had taught her, she opened the book in various places to break in the spine.

She announced with enthusiasm, "This is a great book, Mom!"

As they began the drive back to the Colony, Alissia plunged into *Old Granny Fox*. Eddie had gotten the latest in the collection of Hardy Boys books. Cynthia used the series to encourage his reading, but he started out with his new comic book. When she finished with Granny Fox, Alissia would bargain to read the Hardy Boys book--boys got into great scrapes. She'd get to Eddie's comic book, too. She had become a voracious reader and it did not take much time for her graduate to more advanced writing that stimulated her appetite for the nonconforming and the longing she still had for adventure and travel.

Alissia would not tell her mother if she finished her Burgess book today, or even tomorrow. It frustrated her that Alissia finished a costly new book so quickly, but she could make her mom think it took longer. Besides, Alissia read and reread her books. She loved entering that state of such total absorption that she did not even hear someone speak to her. When she entered the world of a book, she completely abandoned the present. This put her in jeopardy if her father were around. He got inexplicably angry when she disconnected like that. He told her that she was being lazy just doing nothing and he didn't believe that she really did not hear something that was said. Attempts to explain to him he took as confrontation—not a good position for Alissia to put herself in. She could not win. Whenever she could foresee that something might irritate her father, she had learned that her best defense was invisibility. It occurred to her that, as long as she did not become conspicuous by her absence, it would be better to read where he would not see her.

Alissia climbed up the Seagrape tree with the book stuck behind her in the waistband of her shorts. She straddled the familiar, big fork that cradled her as she looked out to sea, book in lap. She sat for a moment, trying to push away a sense of sadness. Maybe she was disfigured like Eddie, she thought, but on the inside. It was a worry that would long stay with her. Alissia put her head back against the trunk of the tree and closed her eyes. When she opened them again she saw brilliant sunlight dance on the white froth that marked the little reef, a glittering line that frolicked across a backdrop of water-and-sky-blues. On the bungalow side of her roost, two large branches curved down behind her. The tree shielded her from view with its whispering saucer-leaves. She opened her book and the Aruba wind stroked her as she entered the story. Alissia's multivalent Seagrape refuge was a part of her island wonderworld. It was a good place for her--a niche where she could be safe.

VIII

Predator

Survival is not about being fearless. It is about decisions.

–E. M. Grylls

CHAPTER 60
SEAGRAPES

Alissia sat discussing her dilemma and her anguish with Rika, carefully skirting some nooks and crannies of the past. Rika went straight to the crux of the matter.

"Are you happy, *lief*?" she asked.

"I have the job I want. That's one of my goals. The other is marriage, to buy my place in the world."

"Buy?" Rika said with a questioning look. Then she repeated her question. "But are you happy?"

"I should be."

"But?"

Alissia squirmed around in her chair, trying to get more comfortable. "Tom's my anchor in a safe harbor."

"Ach. An anchor. I see. Is it then an anchor you want?"

Alissia looked down at her hands and lifted one briefly to examine a fingernail. She sat still again and laced her fingers together so tightly they turned white. She became aware of what she was doing and released the tension. "I *will* find my answers. Being here helps me," she said.

That afternoon at Big Lagoon, Alissia gazed down from the cliff to watch herself flop and splash around in in a laborious dog-paddle. She saw how she had struggled to stay afloat and make it from one dock to the other. She then began to thrash around in a paddle through memory, fighting errant currents that tried to drag her off course. There was no one to correct her stroke, no one to throw a life buoy and haul her in. *I have to make it. I'll make myself deal with my problems or I'll drown in them.* She threw her arms up. Syllable by syllable, she called out to the wind, "Tell me. Tell me what I should do.

Alissia sat down and looked out over the sea. *Life here was so different from my life now. We were protégés with little thought of the outside world. Aruba sheltered us from most external dangers.* A new perception honed her focus. *We paid a price for our privileges.* She leaned forward and put her chin in her hands. *There is always a price. We lived subject to the constraints of a diminutive universe. Although there were local dangers, we could deal with most of those. If we would need to swim, we learned to swim.* It was true that most of the events that segmented the daily routine of living were benign, but not all, even though life should have been perfection for her in paradise.

The children who attended the Colony school looked forward to having a week off for Easter. For the second year, Nessa and Cynthia had planned a joint Easter sunrise picnic at Seagrape Grove. There would not be another person in sight in any direction. It was elating to see Easter day begin on the windward side of the island. They would watch the horizon to see the sun rise out of the sea, filling its daily promise of rebirth. Everyone looked forward to the celebratory event in such a beautiful and awe-inspiring setting.

On Saturday, Nessa and Cynthia coordinated the last details for the Sunday breakfast picnic. The men planned the bonfire, since building a fire was a manly activity. Although Stass could barely boil water and Gil was not much better, the two would happily cook pancakes since they could carry out this operation over an outdoor conflagration.

"Alissia, wake up. It's time." Her mother shook her gently.

Alissia sat up, groggy with sleep. She put on shorts and a T-shirt and, as usual, did not bother with shoes. The Saxtons bundled the children into the car which sat loaded and ready on the street. Gil signaled Stass with his headlights and in the dark the two cars headed slowly off on the two-mile expedition.

Seagrape trees—*druif,* the *Coccoloba uvifera*--grew in many places on the island. The native trees are wind resistant and highly tolerant of salt. Alissia and Eddie loved to climb their fat, stubby trunks and out onto the limbs of smooth grey bark. They also loved the seagrapes, purple berries the size of marbles. They would lie on their stomachs straddling the branches to pluck and eat the sweet, plump orbs, staining tongues, teeth, and mouths, while they dripped the dark purple juice from their fingers onto their clothes. They spit the large round seeds out onto the ground below. Seagrape Grove was at the beginning of the stretch of sand that locals had named B.A. Beach after the couples who sneaked off to this deserted spot to kiss and luxuriate—"bare-ass," as Alissia now understood—in the sun.

On arrival at Seagrape Grove they piled out of the cars. The special occasion, the pounding of the surf and the strong wind excited the children who bounced around like popcorn on a hot skillet. Alissia immediately joined Eddie. "Do you have your flashlight?" she asked.

"Yeah. I'll get it."

They darted into the dark grove of Seagrape trees. They found themselves among eerie moving shadows. The trade wind flapped large, round, leathery leaves with a dry, rattling sound. Alissia and Eddie shined their flashlights on the sand, narrow beams darting here and there in a search for land crabs. They could smell the arthropods' carrion stench. The children climbed around the trunks of trees and snapped through a confusion of fallen branches. Fallen leaves crunched under their footsteps. Disturbed by the intruders, large crabs skittered around in alarm, long legs and claws stirring up the crisp leaves to make small crackling sounds. The two children chased them. Alissia grabbed one, but it slipped out of her hand. Another lucky crab escaped as she snatched at it. Eddie jumped over a fallen branch and lunged, landing on his stomach in the sand where he seized and clutched the crustacean.

"I got it!" Victorious, he grasped it firmly. Through experience they had learned to take hold of a crab from the back, out of reach of the waving pincers.

"Great! What'll we put it in?"

"I guess we need our Klim can." He ran off brandishing his prize.

Alissia walked on alone through the gloom, pointing her flashlight here and there among distorted shapes, some of which moved with the wind. As she moved around a tree trunk a dark form loomed over her. A hand grabbed her roughly by the arm. Terrified, she twisted and turned. As she began to slip from her aggressor's grasp, he clenched her harder and when he grabbed for her with his other hand, bony fingers clamped on tender flesh between her legs. A hurt-puppy whimper pushed up from her throat. She writhed and pulled and wrenched herself free. She was a wiry and agile seven-year-old. As she turned, in the dim light of impending dawn, she looked up into the face of Gil Williams. She zigged-zagged as fast as she could go through the grove, ducking under tree limbs. Her scalp and the skin on the back of her neck prickled. Her heart beat crazily like that of a trapped bird. *Why? Why did he do that? He hurt me.* She burst out of the grove and ran up to the family group. She was panting, but no one took particular note because children running and being out of breath was nothing remarkable. Alissia huddled silently with arms tight around her knees next to the fire that had been built in a hollow in the sand. She rubbed the abraded area on the wrist she had wrenched free and she pressed her knees tightly together. She made herself small and watched the fire burn and snap. Long tongues of orange flame licked out with menace. She wouldn't tell anyone because everyone would get mad. Her dad would yell. He would yell at her—he always blamed her for everything. And her mom probably wouldn't let her run around outside all the time anymore. She couldn't stand it if she couldn't go outside to just wander and be by herself. *Mom always tells me I'm supposed to be responsible, but I was just playing. I wasn't irresponsible, was I?* It seemed that not making anyone mad was being responsible. She pressed her hands to her temples. It was all very confusing.

Eddie came over and hunkered down beside her, clutching the large can where the land crab scratched around inside, attempting vainly to climb out to freedom. Alissia saw him put a hand in one pocket and the movement made as he slowly rolled a couple of his ever-present marbles around in his palm. Then he tipped the Klim can toward her, so she could see the crab but Alissia had turned herself off, like her flashlight, and she didn't respond. She didn't even look.

After a while Eddie asked, "What's the matter?"

She stared at the fire. "Nothing," she said in a subdued voice.

The sky began to lighten. Alissia glanced at Eddie. She saw the thick and lumpy birthmark, the color of purple Seagrape juice, on his upper lid, extending around and well below his right eye where it disfigured most of his cheek. It seemed like she was always on his right side when they were together, as if she could shield him and his blemish from the rest of the world. They both watched the rush of flames grow higher and felt their heat.

The two sat silently. Then Eddie said, "Let's put the crab in the fire."

After a moment, Alissia replied "I don't know. Maybe we shouldn't."

"It's only a dumb crab. Let's see what happens." He dumped the crab into the hot flames. The creature darted around madly for a few seconds and began to crumple up. Its flesh hissed and popped, and the shell cracked, oozing liquid. The two children watched in horrified fascination until there was nothing left but a charred lump.

"It smells awful," said Eddie.

Alissia grimaced and wrinkled her nose. "Ugh. Yeah. Let's go down to the water."

The pair took off running to the water's edge where rough waves boiled up onto the sand and then receded. They stood looking out over the sea at the red-orange globe that rolled up the horizon to take command of the day. The wind of this untamed windward coast misted the two children with salt spray as they watched the sun move higher into the sky. Alissia tipped her head back to let the driving breeze blow up her nostrils, forcing oxygen into her lungs. It made her feel giddy, full of air, inflated with infinite possibilities. Then she put both hands around behind her and reached as high up her back as she could, her elbows forming downward V's. The position made her shoulder blades stick out and with her fingers she hopefully explored the bony bumps. Today she wanted to think the protuberances were sticking out with more promise. It seemed like wings were really sprouting and she crossed into the special world in her head. She began to fly and sail free on the Aruba winds.

Nessa and Cynthia called the children, and Alissia descended back into reality. "Time for breakfast." Everyone gathered in the lee of a dune by the fire. Nessa nodded, all bowed their heads, and over the sound of the wind and sea, she prayed.

Lord,
Thank you for the riches that you give us,
That delight and comfort us.
Thank you for family and friends,
For life, this place and this special day

To remember your renewable bounty
Which we commemorate at Easter.
Amen

Gil and Stass began to shovel pancakes onto plates from the iron griddle set up over the fire. Nessa served Alissia's little brother, Duncan. Alissia hung back. Cynthia called to her. "Alissia, aren't you hungry?" Cynthia put pancakes and fruit on a plate and took it to her. "Here, honey."

Eddie and Alissia greedily ate hot pancakes running with syrup and salty canned butter, ripe banana pieces and sections of sweet oranges. Each drank a glass of the sweet-tasting milk that Nessa had mixed with a hand beater from Klim powder, all frothy on top and served at ambient temperature. Then, bellies pleasantly full, they wandered lazily off to quest for the hermit crabs that crawled down the beach dragging their shell fortresses on their backs.

That night Alissia flew again. It was really easy; people just didn't know how to do it. She could probably teach anyone. She started out upright, slowly treading air just like water. She ascended to just above the roof tops of the one-story bungalows, never higher. Then she flattened out horizontally and gently fluttered her trailing arms and legs to move lightly forward on her stomach, riding the breeze. She watched kids play in the street and neighbors tend to their yards. She floated on the air face down as if she were on the surface of the lagoon, moving slowly forward to look down at coral and fish and waving seaweed. She felt good up there, above and away from everything, effortlessly directing and controlling her movements. People could easily have seen her not far above their heads, but they never looked up. Alissia always awoke in the morning feeling special and safe after a night when she flew. She would reach back to touch her shoulder blades with her fingertips. She liked knowing that with little effort she really could fly anytime she wanted. She probably could fly away anywhere.

CHAPTER 61
VILLAIN

It was 1949. The day began as unexceptional. Cynthia and Nessa went to have coffee and exchange recipes with friends. Stass Saxton had gone to Big Lagoon to work on the outboard motor of his small boat. The engine did not have any specific problem, but Stass spent many happy hours just fiddling with it. Alissia perked up when she heard Stass was going. She loved Big Lagoon, to see the boat and to watch her dad fix things. She always hovered around his shop in the garage when he worked in there in the hope that he would show her how something worked. She followed him around as he put together the tools he was going to take.

"What do you want?"

"Uh...nothing." She continued to follow and watch.

He stopped. "What?"

"Well..."

"Speak up."

"Well..."

"Well what?"

"Can I go with you, Dad?"

He put his hands on his hips and looked down at her. She waited.

"No. You stay home."

She knew better than to ask again.

Her father left and took Duncan. For a time Alissia sat in the patio. Why didn't he want her to go? She did her chores. She got good grades. She hadn't done anything. Why didn't he want her? She tried to swallow and felt like she had a big Seagrape stuck in her throat. After a time, she stood up. Maybe she could play with Eddie. She knew Miss Cynthia was with her mom and so she couldn't claim that she thought Miss Cynthia was at home. Her mom was strict about rules but Alissia elbowed aside the thought. She made a deliberate decision to disobey the Big Rule: a mom should always be at home if Alissia went to a bungalow. Her breathing quickened as she marched across the street to Eddie's. She entered the shady patio surrounded by high cement walls. Standing on the step at the threshold of the house, she tapped on the screen-door of the kitchen. Her eyes were still adjusting from bright sun to somber penumbral seclusion when the figure of Eddie's father came to the screen door and loomed over her. Alissia hesitated, undecided. She almost fled but she just backed down one step. She should have listened to her mom. Wary, she asked, "Can Eddie come play?"

Gil looked at her. "Well, well, it's Miss Alissia," he said in a funny voice.

Alissia hesitated. "I was just looking for Eddie."

"He's not here right now." Gil's mouth spread wide and his lips drew away from his teeth into an ugly grin. He pushed the door open a few inches, reached through and locked onto her hand. "I can help you." Alissia pulled back but he dragged her hand toward him. He fumbled and then with the other hand pressed something hot and squishy into hers. He folded her fingers around it and squeezed her hand with both of his. Alissia tried to extricate her hand. Her neck hurt and her heart pounded. She frantically tried to pull away. It was his thing, she realized with shock. He had put his *thing* in her hand. She panicked. He tried to haul her in through the door. She jerked and pulled silently. The edge of the screen door scraped some skin off her shoulder. Her loud howl filled the air as she raked Gil's upper arm with four fingernails of her free hand. She left deep, bloody tracks.

"Quiet!" Gil hissed and let her go. In reaction to the yell and scratches, Alissia sensed a minute give, the snap of one thin thread in the taught rope of Gil's menace. Gil's voice and face reverted to his own.

Alissia ran out of the patio and across the street. The next time Gil did something, she thought, she would scream and scream and never stop. She would bite him. Hard. She would scratch his face with both hands. She scrambled into the house and ran to her bedroom. She slipped into the quiet dark space of her large closet and huddled on the floor in a corner. She wept quietly. She felt betrayed and alone--confused. She knew that what Gil did was bad. It would cause big trouble if anyone found out. Maybe her dad and Gil would get mad and yell at each other. Her dad would figure out something that she cared about and take it away. Her mom would be angry and punish her, too. Her mom was strict about rules. Maybe she would never allow Alissia to play with Eddie or go to Miss Cynthia's again.

Alissia knew she had been really bad. She knew she was sneaky and she felt guilty. She was ashamed because she made the bad thing happen. What if people found out? It was her fault. She broke the Big Rule on purpose. It served her right. It was punishment for just doing what she wanted when she knew she shouldn't. Tears ran down her cheeks. She pulled up the bottom of her T-shirt and used it to wipe her face and blow her dripping nose. *I'm supposed to be responsible,* she thought. *I was not responsible.*

Alissia laid down and curled up on her side. She closed her eyes and began to think of flying. In her head, she willed herself to rise slowly into the air. She began to tread air just like she did in water and soon she floated above the roof tops. As she flew weightless through the sky, above everything in the Colony, she looked down on the houses, passed them, and on the steady breeze she floated out over the lagoon toward the sea. She could go really far, riding the wind. Her breathing slowed. She quieted.

Suddenly she opened her eyes. She must have dozed for a moment. She felt calmer, but heavy sadness spilled over her. She couldn't tell anyone. She couldn't. Then she realized that someone would soon come home and she had better get out of the closet. She had to look like nothing was wrong. The scrape on her own arm would pass for one of the usual results of her tomboy play. Then, for a fleeting fraction of an instant, just a thin, sharp sliver of that awful moment--her yell, the scratches--seemed somehow like they were a responsible thing to do. She was not powerless. It would be her secret.

CHAPTER 62
MISGIVINGS

"Gil, what's wrong with your arm?" Nessa asked. "Those scratches look terrible."

"They sure do." Cynthia grasped his elbow to look more closely. "I think you need to disinfect them. What happened?"

Gil yanked away and clapped a hand over the angry scratches on his upper arm. His short shirt sleeve didn't quite cover them. "I ran into something working in the garage. It's OK. I used peroxide."

"But what--"

"Forget it, Cynthia!" He wheeled around and stalked off toward Stass, ending the conversation. Gil's glance caught Alissia glaring at him with a fixed look. She did not drop her eyes. He averted his. At that instant she realized that she was not totally powerless. She would not forget.

Cynthia stood with her hands on her hips and frowned. She watched Gil walk away. Her brows drawn together, she pursed her lips. Barely audible, she muttered to herself. "What in the garage would leave parallel scratches like that?"

IX

Rosa

CHAPTER 63
GONE FISHING

Red Burns was up early. Dawn was fast approaching and it would soon be time to leave. He had taken a few days off to go fishing. He would ride to Oranjestad with his fishing buddy, Swede, and leave the car for Rosa. Three days meant a lot of idle time for Rosa. A horn tooted out in front of the bungalow.

Red walked into the bedroom and gently shook his wife's shoulder. "Sweetheart, I'm off."

In bed, Rosa stretched sleepily. "M-m-m-m?"

"Rosa, I'm leaving."

"*Sí, amor.* Bring fish."

"Aye, I shall. Love you."

Red bent over, smoothed Rosa's hair back from her face and kissed her on the cheek. He went to the front door where his fishing gear sat waiting. He picked it up and went out. Red whistled a happy tune and broke into a few steps of a Scottish jig as he headed to the car. Through the open car window, Swede called out "I see you are ready."

Red laughed and called back. "Aye, that I am."

Red and Swede had hired Hermenegildo in Oranjestad to take them out to fish for three days on the Sirena, a 28-foot single-masted sailboat with mainsail and jib on which they had made a number of good trips. The craft was somewhat less alluring than its mermaid name, but it was good for fishing and Hermenegildo handled her well. For calls of nature one used the boat's downwind side and for light there was a kerosene lantern. They would go as far as Maracaibo.

Aruba was a great place for fishermen. It is the only ABC island that is part of the Venezuelan continental flat. In the waters between Aruba and Maracaibo, Red and his fishing buddy would angle for catch as varied as sailfish, white and blue marlin, wahoo, amberjack, kingfish, bonito, blackfin and yellowfin tuna, and red snapper. The men might even catch a feisty, fast barracuda. There were few things more gratifying than fishing and sailing on a fine day at this latitude. The sky stretched azure from horizon to horizon, with scattered puffs of clouds. Red stood with his feet planted apart on the deck and let his body rise and fall with the scend of the sea. He threw back his head and with all the power of his lungs yelled a prolonged "yahooooo" to the expanse of blue above. Hermenegildo and Swede looked at each other and laughed with the pleasure of life.

Trolling was a practical way to fish in the choppy water and the fishing was good. The two men let out a seven-hundred-foot line with four hooks to bottom-troll for snapper. They are fighters. At the feel of a bite Red jerked to set the hook. When he could feel that he had hooked at least two more fish he called out, "Hermie, slow it down. I'm going to haul in." Hermie slackened sail. Red hauled in two large snapper. The third got away at the surface of the water. Later Swede brought in a barracuda.

Hermenegildo quenched his thirst with water he carried in a barrel. It had a four-inch hole cut through a stave on top that he had covered with a flap made from an old inner tube. Red and

Swede carried water of less dubious potability in a couple of jugs. That evening, Hermie anchored the Sirena off the Venezuelan coast. They wanted to wait for daylight and high tide before navigating through the sandbars to enter Lake Maracaibo. After a long day of fishing, the stop was a welcome respite. For dinner, they ate fresh fried snapper. Well satisfied, they stretched out and went to sleep on deck with the tang of the sea in their nostrils, lulled by the creaking of the rigging. They dreamed with satisfaction of more and bigger fish.

The three men were plunged deep into a slumber full of images of catch when suddenly their fantasies erupted into a barrage of real yells and gunshots. The fishing *aficionados* were being attacked by Venezuelan fishermen who swarmed onto the boat and held them at gunpoint. Hermenegildo tangled his tongue with nervous explanations that the Sirena was on a fishing trip. He gathered from the attackers' disorganized comments that the government would pay them for the capture and delivery of anyone who might be running contraband. He relayed this to Red and Swede. Red told Hermie to offer the men some rum. This slowed down the torrent of words, the pace of which far outran Red and Swede's knowledge of Spanish. The intruders accepted drinks and their tense postures began visibly to slacken. Further discussion ensued in rapid-fire delivery. The unintelligible stream of words sounded to Red and Swede like an escalation back into heated argument. At its peak, Hermie poured more rum which was downed. A lot more rum was consumed. Hermie took advantage of a lull to tell Red and Swede their by now relaxed captors had been explaining the best way for the Sirena to sail in toward Lake Maracaibo in the morning. By the next day the dilettante mercenaries, anchored alongside the Sirena, smiled and waved to the trio from Aruba, who were now their great *amigos*. Everyone went back to the serious business of sailing and fishing.

The Sirena put into port in Las Piedras near the entrance to Lake Maracaibo. Red treated Hermenegildo to a couple of hours off and some cold beer at La Cantina, a bar that sat in a row of dilapidated bars. The men were approached by two pathetic prostitutes who looked tired. Red and Swede managed to convince the women of their staunch disinterest. Red's interest lay only with Rosa; Swede probably had too much good sense; Hermenegildo said he didn't want to spend the money. Red's treat to Hermie only extended to beer. For most Aruba visitors it was not a question of virtue or resisting temptation. Most—but not all—of the refinery men who visited would spur each other on, with dares to pick a girl. They would joke that to even consider the prospect of an encounter with what was being proffered would make any successful engagement physically impossible. The unfortunates looked so scruffy they scared off all but the most drunk or foolishly intrepid. Tex was reputed to have once said, shaking his head with real sympathy, "Them gals look like they was rode too hard and put away wet."

In Aruba, the trade wind carried on its rustling conversation with the leaves and flowers in Red's garden. Rosa Pérez de Burns had her own plans.

CHAPTER 64
FOLLY

Rosa rolled over and curled up on her side. She slept a while longer. After lunch she leisurely showered, washed her hair and groomed herself from head to toe. She rubbed lotion into her skin and splashed gardenia-scented cologne on her neck and breasts. She thought about her evening plans and felt a brief, nervous flutter in her belly. She would go, at least for a little while. Rosa knew she shouldn't, but she liked the attention and especially playing the game. It couldn't be that bad to flirt a little, she rationalized. The prospect tantalized her.

At dusk she walked out of her bungalow in the Colony, climbed into the Chevy coupe and headed for Seagrape Grove. When she arrived, she parked on the sand next to the car that was waiting near the Seagrape trees. Máximo Hirsch sat in the front seat smoking a cigarette. He motioned for her to get in. Behind them the horizon swallowed the sun. Sitting side by side Rosa and Máximo watched the evening light wane over the sea and listened to waves break on the beach. The fresh breeze blew through the car across their arms and faces and into the grove where it rattled the saucer-like leaves. The wind tickled Rosa's skin and she shivered involuntarily as the fine hairs on her arms prickled up.

"Let's go," said Máximo.

"All right," Rosa acquiesced.

Máximo flipped his cigarette onto the sand, started the car, and drove slowly back along the road on which Rosa had come. Night fell. The evening temperature was delicious and the pair enjoyed the slow ride without talking. Moonlight softened bristly cactus and transformed a divi-divi into the shape of a tempting woman. Rosa drank in the lucent night landscape, a perspective of the *cucunu* that she rarely saw. Then Rosa realized that they were going back to the outskirts of the Colony. She had thought that Máximo was going to drive her out through the *cucunu*, where there were few people and houses, then over to Natural Bridge on the windward coast.

She tensed. "Where are we going?"

"To my house."

CHAPTER 65
SEDUCTION

"I thought we were going for a ride." Rosa ran her fingers through her hair, pushing it back. She shifted in her seat. Her throat tightened and she swallowed. "Not your house. Someone might see us. The Colony is small." This was not what she had envisioned. She had pictured a country drive and strolling on windswept sand, flirting to the sound of waves.

Máximo glanced at her. "I want to show you some photos. Don't worry. I'll park in the garage. No one will know. It's dark now." When they arrived at the house Máximo pulled up to his garage, drove in through the open doors and pulled them shut. They exited through the side door. Rosa could smell the perfume of Night Jessamine floating on the evening air. They entered the house through the back and walked through the kitchen into the living room. A small lamp had been left on next to the couch. All of the wooden louvers on the screened windows were tightly closed even though people usually left them open to let the island breeze cool the house. Máximo turned on another lamp. He led Rosa over to the couch by the arm. "Sit down. I'll get something to drink." He went into the kitchen.

Rosa sat down on the couch and looked around the room. A painting that depicted flamboyant Colombian vegetation with forceful strokes and bold colors hung on one wall, and handsome frames displayed a number of black-and-white photographs. Máximo had an eye for both subject and composition and took striking pictures. His framer in Oranjestad did meticulous work for him. A few feet away from Rosa, facing the couch, a camera with flash attached loomed stolidly in wait on a tripod. The dark eye of the lens watched her. Máximo strode with purpose back into the living room carrying two glasses of Coke and rum with ice.

The ice in the glasses clinked as Máximo handed Rosa hers. He sat down close to her on the couch, pressing his thigh against hers. He lifted his glass, said "To you," and drank. Rosa sipped her beverage and sat back. Máximo set down his glass and put an arm around her. Without preamble, with his free hand he grabbed a breast. Pulling her close he kissed her. At first she resisted, but he was insistent. He ran his hands expertly over her body and she began to respond. After arousing her shamelessly, he stood up.

"Stand up." He pulled her to her feet. "Undress."

She tried to push away but his hands had already snaked behind her and unzipped her dress. It dropped to the floor. In no time, she stood naked in front of him. He cupped both her breasts with his hands. "You are as well rigged as a fine schooner." He reached behind his neck and unfastened the gold chain with the Colombian coin. He put it around her neck and the antique gold with the condor nestled between her breasts. "I will have you, but not yet, my beauty."

Rosa stood frozen as Máximo walked over to his camera. He began snapping shots. He was so quick and assumptive that any protest went unnoticed.

"How shall I take you? So slowly that you beg, or hard and fast? What do you like?" He stopped and looked at her. "Sit down." She hesitated. "Sit down. Now!" She sat. "Bring one foot up under your thigh on the couch. That's it. Show your curly love nest." He snapped three more photos. "Good. Now come here."

Rosa walked over to him. He picked her up, carried her into the bedroom and dropped her onto the bed. He removed his clothes quickly and was on her forcefully, levering her legs apart with his knee. He was a strong man and worked her until she moaned and cried out. Afterwards they lay still on the bed. Eventually Máximo roused himself and reclaimed the gold chain and coin from around Rosa's neck. "Put on your clothes."

He drove her back to her car at Seagrape Grove where he motioned for her to get out. "I am sure we will see each other soon. It's a small island." He nodded to her. She stood and watched him as he drove away.

At first Rosa wept in her bed, but the sobs didn't last. She began to think about how Máximo had wrested control from her and the intensity of the sex that was almost forced on her. She lay on her back and replayed in her mind images of Máximo's body over hers. Waves of desire again swelled and flowed down her belly parting her knees but, finally, she was able sleep. When she awoke in the morning, her first thought was of Máximo. She didn't want it to be just a game or flirting. She really liked him. She *more* than liked him. She could picture herself spending her life on the arm of this handsome, polished man. She fantasized about what it would be like to be married to him. She had only felt this way once before in her life--before Red—and this time she had really fallen hard.

The day before Red's return, as Rosa walked through the living room to the kitchen for a cup of coffee, she noticed something white sticking in under the front door. She went over and picked up an envelope that had been slipped underneath sometime during the night. Nothing was written on it. Opening it, she found inside a single black and white photograph. She looked at the image of herself, cropped to face and torso. A gold coin glinted from between her bare breasts. A painting that depicted heavy vegetation looked out from the wall in the background. The photo showcased her good looks and sultry expression. The reminder of what she had intended to be just a tryst not only made her long for Máximo physically, but also to spend ordinary days with him, doing the ordinary things that people do. She took the photograph into the bedroom and for a while sat on her bed looking at it, wishing she could see him. Then she slid open the drawer of the night table where she kept a flashlight, a few odds and ends and a Spanish-English dictionary. She cached the photo between the pages of the dictionary.

CHAPTER 66

FORAY

Alissia was, as usual, out roaming in the very early morning. The sun rose up from the horizon to dilute the pink rays of dawn that streaked the sky as she marched down the street with her wheelie. She was intent on counting to see how many steps there were in a block, when she happened to observe something quite odd. It was Máximo Hirsch. She halted and through the bushes watched him slip into Red Burns's bungalow. Máximo did not knock. Alissia knew that Red was at work with her dad. She resumed walking but had lost count of her steps. She was curious. She circled around the block. When she got back to Red's bungalow again, everything just looked peaceful and quiet, as if Rosa, as usual, were still in bed, sleeping late. She stood for a while, looking at the bungalow. The time and place for Máximo did not seem right. Finally, she shrugged and tucked the circumstance away in a niche of memory to be retrieved at some later time. She moved on. She did not mention the odd occurrence to anyone. She had learned to be very circumspect, devious in fact, to protect her forays and her freedom.

X

Betrayal

Death of illusion.

CHAPTER 67
FOUND OUT

Red could not remember the word for fishing-hook in Spanish. It just would not come to him. Rosa was not at home so he would have to resort to looking it up. The easiest dictionary to find was always the one she kept in the drawer of her night table. He went into the bedroom and sat on the edge of the bed. He extracted the book from the drawer and opened it to the English-Spanish section. There was something in the dictionary, perhaps inserted as a bookmark. When he took it out, he froze and stared. Rosa looked back at him with that sultry look she could get, her back straight and naked breasts lifted. The glint of the gold coin stabbed him with recognition and he winced as if from physical pain. He knew that painting and the photograph of the schooner on the wall. Looking at the living room that was not his, he sucked in a deep breath and from deep down in his gut emitted a drawn-out howl of anguish that filled the room and hung thick in the air. He threw the photo and dictionary on the bed. He sat there, bent over, head heavy in his hands.

Finally, he stood up and on unwieldy limbs he lumbered through the house and out to his car. He jammed it into gear and drove straight to the bungalow of Máximo Hirsch. He pounded on the front door and waited a few seconds. Nothing. He tried to open the door but Máximo must have left through the back because it was latched. He took a step back and with the whole weight of his body crashed the door open. He looked around the orderly living room. The only thing that caught his eye was the oil painting. "Máximo!" There was no answer. "Máximo!" He walked into the bedroom which was neat and spare with no clutter. Nothing in particular stood out. The closet door was locked and with two hard kicks he broke it open and in a glance he took in the darkroom. The Morse code transmitter that sat on top of the file cabinet immediately caught his eye and he stepped over to the cabinet to pull open a drawer. He hauled out a file, opened it and jerked with shock. With disbelief, he examined photos focused on details of the refinery, the harbor, the ships. Mixed in with the photos there were sketches and pages of notes, handwritten in German. Another file contained photos of women. A realization struck Red, sending anger coursing through him. His face hardened *He's kept all this all this time as trophies, the arrogant cur.* Then he came to the photos of Rosa. Each image knifed him in the gut as he looked at it. He threw Rosa's photos to the floor, doubling over in pain. He crossed both arms and clutched hard at the iron spasms that seized his abdomen. They finally subsided enough that he was able to straighten back up. Red's mind began to race.

Máximo was the bastard responsible for that terrible night in 1942. How did he get away with it? The men had all worked together as a team. They supported each other in their daily work, watched out for each other in times of dangerous emergencies. They all had a common and important objective. How could it be that they had never known? They had never even suspected. Máximo socialized with them, worked side-by-side with them, made them believe that he was working for the same goal they were. The man whom they admired for his knowledge and respected for his competence had deliberately betrayed them and he had gotten away with it.

How could they all have been so gullible? How was he able to dupe them all for so long? Well, no more. Red's co-workers had the right to share in this, but he had uncovered two betrayals and one of them belonged to him only. Red made himself take some long deep breaths. He needed to figure out the best way to handle this, consider all the ramifications. He should take care of the men first, his team, he thought. He owed it to them. Then he would take care of himself. Red ran to his car. He hit the gas pedal and the tires shrieked as he took off, driving with dangerous oblivion out of the Colony and on through the barren *cucunu.* Before he acted, he knew he would need to slow down. He needed to be able to think clearly.

Outside of Maximo's bungalow, the trade wind blew. Máximo sat in his car and watched Red leave.

CHAPTER 68

SUBORNATION

Máximo entered the bungalow and with a glance assessed the situation. He had become comfortable in his life here. The climate was most agreeable, he liked his job and he liked the good pay. He enjoyed his status at the refinery and his social standing in the community, but now he had to get away and it had to be fast. He needed to buy time because it would take at least a day, maybe more, to find a particular sailboat in port in Oranjestad. The captain had acted as a courier for him before, which would not be something the man would want to be known and, for the proper fee, he would be, as always, quick and discreet. No one would know how Máximo left or where he went.

Máximo drove to the Burns's bungalow. Red's car was not there; he had seen Red head in the direction of the Colony gate. With deliberation, Máximo walked to the front door. He paused and squared his shoulders. He assumed an expression of concern and burst in without knocking. He found Rosa, who had just arrived from the Commissary, in the kitchen. "He knows."

Startled, Rosa looked up. "What? Red? About us?"

"Yes. There's no time. I'll explain later." He grabbed her by the shoulders. He looked her in the eyes. "Come with me to Colombia."

Rosa gaped in astonishment.

"I have connections there. I can find work and we can live well. Leave this god-forsaken place." He kissed her roughly. He hesitated only briefly before saying, "We can get married."

"Married? Oh Máximo, you will marry me?"

"Yes, Rosa. I will give you the life you deserve. A proper house with servants, money. You will have status and respect. We can't let him stop us. Say yes," he cajoled. He shook her. "Say yes!"

Rosa looked up at Máximo, wanting to believe in his intensity. "But how? Now?" she asked. "What do we do?"

"Rosa." He held her facing him with a hand on each of her shoulders. "He found your photos at my bungalow. He took them," Máximo lied. "He's enraged. He'll make everything public. It will be in the mouth of every refinery worker, every resident, every sailor. Talked about in every port in the Caribbean. The photos will be passed around. It means your ruin. You can't stay." He pulled her hard against him. In her ear he whispered, "You need to take care of this." He pulled back and again looked her in the eyes. He gripped her shoulders. "Use oleander leaves."

Rosa looked aghast. "I can't!"

"You have to. He'll hunt us down. He never forgets, good or bad. And he never forgives." Máximo softened his tone. "He's a passionate friend and a vengeful enemy." Máximo pleaded with Rosa. "It's our only chance, Rosa. When he can't find me he'll come to you. Beg him for another chance. Tell him you need to talk. Fix him a drink. The oleander will make it look natural."

Rosa shook her head. "No. I can't. I can't do it."

Máximo had to convince her. He gambled that he knew Red well enough to know that he'd first come to Rosa and afterwards go to deal with the situation of the torpedoed ships with the refinery men. It was the truth about the attack that was the real danger to Máximo. Máximo could not make his escape if the men came after him. He had to buy time to get to Oranjestad, to find the boat at the quay. He seemed to cave in.

"That's the risk I took. Gaining you and losing you. I thought you loved me."

"But I do— "

Máximo shook his head and audibly blew out his breath. "You don't understand." He continued with a torrent of words. "When Red gets angry he's a wild Scot. Maybe he'll calm down if I leave the island. He might forgive you." He dropped his gaze. "I have to go." After a moment he looked up. "*Adios,* Rosa." He turned, rounded his shoulders forward and walked toward the door.

"No, wait. Wait."

Máximo stopped and turned back to her. He waited.

I will." Rosa caught her breath. "I'll go."

"When it's done, come to me at the bungalow. I'll wait for you there. Don't bring anything. You won't need it."

CHAPTER 69
OLEANDER

Alissia was rolling her wheelie down the street when she glimpsed Rosa doing something with a plant in the garden. Rosa never did any work in the garden. She stopped to watch, spying through the screen of the hedge. An erratic gust of wind blew her hair into her eyes and she brushed it back. One by one Rosa plucked oleander leaves. When she had a big handful she took them with her into the house. How strange. Alissia hoped Rosa knew not to put her fingers in her mouth after picking oleander. White, sticky stuff always oozed out of the flowers and leaves and got on your fingers. It was poison. Everybody knew that. Even kids knew it could kill you. And it was supposed to be especially bad in drinks with alcohol. She had heard grown-ups joke at garden parties about what would happen if a leaf fell into a glass. Since Rosa had gone inside, there was nothing more for Alissia to nose into here at Red's. She shrugged and continued on, rolling her wheelie along the asphalt street.

If Alissia could have seen inside the house, she would have observed Rosa busy in the kitchen with the oleander leaves. Rosa first crushed and bruised them by rolling them hard in the palms of her hands. She then placed them on a cutting board and pounded them well with a meat hammer. She tore the leaves into small pieces and dropped them into a glass. She poured in the rum. She stirred the mixture well and hid the glass in a corner of the cabinet under the kitchen sink where she left the oleander to steep.

Out in the *cunucu* Red careened around curves on winding roads. When he reached the windward side of the island he got out of the car at Natural Bridge. He walked across sand and rock next to the sea and then up onto the rock formation where he sat down. Wild waves pounded on the shore in countermeasure to the pain that throbbed in his temples and stabbed into the core of his being. He looked out over the water to the horizon where blue space rose up into the infinite. Friendship and love scattered around him in shards. How did Máximo hide it for so long? The deaths of all of those men. That's how the submarine knew when and where. And Rosa. Máximo had defiled Rosa. *I was a fool,* he thought, *to think I could make her happy. I trusted her.* He grimaced. *I loved her.* With his forearms he flung away the moisture that began to pool in his eyes.

Anger welled up again to replace his pain. He knew what he had to do. But first he had to see Rosa. Afterwards he would deal with Máximo. Revenge for the lost men could not be his alone. They could quickly organize.

Rosa bent down and took the glass of leaves and rum out of the cupboard. On the counter she strained the brew with the strainer that she used to make Red's hot tea. She threw away the detritus. She set the glass on the kitchen counter and checked to make sure there was Coca Cola in the refrigerator. She went to her bedroom. On the bed she saw the dictionary and photo. It had been stupid of her to keep the photo. A ruinous vanity. She put the dictionary away, then tore the photo into little pieces. In the kitchen trash she disposed of the torn scraps under wet peelings and tea leaves. She returned to her bedroom where she untied her hair and brushed it, arranging it down around her shoulders. She heard Red's car pull up in front of the house.

Alissia was coming back down the street when she saw Red arrive and slam the car door. He looked upset. She saw Rosa standing in the open front doorway. Alissia couldn't hear what Rosa said but she saw her start to cry. Rosa put her hand on Red's arm and he jerked it away. They acted angry. Their voices rose. She dragged by the bungalow slowly, straining to hear what was said. The door smacked shut and the loud voices faded. What was going on? Red never got angry with Rosa. She had overheard her folks talking one time and they said that Red spoiled Rosa too much, that she could do whatever she wanted.

When Rosa opened the door, she pre-empted anything Red could say with a torrent of words. "I found the photo on the bed. I'm a fool. You are right to be angry." Her voice quavered, then lowered. "You can throw me out. Oh, Red, I have made a terrible mistake. *Perdóname.* Forgive me." She began to cry. "I need to talk. Sit in the living room. Please, *mi amor.* I will fix us both a rum and Coke." She disappeared into the kitchen and returned in a moment with two glasses. She stood holding a glass in each hand for what seemed like a very long time. Then she half-turned, as if to go back to the kitchen. It seemed as if she didn't know whether to go or come.

For an instant Red looked puzzled, then his face contorted back into anger. "What's the problem?"

"Yes. Well, no."

"What?"

"No. Yes, I mean I'm all right." She looked down at both glasses, hesitating, then with care she handed the glass in her right hand to Red. She seated herself in a chair opposite him on the other side of the coffee table. The two looked at each other. They sat in silence as they drank.

Rosa shifted. She looked down, then looked at Red. "Aruba has been hard for me," she began. She cleared her throat. "Life is not like Cuba. I was wrong. I was weak."

Red sat, his face as hard as pillow coral. He held his left hand clenched into a tight fist, his fingernails biting into his palm. He raised his glass and downed the rest of the rum and Coke in big gulps. He sat for a long time and stared at the floor. He looked uncomfortable. After a while, he put his hand to his chest, then let it drop.

Outside, Alissia again walked slowly down the street, feigning detachment. She examined one hand, she looked at the sky. She stopped and pretended to take a sticker-burr out of the bottom of her foot, hopping a little to maintain her balance. She kept taking quick glances at the Burns's bungalow as she passed but now she couldn't see or hear anything. At the corner she turned and started around the block again.

Inside, Rosa watched Red. Then she spoke again. "I didn't mean to," she told him. "It was his fault."

Red leaned back and looked up at the ceiling. Rosa saw his breathing become labored. He closed his eyes and put his hands up to the sides of his head and pressed, as if trying to hold up its weight. He took his kerchief out of his pocket and, resting elbows on knees, he cradled his face in the kerchief spread on his open palms. He sat immobile for what seemed a long time, then mumbled through the cloth. "Going to the loo."

A hard knot of apprehension rolled up from Rosa's feet through her body. It socked into the base of her skull.

Red pushed himself to his feet and walked toward the bedroom. He clutched at his chest, then stumbled through the door. Rosa heard a heavy fall. She ran into the bedroom and found Red on the floor. He lay collapsed in the doorway of the bathroom. His legs lay askew inside on the tile and the trunk of his body sprawled out on the wooden floor of the bedroom. His eyes rolled back as he gasped. His body stiffened and arched up and then all of the muscles let go and he lay limp. Urine leaked out from under his hips forming an impotent little pool.

Tears welled up in Rosa's eyes. She crouched down next to Red and hesitated a moment as she reached one hand toward him. There was no turning back now. She slipped the car keys out of his pocket and ran to the front door of the bungalow.

CHAPTER 70

LEFT

Alissia watched Rosa run out of the house. She left the front door wide open and Alissia had a bad feeling. After so much commotion and strange behavior, the bungalow sat still and silent. Alissia wanted to go look inside the house but now the wife was not at home and she knew the Big Rule. But Mr. Burns was her friend. He was her secret uncle. She would just look. From the front doorway she could see nothing. She took a few steps into the living room.

"Mr. Burns?" No answer. More loudly, "Mr. Burns?" She turned and sucked in her breath. She could see his head. He was lying on the floor. She ventured to the door of the bedroom. Then she stepped into the room. What was wrong with him? She saw the wetness on his trousers and the floor and thought she saw one finger twitch. She should do something. What should she do? She didn't know how to help. He needed help, but she felt paralyzed. She wasn't supposed to be in there. She felt embarrassment for this grown man lying in a puddle because he wouldn't want her to see him like that. She knew that sometimes people who drank a lot fell down, but Mr. Burns wasn't like that and he had not been home very long. She had to get out. Rosa might come back. Someone might see her in the Burns's house and she didn't want to get caught.

Sliding one foot back at a time Alissia edged out of the bedroom. Outside the house she looked both ways, then slipped out of the yard. She started to run down the street, but remembered the wheelie she had dropped in the street in front of the bungalow and went back. She grabbed it up by the handle and headed for home dragging it on its side behind her where it bounced and flopped. She was in turmoil. She didn't understand what was going on, what had happened. With every step she took toward her house the words hammered at her. *He needs you. If something happens to him, it's your fault. You're supposed to do something.* But she wasn't sure what to do. She felt confused, afraid. The other time she had broken the Big Rule she made something very bad happen. She had to get away from Red and Rosa's house before she got into really big trouble.

When Rosa pulled up at Máximo's, the broken front door hung ajar. She went in calling for him. The living room was as neat as always, but he was nowhere to be seen. She proceeded to the bedroom where she could see the shambles in the closet darkroom through its open door. The photos of her lay on the floor like bizarre, naked reflections of herself. She stood looking down into images of her own fixed eyes that stared back to accuse her. She looked around. Drawers hung out of the dresser, crooked and empty. Máximo was gone and she understood. Her heart leaped in her chest as panic drowned all reason. She had to hold herself together. She had to get home.

Its sails filled with wind, the small sailboat was now outside the reef. Only the captain and one well-paying passenger were on board. Indeed, as Máximo had told her, Rosa had not needed to take anything with her to his bungalow.

Everyone said that the widow took Red's death very hard. They had rarely seen anyone so overwhelmed by grief. Red was such a nice guy--and crazy about his wife. The neighbors who heard the tumult found Rosa inside. She was sobbing hysterically and bersek, banging on doors and walls with her fists and head until she was black and blue. She was incoherent and irrational. From what little she said two days later, when the sedatives that Dr. Ritsema injected wore off, Red must have just dropped to the floor. On the day that Red died, the only words that anyone had been able to understand in Rosa's crazed Spanish-English babble were "*Se fué.* He left. He left me."

CHAPTER 71
TRAUMA

When punctilious Máximo did not show up for work on time for his shift, the small group of men looked at each other with visible disbelief.

"Maybe Mr. Uppity ain't so perfect, after all," commented one.

"Well, we *are* here," said Stass, "so quit standin' around and get your rears in gear." The cluster broke up, each man heading in a different direction.

A little later, Tex checked his watch. Half an hour had passed and he went to find Stass. "I'm going to check on Máximo," he told him. "The guy's never late."

At Máximo's bungalow, first Tex went checked the kitchen, then he walked through the living area to the bedroom. At the doorway he stopped with a jerk and stared in disbelief at the dresser drawers, hanging half open and empty. *What the hell?* The guy was obviously gone. He saw clutter on the floor by the closet and walked over to look at it. For an instant he froze. Then he saw the Morse Code transmitter and recognition hit him like an electric jolt. He crouched down to examine what was on the floor and winced at the photos of Rosa. He stood back up and yanked open the file drawers full of refinery photos and reports. Sick, instant comprehension saturated his body. He gathered and stacked all the refinery photos and reports in a pile, put all the photos of Rosa to one side in a separate stack and then, with a bundle under each arm, he left.

It was a traumatic week. Tex shared the information about Máximo with the refinery men, who were outraged. He did not mention the photos of Rosa, which he destroyed. That was not how he wanted Red to be remembered.

The suspicion of espionage was confirmed and the people in the Colony learned that Red Burns was thought to have died of a heart attack at home. Alissia Saxton heard someone say that if Red had gotten help right away he might have made it. She got very sick.

Alissia lay curled on her bed, face to the wall. Nessa took her temperature to rule out fever. She had Dr. Ritsema come to check her. Hendrika came also to check on Alissia and to comfort Nessa.

"I think it is not serious," Dr. Ritsema concluded. "Give her much water and let her sleep. She is healthy. She should soon improve."

But Alissia wouldn't eat and she wouldn't get up. Stass hovered, ever gruff, in the background.

Nessa went to Stass. Tears filled her eyes. "I'm so worried. She's always hungry and she's always busy. It's like she doesn't hear me when I talk to her."

Stass tromped into the bedroom. "What the hell is wrong with you?" Alissia did not respond. "You answer me when I speak to you!" Nothing. Feet apart, hands on hips, Stass furrowed his brow and observed the limp form on the bed for a few moments. He went to the kitchen. "I've never seen the kid like that." He put his arms around Nessa. He swallowed noisily. He put his head down to Nessa's and in her ear whispered gently, "It's OK. If we need to, we'll fly her to Curaçao or the mainland somewhere. Just tell me what you want. We'll take care of her. Whatever she needs. We can use our savings."

That night Dr. Ritsema told Hendrika, "I've never seen Alissia like that. She never holds still. She wears people out with enthusiasm. Now she acts like a person in shock. Since I find no specific symptoms of illness, I think just rest will take care of it. We will watch her."

Nothing had ever laid Alissia low for so long.

XI

Exodus

All changes...have their melancholy; for what we leave behind us is a part of ourselves...

–Anatole France

CHAPTER 72
INSECURITY

Times change. Residents of the little Lago Colony, accustomed to their cocooned island life by wind and sea with only one world of employment, became aware that evolving circumstances might bring into the familiar routine of their lives a move they had never before had reason to consider. To even think about the possibility of ejection into the vast, unknown, outside world provoked acceleration of pulse and breath. Anxiety locked necks and shoulders into heavy, immobilizing rigidity. To be thrust into such foreign territory meant trying to find their way on unknown paths in unexpected directions. For Alissia, it meant that she might end up in a place and circumstances she had never contemplated.

Due, in great part, to the Standard Oil operation, in the 1940s the total population of Aruba grew to nearly 47,000. The Lago refinery employed a work force of 8,300 men, from rough-necks to university graduates. They came from 53 different countries and some 600 were American. Despite such precipitous growth, sixty percent of the people on the island still spoke Papiamento as their mother tongue. Then, over time, the mix of men working at the refinery began to change as the Dutch government formally required that Lago hire more and more Arubans, training some for technical positions. As the decade of the 1950s opened, due to automation and ever-better production techniques, a worrisome decline in total Lago employment numbers began.

By 1951, rumors bruited about the office of the refinery manager. Worrisome talk of reduction in the jobs that had been the mainstay of Aruba's economy for so many years filtered down to high-ranking supervisors. Even though the subject was all hush-hush, this type of secret always leaks out.

There were a number of men like Stass Saxton. He and Nessa had both grown up on the island with parents and friends, immersed in familiar activities, in an environment that they knew in breadth and in depth. Talk of change in his familiar, insular microcosm intimidated Stass. He knew no other work, no other place, no other system and he began to worry about how he could support his family if he were let go. He had never looked for a job in his life. He knew nothing but Aruba's refinery where he had gone to work just like his father. Here he was valuable and competent. It sounded like a lot of men might be sacked at the same time and he feared that would make it even more difficult for him to find work elsewhere. There would be a flood of experienced people all seeking jobs.

Stass was a "process" man and he performed the duties of a chemical engineer. He understood in minute and specific detail every procedure of refining oil that was used in the Aruba plant. He knew the Lago Refinery intimately and could picture its details with his eyes closed. He decided to take the risk of answering ads in the industry's Oil & Gas Journal. The hand-written résumé he prepared to send out with his job applications was just as specific and detailed as his knowledge of processing petroleum. But he had to be careful. Aruba was small, Colony residents nosy. Everybody minded everybody else's business. Any mail he received from an oil company would scream for attention when sorted into his box at the diminutive post office. To make sure that responses to his inquiries would go unnoticed, in all of his application letters he stipulated that the reply be mailed in a plain hand-addressed envelope bearing only an individual's return name and address. Then there was the question of mailing his letters. He gave them to Tex, who could be as close-mouthed as needed. He mailed the applications for Stass in Curaçao, where the sender and recipient names on the envelopes were of no interest.

Within several weeks of having his letters posted, Stass, who had never given much attention to receiving mail--since he almost never received any—began to make regular stops at the Colony post office near the refinery gate.

The idea of working somewhere else stressed him. His short temper grew shorter and he walked around in a thick miasma of irascible mood. Nessa tiptoed around him; she kept the children out of his way as he contemplated imminent departure from his island sanctuary.

CHAPTER 73
DECISION

"Nessa, where's that atlas?"

The wait had seemed interminable. His first job reply was not of interest because it did not call for his skill set and the pay seemed low. He set it aside. A week later, two more responses came in. They were both for a position in processing, his specialty, both in Louisiana. The fourth response that came in yet another week was to work in a refinery in a place called Cubatão. From the information enclosed he gleaned that this was in the state of São Paulo, Brazil. The name and location seemed very foreign, but he really didn't know that much about Louisiana, either. He sat at the dining room table and contemplated the three offers.

Nessa brought the atlas. Together they examined a map of the United States. The two refineries in question were on the coast. They knew where Louisiana was, of course, but that was about all they knew, except that there was a local French influence and, from time to time, Stass heard discussions about the refineries there.

Alissia stood behind them and looked over their shoulders.

"Alissia, you know this is our secret, right? No one can know Dad is looking for another job."

"I know, Mom."

"I don't want you talking about it with Eddie."

"I won't. I won't tell anyone."

They examined the map of Brazil. "Jeez. That is one hell of a big country," Stass exclaimed. "It practically fills South America." He pointed to the speck on the map that represented Aruba. "Think Brazil's bigger than Aruba?" he asked Nessa with a straight face.

Nessa adopted the same expression. "Oh, not much."

That night, when the children were in bed, they talked more. The pay range for the job in Brazil was good, very good. It was a lot more than Stass made now. And the job and plant specifications sounded familiar, despite the alien venue.

The next morning Nessa picked up two geography books on South America from the school library along with a book on Europe, to disguise her real focus. As she checked them out, in response to the librarian's rhetorical question, she said "Oh, you know Alissia. She's always got questions I can't answer, so we'll look at these together. I always learn something, too." Although the presentations were simple, the children's books gave a quick overview of Brazil, which they supplemented with details from their Encyclopedia Britannica. Checking, they found that the area of Brazil was larger than the continental U.S. The country's sheer size was daunting--3.3 million square miles.

Stass shook his head. "I can't picture even a thousand square miles. Maybe a hundred?" When he thought of the comfortable seventy-seven square miles he had always lived in, his stomach knotted. He could not have been more unnerved if he had been asked to travel to the moon.

That evening, Stass asked "What do you think?"

To Nessa Brazil was enticing, exciting, vast. With forced passivity, she replied, "Well, the job has to be right for you, Stass." She shrugged. "If you think it is, I suppose we can make it work."

"The refinery is a project of the Brazilian government. They have a company called Petrobrás. That plant is big but I know the work." He sat without moving. Then he said, "You saw they speak Portuguese there." He slumped forward and looked even more dejected. Nessa kept quiet. Usually Stass got angry when something bothered him, not pleasant, but this was worse. Although sometimes he might look tired, exhausted, now he seemed knocked down, like there was no fight left in him. He looked so vulnerable. She wanted to protect him.

Finally, Stass looked up and said in a beaten tone, "Hell, even my Spanish is rotten. Half of it must be Papiamento. Not that any of it would help me in Cutaban or whatever the hell that place is called." He pushed himself up to his feet as if his body were too heavy for him. "Shit. I don't want to move there. I'll make an ass of myself. I'm going to bed."

Stass usually fell instantly into a deep sleep that lasted through the night, but going to bed didn't relieve his tension. He didn't think it was possible to sleep so little. He knew he slept a few short stretches because all sorts of horrible fiascos on the Brazil job streamed in hellish hallucinations through his head. Stass saw life in black and white and dealt with events decisively, right or wrong, but he could not turn off the unruly tumult of thoughts. When he got up in the morning he felt terrible; he had a hangover from worry.

When Nessa served him his coffee, he said "I had one hell of a night, I can tell you."

At work that day there was more news of layoffs. At dinner he told Nessa, "Bobby Blackfoot was laid off, and Swede. I have to make a decision." He sat quietly for a moment. "What do you think?"

Nessa weighed her words; she knew what she would like but she truly wanted Stass to make a decision he could live with. "If you think it's best, we'll manage."

"What if it doesn't work out?" said Stass. "Then we'll be in a real mess."

"I'll *make* it work for the family, but the job decision has to be yours."

"Well, I've gotta do something. Sounds like they'll hire me, so I guess I'll go. I gotta have a job. I'll write a letter tonight."

"Oh my gosh! Neither of us has ever lived anywhere else. I don't know if I'm excited or terrified," said Nessa.

CHAPTER 74

THE OFFERING

It was on a Saturday when Alissia found them--not long after her father made his big decision. She had hovered around the kitchen with anticipation as the earthy aroma of baking bread spread through the Saxton bungalow and her expectations were fulfilled. She consumed warm, thick slices slathered with salty butter and then, one by one, fried doughnut holes which she dipped in sugar. Comfortably satisfied, she headed for her Seagrape tree in the yard.

Outside she looked up. The clouds traveled by and changed shape as they headed for some unknown destination. She gazed out over the azure lagoon and the deep blue of the sea. It was a clear day and she could faintly discern the high peak in Venezuela. Her Dad said that Santa Ana Mountain was ninety miles away. Just outside the reefs, small sailboats plied short distances up and down the Aruba coast flashing triangles of white sails. She clambered up to her usual perch and when she reached it she discovered an object tucked in the tree fork she habitually straddled. She picked it up and settled in to examine it. It was a small scrap of blue denim with the corners tied into a tiny bundle. She carefully untied it. Inside she found two marbles. The brilliant orange inclusion in the ink-black cat's-eye winked up at her; the other marble was an oversize green aggie shooter. She enclosed the smooth spheres in the palm of her hand and rolled them around. They felt cool and comfortable. They were Eddie's two favorite marbles. She would take them with her.

CHAPTER 75
FLYING AGAIN

In her mind, Alissia could always fly. When her family left Aruba, she felt the plane move through the air away from the *vientos alisios*, the faithful trade winds, toward a new destination. She soared with exhilaration. A disparate thought flashed through her mind. "Oh. Klim is milk spelled backward." It was 1952 and at Aruba's Dakota Field the Saxtons had boarded KLM for the short hop to Curaçao, the first leg of their trip.

Duncan fell asleep instantly in Nessa's arms. Alissia looked at her mother. Nessa's eyes danced with anticipation. She leaned close to Alissia and whispered that she could go to a Brazilian school. Alissia's excitement grew. She would enter a new place, a new language—she would explore a new world with different rules.

On the plane, Nessa turned to Stass. Her capable, strong-willed husband looked wilted. He was always certain about everything, even if he was wrong, yet now he slumped with uncertainty. He was leaving the only life he knew. He cleared his throat and turned to Nessa.

"I've been thinking about it. When we get there, I can get blueprints for the Cutiban plant first thing," he said. He looked out the window and after a moment turned back. "I'll study them. I figure I can memorize the layout pretty quick."

Nessa nodded. "Stass, you'll know that refinery in no time."

Stass sat for a moment without moving, then placed a hand on Nessa's forearm. "You are a good woman, Nessa." His voice quavered.

Nessa looked up.

"I can always count on you," Stass said quietly.

Nessa's eyes widened with surprise. She leaned over and kissed her husband gently on the cheek. For a few seconds, he sat immobile and then appeared to subside back into his gloom.

Alissia gazed out the window of the aircraft and her mind flew ahead through the air. The vast expanse of sky and sea made her feel giddy with adventure.

XII

Set Free

Return to paradise.

CHAPTER 76
CLUES

Now Alissia stood on Pink Beach and the trade wind cooled her. She watched the clouds sailing by overhead and envied their freedom. In the morning, she would leave the island for the second and what would be the final time. She had the answers from the past that she had returned to Aruba to find; now she needed the answers to her present. She had an immediate decision to make. It was urgent, critical to her future.

Now, years after her family's exodus, she stepped for the last time into Baby Lagoon to let the warm water caress her ankles. She stood and contemplated her family's diminutive, twenty-mile-long world. As an adult, back here on her island, she understood that the prospect of leaving this place must have been inconceivable to her father. She had seen him as omnipotent but now apprehended him as fallible. He had the strengths and foibles of just being human. It jolted her to understand that this strong-willed man had been afraid. Moving to the outside world ripped him out of the only system he knew, he who endeavored above all else to impose order and control on everything in his life.

But there was another aspect to the island, she thought. For those of us who lived here, Aruba's sheltered protégés, the essence of this place permeated to the marrow of our bones. We carried the memory of the people, the draw of a farrago of nationalities and languages and cultures.

She pictured how people greeted each other. Some said hello and shook hands and some just said hi. Others hugged and kissed each other on one cheek or both and got all excited about seeing somebody that they had just seen the day before. You didn't think about it, you just got a feel for it, like imitating the steps to a dance. The people who spoke Spanish were all huggy and kissy and touchy. Americans didn't touch so much and the English didn't touch at all. Russians kissed each other on the mouth. Even men.

People are different, she reflected. It wasn't really about how they looked or sounded. It was because Dutch, English, Cubans and who-knows-what didn't *think* the same. Alissia had reveled in her polyglot, multicultural world. With the astounding plasticity of a child, she watched, observed and mimicked. She also learned that to fit in can protect, and that to stand out may be dangerous. There are different rules about how people are supposed to act in different cultures, she thought, and one can learn them just like one learns another language. Being a chameleon can give one entrée anywhere. Her imminent marriage to Tom seemed to fit what she knew about how to fit in. Maybe it would help her at her job. Tom. *What do I do about Tom?* she asked herself.

In the Colony, the pervasive smell of the refinery had been comfortable and familiar. A whiff of that acrid odor anywhere always provoked nostalgia in Alissia. There were the interesting excursions, the fruit and fish and vegetables with different colors and scents that came into Oranjestad on sailboats, the press of people and the chatter of different tongues. The Indian pictographs in the caves at Fontein bore witness to a long-lost people; adventures down into the Colony cave revealed the uplifted limestone of the island. The bats and the ocelots, the Shoco owls that nested in their ground burrows, the pretty little bananaquits with their trills, the garrulous and hyperactive *chuchubi*s that cavorted about and churbled jumbled phrases from all the birdsongs they had ever heard, as if they too mixed languages in a winged Papiamento. Wherever people from the Colony have scattered, thought Alissia, in their heads they carry images of placid green iguanas and busy little goats in the branches of divi-divi trees, of lava and coral that formed distinctive textures and shapes across a well-remembered landscape. With closed eyes, she could still feel big, warm drops of rain fall on her face and arms, released by a sudden squall. She re-inhaled the steamy smell that rose from the ground, saw rainbows that formed when the rain stopped. After a good rain the frogs would croak their chorus; sometimes at night one would sound like the distant foghorn of a ship. She saw a fiery red globe extinguish itself in the sea at sunset. This place. This vast sky filled with stars and falling stars. The bright light of the full moon. The sea. Teeming fish and small creatures when she and Eddie probed the reef that cradled Baby Lagoon. The warmth of shallow, turquoise water with gently lapping wavelets. The pounding of waves crashing on the wild northern shore and skyward spouts of water shooting up into the air from blowholes. The feel of salt spray and the scent of Caribbean water. The wind that seemed to shape lives like it shaped the divi-divi trees that inclined before it. The constant wind. Especially the wind.

CHAPTER 77

RELEASE

On her trip back, Alissia had gorged on the sensory pleasures of island life, the extraordinary aspects of her wonderworld. But the right side of paradise did not suppress the other side. With fondness, she thought of Tom—good-looking, a good man—which summoned back the demons of guilt that were destroying her chance to fit into the life she believed she needed to live. How did she fix her future? With no special aim, she drove around the Colony one last time before leaving. In front of a bungalow she saw a man standing, bare feet dusted with red kaliche, and she stopped.

"Hello," she said in greeting.

"Hi."

"My name is Alissia Saxton." She laughed. "Actually, it's Alissia Aruba Saxton. That probably tells you something. I've been gone a long time. I have a question, if you don't mind."

"Sure."

"Do you by chance know if Tex is back from Venezuela yet?"

The man thought a moment. "Yeah, I think he got back late yesterday."

Excitement shot through her. She would get to talk to Tex before she left. "Tex used to always come to our bungalow with the refinery men to have a beer with my dad." She shook her head. "I can't believe Tex is still here. He was always threatening to retire."

"Oh, he still sings the same song, but he married a Dutch woman, a widow, and stays on and on. When he's not in his bungalow with the radio and his wife, he hangs out at the refinery or checks out things in Maracaibo. He must be sixty-something now. Even with its reduced operation, the refinery just hangs on to him. The guy's a walking reference manual."

Tex knew Alissia's name and invited her in. His wife, Lotte, served coffee.

"We're both older," Alissia began.

"Yep. That's a miracle," he drawled, "after drinkin' that water with rainbows of heavy metals all those years."

Alissia laughed. She well remembered the deceptive whorls of pretty colors.

They made small talk, and then Alissia asked, "Tex, what ever became of Eddie Williams? He was a kid my age. I used to play with him. You know, I still have something he gave me." She reached into a pocket, then pulled her hand out and extended it toward Tex. In her palm lay two marbles.

"Quite a treasure you got there."

"Indeed." Alissia smiled.

"Yeah, little Eddie. That'd be Gil Williams's boy. I remember he was kinda odd. Heared he started college in Louisiana. But he'd only go to classes he liked and to heck with the rest. He up and quit the first year. Gil worried a lot about him. Turned out, though, that he's some kind of genius at electrical circuitry. Got hisself a really good job."

Alissia was pleased. She felt relief, as if a latent responsibility had been removed from her.

There was someone else she had to know about. The comments she had always heard about him were never straightforward; they were always loaded with allusion and innuendo, without precise details she could grab onto. "What about a guy named Máximo? I forget his last name now. A few times he came to our bungalow to hang out with the men and talk. I heard somewhere that he bolted in a big hurry for Colombia just before we left."

Tex sprang up, startling her. He walked a few steps and turned around. His face had turned Seagrape purple. He exploded. "That son of a bitch! He took off like a bat out of hell. I found photos and stuff all over the floor at his place. He was the damned traitor."

Alissia cringed at Tex's anger. She let it settle a moment. "What do you mean?"

"Máximo was the gol-durned spy. We knew there had to be one. He got those guys cremated in the harbor."

Alissia had heard talk about a spy but mention of the harbor disaster punched her in the gut. *Uncle Ruddy, the uncle who died and I never knew,* she thought. All the stories of that night of mayhem were still horrifying.

Tex became silent. Then, dammed up for so many years, it gushed out. "That's not all. I can't believe what that bastard did to Red."

Laughing, tender-hearted Red. Her secret, surrogate uncle. Her muscles clenched in knots.

"Us guys all worked together, helped each other out," he continued. "We was buddies." Tex cleared his throat. "Lot of us thought Máximo was a cold fish. But Red's wife musta thought he was hot stuff."

She must have shown her shock. Tex paused.

He covered a dry cough with his hand. After a moment he said in a low voice, "He took all kinds of naked photos of Rosa."

"What? Rosa?" Red's beloved Rosa? With Máximo? Then Alissia recalled prowling in an Aruba dawn with her wheelie. She pictured Máximo sneaking silently into the bungalow. Red was still working the night shift.

"Máximo was a double bastard traitor. Red was a good guy." He cooled down some. "Sorry 'bout my language. I use worse for him."

Máximo, Red, Rosa. A small, faint image slid into her mind. It grew larger and when it became distinct she examined the clear, still picture. Rosa stood in the garden picking oleander leaves. Oleander...

"Tex, you know how everyone always said to be careful with oleander, that it's really poisonous? What exactly does it do, do you know?"

"Does somethin' to the heart. That's what Doc Ritsema said. Acts just like a heart attack."

She started, then froze. She remembered standing at the door of Red's bungalow, trying to find the courage to go in—to again break the Big Rule. Her hair prickled at its roots and she relived fear. From the door of the bedroom she regarded the figure of the gregarious, delightful man who lay inert and impotent. Bits of information scuffled around to rearrange themselves for her, each putting itself into the right niche. Suddenly she felt cold.

"It wasn't me," she exclaimed without thinking. She shook her head. "Not me," she said softly.

Tex looked confused. "What? What about you?"

"Oh, I'm sorry. Nothing. I was thinking of something else. Sorry." The feelings of helplessness and confusion that she carried began to recede. Comprehension filled her chest, then expanded up to fill her brain. She leaned back and closed her eyes. She couldn't seem to move.

Tex's face puckered with concern. "Are you OK?"

"Oh, uh, yes." She sat up straight. "I was just a kid but Red Burns was really good to me. His death"—she searched for words—"his death was a shock." She looked around. "Excuse me, but may I have a glass of water, please?" She tried to joke. "No heavy metals, please."

She swallowed some water and continued in a tone that she forced to sound normal. "Didn't Red die of a heart attack?"

Tex replied. "That's what the doc said. Red hadn't complained. He musta just keeled over. At least that saved him from finding out about Máximo and Rosa. That woulda killed him from a broken heart, anyways."

She couldn't formulate her next response. She still pictured Rosa in the garden. She was too overcome to talk about what she had seen her do. As a child, that second horrifying consequence of breaking the Big Rule had burned belief in her own guilt into her psyche. Guilt at having abandoned Red still filled her.

Tex went on. "Rosa went back to Cuba soon as she could think straight." He shook his head. "Máximo and that Venezuelan guy was a bad mix. They was always chasing after other men's women. Máximo was damn good at his job but he was a real mean varmint."

Máximo, Rosa, Red... Alissia wanted to bolt. This was too much at once. She didn't want to talk about what she had believed for all those years. She would need some time to sort everything out. She dissembled her agitation and remembered to be courteous. "Well, Tex, Lotte." She nodded at each. "Thanks for the coffee." Steady Tex's company had been somehow comforting. "I remember when you used to come over to see my Dad, Tex. It was a good feeling, to hear the refinery bunch talking and laughing. Dad always shooed me away when he saw me hanging around. He didn't want me to listen but I did. I used to hide where he couldn't see me." She stood. "I'll take one last look around the Colony, then drive back to Oranjestad. I leave Aruba tomorrow." She hesitated. "Tex, there might be something I need to tell you, but first I need to think it through, get my thoughts straight."

Tex looked quizzical, but nodded. "Sure. Take your time."

"If I figure it out, I might make a quick stop by here before I leave. If that's OK."

"We'll be here. We're not going anywhere."

In front of Red's bungalow, Alissia stopped to contemplate the familiar dwelling while she processed what she had learned. A little girl sat cross-legged in the hedge to watch a sprightly bananaquit trilling and eating sugar. The girl faded in, then out. Being at that place adjusted her perspective of vivid memories to the reality of the time. *You were just a kid*, her rational mind whispered. The memory of Red's death loosened its choking grip around her neck. She had thought that she was a coward, that to save herself she ran out on him, just so she wouldn't get into trouble. She knew she had broken the Big Rule a second time when she went in. She thought she was supposed to rescue him and she believed that she could have. It wasn't a heart attack and it wasn't her, it was Rosa. The new reality dulled the sharp edge of her pain over Red. Rosa had willfully poisoned him. Rosa did not deserve that good man. How appalling. *But I was not responsible*, she thought. *It was Rosa.*

Alissia felt light. Above her, the sky turned a brighter, more luminous blue. It was vibrant. Then, like a kid, she went to run one last time toward the beach.

"It wasn't me," she called out to the blue sky and sea. "Not me. It was never my fault," she told herself as she continued to run toward the lagoon.

Alissia had one more thing to do. Before she left the Colony to return to Rika's, she needed to face the final demon. Slowly she approached Gil Williams's bungalow where she saw the shadow of the small girl of the past cross the street. She did not provoke what happened. She just went to play. With gentle compassion Alissia, the adult, absolved that child and passed the guilt to the man. *I was so young*, she thought. *I saw in opposites of black and white where there was a continuum of shades and colors. And I did not have all the pieces. I learned the wrong lesson. Fragments of what happened misassembled into a damning hallucination of what the reality was.*

It was time for Alissia to leave the island. Before going, she would talk to Tex and Rika. She would tell them about the oleander, what had really happened. Then, with power and will, she would choose her future.

CHAPTER 78
DOWNWIND

Alissia's return to Aruba had given her key answers. Her understanding of the past now more closely represented what the reality had been. *What has been fueling the conflict that is destroying my life,* thought Alissia, *is that I believed I had to press myself into an acceptable mold to atone for past sins. Sins I did not commit,* she again told herself. She also understood that it was more than that. She had feared that if she did not play by the rules, her real character would be exposed. She had been afraid to admit to others, but especially to herself, that she still wanted to circumvent convention. *I don't want to conform. I want to escape.* She had believed that revelation of what she really wanted, non-conformity, came with a terrible price. It would confirm her as derelict and a coward, worthless and self-seeking. She would never belong, never fit in. But in reconciling the two sides of her wonderworld, the events of her island life no longer warred. They took their place, as they should, along the extraordinary-ordinary continuum that is life.

Alissia willingly claimed her many childish pranks and transgressions. They were a part of who she was. She had also unmasked and freed herself from the phantoms of death and evil that had stalked her—they no longer had power because she understood that she was not responsible for the shameful violation or for Red's death. She wanted—she needed—to fit in somewhere, she thought, but it did not have to be into the system of her current life with its tight set of rules. She did not have to force herself into a cold and grey, ill-fitting slot. If she did so she would damage herself by living a lie. She would also damage Tom. Their relationship had been good and in good faith. They had cared for each other and each had enriched the life of the other and they would always keep that. They had done each other no harm and she again had to do Tom no harm. She understood that they must each take their own path and she began to formulate how to tell him.

Alissia well remembered the day she raked Gil Williams's arm with her nails. She would use that bravado. She also remembered how willful she was as a child. She would use that willfulness. Fingering her shoulder blades, she claimed the right side of paradise and embraced who she was. She would jump ship. She craved adventure, the excitement of the smell and feel and sound of an exotic new place. She was finished with the chill and dreary environment she had forced herself to endure, with the commitments that confined her. She would gaze at blue skies with white scudding clouds. She would listen to other languages play their sweet music, take pleasure in new tastes on her tongue and swim in azure, warm lagoons. She would again wrap herself in tropical nights and wear the sweet scent of flowers. She chose to roam unfettered and she exhilarated in reclaiming her freedom. Once again, she would ride the wind. She was not powerless now. She could fly away anywhere.

ABOUT THE AUTHOR

In the early 1900s, few people had ever heard of a speck of land called Aruba. Life there in the mid-twentieth century and the role that the island played during the nascent era of Black Gold--as petroleum was often then called--as well as the long reach of World War II—have been part of my family lore for my whole life. I was born on the island where three generations of my family lived in the Lago Colony; a pack of my first cousins lived next door. For the setting of this fictitious story I draw from personal experience and from family conversations over many years after our exodus. When I gather with family today, we still laugh about pranks and reminisce with nostalgia about life in Aruba at a time when few people had heard of our speck of land. In addition, over decades my uncle recorded and transcribed the oral memoirs of many people of his and older generations who lived in the Lago Colony. My cousins posthumously and privately published his transcriptions and I have a copy of this work, as well as miscellaneous "Lago" publications of the time that belonged to my father. My extended Aruba family shares the characteristics of being voracious readers and strong swimmers—our principal pastimes in those days. My mother really did take us for midnight picnics on the beach under the full moon.

The size of Aruba is a simple concept. However, when I returned to the island as an adult, with the distance of time I was able to appreciate its size relative to a vast world. Three generations of my family lived at one tip of a microcosm that was six by twenty miles in size. On my visit, I also reflected on the exodus from the Lago Colony in the 1950s. It must have been traumatizing for men who had never looked for a job or worked anywhere else in their life.

Relative to this work of fiction, I have a deep and ongoing interest in language and particularly in how culture affects communication. My books "Intercultural Communication: A Practical Guide" and "Communicating with Brazilians: When 'Yes' Means 'No'" were published by the University of Texas Press. I speak fluent English, French, Portuguese and Spanish and limp along in a few other languages.

And I still feel that as a child I lived in paradise.

NOTES

Potable Water in Aruba

Today Aruba has the second largest water desalination plant in the world. Water-en Energiebedrijf Aruba, N.V. is surpassed in size by only one plant located in Saudi Arabia.

Papiamento

Papiamento continues to be the first language of native Arubans; they also speak Dutch, the language of government and schools. Most speak also English and Spanish. Papiamento is one of the few Creole languages of the Caribbean that has survived to present time. Unlike many creoles, it enjoys high prestige among its speakers and appears to be in no danger of disappearing.

The Papiamentu or Papiamento that is spoken on the three islands of Aruba, Bonaire and Curaçao varies slightly from island to island in vocabulary and spelling conventions. The small variations are mutually intelligible. That Papiamento first developed as a Portuguese-based language is evidenced by many words in its core vocabulary. Some examples, with translations, are:

Papiamento (English) - Portuguese/Spanish
afó (outside) - fora/fuera
batí (to hit) - bater/golpear
bong (good) – bom/bueno
brínga (to fight) – brigar/pelear
fórsa (strength) – força/fuerza
fóya (leaf) – folha/hoja
kachó (dog) – cachorro/perro
mai (mother) – mãe/madre
nóbo (new) – novo/nuevo
pai (father) – pai/padre
papyá (to speak) – papear/hablar
te (until) – até/hasta

Some examples of words with diverse origins are:
watapana, from Arawak (divi-divi tree)
supposed di, from English (supposed to)
bin bek, Portuguese *vem*/English *back* (come back)
wak, from Dutch (watch)
marshe, from French *marché* (market)
kèch, from English (catch)
masha bunita, from Spanish words *mucha* and *bonita* (very pretty)

An interesting characteristic of Papiamento is that plurals are formed by adding the suffix "nan" to the end of nouns. *Bailador* is one dancer; the plural is *bailadornan.*